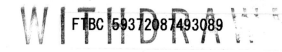

D1616036

The Book on Fire

The Book on Fire

Keith Miller

IMMANION
PRESS
Stafford, England

The Book on Fire
by Keith Miller
© 2009
2nd edition 2011

"City of Bones" first appeared, in somewhat different form, in *The Arabesques Review*.

Author website: millerworlds.com

Interior illustrations by Keith Miller
Design and layout by Storm Constantine
Edited by Storm Constantine

Set in Garamond Premier Pro

IP104

ISBN: 978-1-907737-20-6

An Immanion Press Edition
immanion-press.com
info@immanion-press.com

ACKNOWLEDGMENTS

For assistance in various forms during the writing of *The Book on Fire*, I would like to thank Sofia Samatar, Peter Dula, Lionel Thompson, Edward Miller, John Ashaiya, Mark Sawin, Alaa Bahy, and the inimitable Storm Constantine.

Many texts were helpful to me during the writing of the novel, but I would like to particularly acknowledge the following: *The Nag Hammadi Library*, ed. James M. Robinson; *Cairo: The City Victorious* by Max Rodenbeck; *Christians in Egypt* by Otto Meinardus; *Alexandria: A History and a Guide* by E.M. Forster; *Library: An Unquiet History* by Matthew Battles; "A Study of Shamanism in the Nuba Mountains" by S.F. Nadel; and Michael Haag's wonderful *Alexandria: City of Memory*.

CONTENTS

I

Entrances

CALL ME BALTHAZAR. Call me silverfish, sweet dreams, the end of the rainbow. Call me dust devil, night owl, will-o'-the-wisp. Call me the man in the moon. But call me Balthazar, and place a book in my hands. And what book is that, the book I reach for? Ah, that is why you are reading, of course; that is why I am here, in my thin-soled shoes and soiled leather jacket, a knife in my belt and a coin in my pocket, a wink and a grin at the ready, to lead you toward that book. And to lead myself toward that book, because this is a journey we will take together. You can almost see it, the book of our desires, its green morocco binding tooled in gold, the five raised bands on its spine, the uncut pages like sealed lips waiting to be slit with a dagger, the dagger you use to peel your oranges, slay your enemies. (Because this book is also fruit, is also demon.) Or perhaps it's a soiled paperback lacking a cover, half the pages dyed in blood and wine, every corner creased, the margins filthy with fingerprints, shopping lists, scraps of verse . . .

If you approach Alexandria from the sea, the library is hidden and what grabs your gaze as you near landfall is the lighthouse, steeple of fire, stuck like a spear into the glitter of the bay. So arresting is the beacon that as the boat bucks and you clutch the gunnels you fail to notice the crowded waterfront, the broken ring of the corniche, the bright speckling of other boats around the wharf, until you're almost through the arms of the breakwater. But then you look down and Alexandria is before you, all minarets and a multitude of windows like spaces in a loosely woven fabric, like coarse dusty cotton folded and twisted and crumpled, the colors ink watered to barest cinnamon, faded rose, jaundiced lavender, the lemon of light through glass. Over the city, like a sprinkling of spices, hangs the dust. If you're lucky you arrive at twilight and the calls to prayer chord and jar and doves scatter, curling up till they break free of earth's shadow and batter the vanishing sun to shreds.

As your boat slips with a flutter and a groan alongside the other hulls and masts, the first scents surface after the day of brine. Cardamom and wet cunt, randy goat and roasted garlic, putrid fish heads, steaming horseshit, frying aubergine, ylang-ylang. All this with the sweat of the dockers and the seaweed reek of the pilings. A brown hand reaches to haul you onto the boards; suddenly stable after the hours in a salt cradle, you lurch to keep your balance. Stevedores bellow in a dozen languages, shrugging burdens onto dunnage. Jarveys in spats and scarlet jackets approach, and touts from seedy hotels murmur prices in your ear, while porters squabble over your traveling cases.

My books stashed in the Pension Scheherazade, I set out that very night to explore the city, entranced and baffled by the graffiti in six scripts and the mishmash of mashrabiyya, minaret, Coptic cross, Gothic arch. Architecture of stone, but also of light: shadows cast by wrought iron, sieved moonlight across marble, shadows thrown on interior walls by unseen inhabitants.

I love encountering a new city, but that first night in Alexandria I was curiously nervy. Though the citizens I passed paid me no heed, I could not shake the notion that eyes watched from every shadowed alcove. I kept flicking round, trying to catch the flag of shadow that always seemed to have just tucked itself behind a pediment or palm leaf. And in the gnash of passing trams or the mutter of waterpipes, I thought I heard a voice whispering my name, whispering the titles of my favorite books.

As I walked I asked merchants and shoeblacks and coconut vendors where I might find the library, but all either smiled and turned away or murmured an enigmatic couplet, till I learned that there was a conspiracy against directing foreigners to the secret center of their city. So I wandered for an hour or two through the tangled streets until, near midnight, I came out from an alleyway and beheld a fragment of another world.

I will not forget that first sighting of the library. After the bells and hurly-burly, the reeks and perfumes, I emerged into the quiet stirring of leaves, the scents of juniper and thyme. Behind iron bars great palms stood, spaced far apart, and long-tailed birds of a species unknown to me beat silently between them. Along the inner perimeter of the fence, like their own shadows, like denser dusk, the librarians paced in their gray gowns: barehanded, shaven-headed, the open book tattooed on their wrists. And beyond the trees and the gray-garbed women the library stood, huge and lovely, with the colossal grace and fissured skin of an elephant. Its original shape was lost, the stone clawed and nibbled by millennia of weather— the infinitesimal lick of raindrops, the scouring of sandstorms—so it resembled a natural outcropping.

As the moon rose, I clutched the bars of the fence, which are the bars of a prison. We are the prisoners: the citizens of Alexandria, the bibliophiles of the world. I stared beyond the passive glances of the librarians to the stone carapace, trying to conjure from dimples and swellings some eroded sculpture— sphinx haunch, archangel clavicle—but all was cloud-reading. The library was windowless. There were no portals carven with winged bulls, no gilded gates attended by liveried guards. The sole entrance was a door set deep in the stone, slightly smaller than the height of a man. The roof of the structure was punctured by narrow skylights that angled pale spines among the minarets, and that must have sprinkled the interior with suns in the day. Librarians walked along the roof as well, restlessly, hands at their sides or clasped behind their backs. From a distance they seemed all alike, sisters of some ascetic tribe.

As I strolled back through the city, my mind so aroused by the notion of the riches within the library that I viewed the streets through a crimson scrim like the aftermath of pornography, I heard from a doorway a voice like sandpaper on iron:

"Sst. What's your desire?"

I peered into the archway. "Who are you?"

She stepped from the shadow with a sound like crushed glass, but did not come more fully into focus, because she wore a blue niqab, veil fringed with silver bells. Indigo gloves up her arms. Only her eyes showed, but even they were rimmed in a domino of slathered kohl. "Call me Zeinab."

"And you want to know what I desire?"

"This is the city of desires. Requited, unrequited. All for a price, of course."

Ordinarily, I don't pick up girls off the street, but, as often in a new city, I craved companionship. And something about the voice, the veil, the bells, gave me pause. To hear that voice again, to make certain it was quite as harsh as it had seemed, I asked: "And what would you cost?"

She named a book.

Reader, this was no ordinary hardcover, nor even a scarce first edition such as might enhance your shelves. No, the title she mentioned was among my most precious possessions, freshly sequestered in my seedy pension. It was inconceivable that she could have known of its existence. Perhaps in shelving it I'd rubbed it the right way between finger and thumb, and this was the veiled djinn I'd summoned.

"Never," I said, and started to walk away. She was beside me—blue rustle, silver shiver—and then, as we neared the sea, disappeared. I turned full circle, gaze craning into every shadowed aperture, but she was gone. I laughed, but my laughter was laced with dread, as if someone had reached out from darkness and touched my eye.

. . .

11

Step with me beneath the painted signs awry on the graffitoed wall, up six spiral flights to the Pension Scheherazade. Past rooms occupied by transients, the rucksacked riffraff who stay a night or a week, festooning the furniture with threadbare laundry before marching off again under their burdens, having notched up another city. Past rooms hired by nervous husbands who spend an afternoon half hour with a fat whore. I sometimes see them leaving, melancholy, slack-shouldered, like men who've lost at cards.

It is not my custom to allow strangers within my defenses; the only people allowed to breach my boundaries are Abdallah the errand-boy, who brings my coffee, and the occasional one-night wench. But, though we have been acquainted only a few minutes, you are no stranger. I do not know you but you are bound to me, closer than a mother or a bride. Our ribs are braided, our tongues twisted to a single cord, your systole is my diastole. You are welcome behind my oiled lock and supple hinges.

This is the robber's lair, the thief's den. Perhaps you wished for cases of knives and drying blood in the washbasin, a bullet hole in the mirror, but I keep a tidy residence. The room contains a desk, a bed, and a wardrobe.

Just inside the balcony doors, on an unvarnished wooden table, are jars of pencils and kneaded erasers and razor blades, Japanese rice paper, bone folders, wooden rulers—the tools I use to refurbish the books I steal, to lift library marks and owners' names, to reset the leather and rebind if need be. I'm not above tampering with my goods, adding false publication pages to transform them into first editions, binding in substitute signatures to lend them the veracity they need to attract point-maniacs and tinkle a few more guineas into my pocket.

But where are the books? you ask. Ah, step this way, over to the wardrobe. The wardrobe? you say. And what's so special about this wardrobe? Let's stand back a moment and examine it. Plain cedar, varnish clinging in chitinous scabs to the grain. Paneled doors with chipped handles screwed on askew. Open them. Sharp-edged cotton—blue shirts, tan trousers—a few mothballs, and shadows. No matter how bright the afternoon, or how wide I fling the curtains, shadows pool in the recesses of the wardrobe like ink spilled in the corners. Come with me, that's right, step up into the wardrobe, sidle past the clacking hangers, loving the caress of cotton, and, if you're lucky, through the shadowy back. Are you still with me? Welcome then, doubly welcome, charmed one, whom the gods and djinns have blessed.

We find ourselves in a room with a kilim on the floor and a portly armchair in a corner, a little table beside it bearing a candle in a brass holder. And beside the armchair a single shelf of books. But where is this room? you stammer. The wardrobe backs onto the wall of the adjacent room, does it not? And do you carry the wardrobe with you? What do you do in other cities? How . . . ?

Hush, best not to pry too hard there, you don't want to wake yourself up. Gently, gently, that's right: slumber, my sweet. Now then, hearken to my lullaby. No, I do not haul wardrobes around. There are wardrobes in every city in the world that will suit my purposes. How does the magic work? That is not a function of the wardrobe, my friend. Of course, the magic does not work for everyone. Some, genuine though their desire may be, knock their foreheads on the back panel, fingertips bristling with splinters. Others may enter the wardrobe only until they reach a certain age, and then the shadows are nailed fast. For some, the wardrobe seems to open

13

and shut on a whim—one day allowing them passage, the next as solid as a coffin.

Anyway, my sleeper, you're inside. Softly now, as we approach the inner sanctum, the holy of holies. Slip the sandals from your feet. Bare and bow your head. Close your eyes a moment and ponder your peccadilloes, for this is sacred ground.

The shelf is not overly long, as you see, shorter than might be expected for the collection of one who has spent decades foundering in pretty typefaces. After half a lifetime in dusty hallways, crouching in shadowed libraries, churning through pages by candlelight, this is what I have surfaced with: a single shelfload more precious, more lasting than a diamond elephant, rarer than the mkoli mbemba. These are my books, these are my books. I never travel without my books. Step forward, reach out your hand, touch one . . .

The cover of a book is a portal you open at your peril, peering into the gloom between ornate jambs. What moonlit ripple in those shadows, what damsels? What nightingales, suzerains, and belly dancers await you? What infidels, hierophants, lepidopterists, prestidigititators, what incubuses, changelings, charlatans, waifs, pixies, pederasts, gourmands, cherubim? Here are the rainbow zebras and indigo octopi, the cherry glowworms and tartan chameleons of the inner eyelid, those demon figments we read when we dream. Here are the cities, the seas. The nights, our own breathing, ten thousand kisses. Here are baskets of suns to be broken like bread and nets full of seahorses and here like strung gemstones the screams of the tortured and moans of the tattooed, the dovecoos of mothers and the caterwauling of a gypsy girl's orgasm.

Do you love to read? I'm not referring to plots and characters, however compelling. Nor to fancy words, turns of phrase. I'm talking about nestling in a pool of candlelight and cradling a book like a baby in your lap and nudging the corner upward with your thumb, the whorls snagging the grain of the paper, and hearing the soft sizzle as the page turns. Do you love to read?

Spend a day with me.

I wake into the pale afternoon and call for a coffee, which Abdallah brings in a jiffy, smoking in its long-handled copper kanaka. He tips the thick liquid into a black-and-gold demitasse and I go onto the balcony and watch the glitter on the sea. I light a cigarette, the air so still in the forenoon that I can watch the smoke a long time as it gently swerves and burgeons into the sky, elegant as Diwani script. It's important to wake up slowly, to keep your dreams about you as long as possible. After a while, I go inside and pull on a pair of tea-colored trousers and a cotton shirt with shell buttons and my thief's shoes. On a wicker chair outside the Trianon, I sip a macchiato and smoke another cigarette and nibble the corners of a croissant and watch the passersby.

Then back to my rooms, where I work at refurbishing my loot; binding, resetting, mending rips, scappling away library stamps. Those I've finished with I parcel up in cotton and brown paper and address to my co-conspirators across the globe, who will sell them at exorbitant prices. You may have bought one of my tampered volumes, or coveted it at any rate, gazing through iron grills and bulletproof glass to where it stood, paper grail.

At dusk I walk along the corniche, slowly, because the enormous cobbles are uneven. Lovers sit at intervals along the embankment. The girls are crying, the boys looking away or trying to explain. Peasant girls sell ragged roses pilfered from municipal gardens. Sometimes I buy a flower and carry it a while, then hand it to a child. If I'm sad, I pull a volume of poetry from my pocket and sit above the shattering waves and read those worn words. When you're sad you must not run, because sadness, despite its doleful eyes, has a mouthful of rusty teeth and a hankering for blood. Instead, walk toward the beast and curl within its paws and let its rough tongue lull you. It is good to be lonely at dusk, as the day falls away in a tinsel mosaic. Then, turning your back on the sunset, you watch longed-for nightrise.

I walk across to Midan Saad Zaghloul. Children play in the empty fountain. The moon, old gold coin, floats free of the minarets and tarnishes to silver, alabaster, at last fragile as a sand-dollar. Swallows crosshatch the sky into darkness.

Imagine a sleeping city, a city of mussed sheets and creased quilts, of pillows embraced and mattresses stained by inadvertent filth. Imagine all the dreams seeping up like iridescent mist. And then imagine a silent tribe, clad in ultramarine, skipping across rooftops, through side streets. In their hands are lock picks, matchsticks, daggers, blood.

Some say sleepers lose their souls, that when we shut our eyes and curl to a pillow our inner animals sneak forth from nostril or ear hole to dance on rooftops and make love to strangers. If so, thieves are dreamers reversed. We're demons on the loose, abroad in night cities, while our souls slumber, invisible, under the sheets. You will be my companion tonight, as we seek books.

Two a.m. A great villa in Moharram Bey. Locked houses

are unread books: lift the hinged lid and you're within, sidestepping somnambulists and late-night urinators, eavesdropping on sleep talkers, stroking cats.

As you ease into the shadows, use your ears, your nose. Listen for snores and sighs, the moans of lovemaking. Often, as soon as I enter a house, still blinded by streetlights and the moon, I'll know if it contains books, and even how lucky I might be, because my nostrils are tuned to that odor of rust and saddlebags native to old bindings and ancient ink. That scent—nothing to match it. Feel the talons at your groin, the sudden blossoming of your heart. You can almost smell the words entering your brain like motes, gusting and prancing as if they've entered a sunbeam. Wait, wait. Though you know from which room or hall the odor comes, first you must step through the house, scouting the terrain. Walk catlike, on padded soles, movements liquid, eyes wide. Touch nothing. You're an ultramarine sirocco, wafted in from the sea, leaving no traces, only rearranging objects a little. Here are the parents, raucous as garroted pigs on rutted sheets, here a child adrift on a raft of dreams. Do not linger. Even the sleeping can feel the weight of eyes.

When you've marked exits and danger zones, move to where your nose has told you the bookshelves are, in some hallway or, in the largest houses, in a room of their own, a room paneled in dusty spines, tooled gold, baroque colophons. You work swiftly, tickling oil into hinges with a dove feather, drawing curtains, bunching silk scarves beneath doors. You light your candle and come at last to the shelves. You can't resist running a finger along the banded leather, tipping down a plump volume, hearing the seashore sigh and gravel crackle as it opens. You read a line, a page. Careful now. This is where a book thief's work is more dangerous than that of other thieves: too easily we lose ourselves in our loot. Many a night I've buried myself in some Russian romance or Arabic ode and only realized as I raised my eyes that a bird's vibrato was not that of a St. Petersburg lark or Yemeni falcon but a hoopoe in the Alexandrian dawn, that I'd been submerged too long and must make haste that I not meet a maid brewing coffee or the bread-delivery boy on his bicycle.

Off to steal I stride along sidewalks swinging my satchel, like a blue-suited businessman walking home from some late-night meeting, but returning from work, if my swag bulges, I exit the house from the top story and step out onto the rooftops of Alexandria, haloed by moths, bat shriek bouncing from my skin, saluting the muezzins seated in their towers, who watch the east for the first bead of dawn. Sometimes, sidestepping dead gulls and sleeping asps, dreaming poets and fallen kites, I encounter another thief returning likewise from an early morning escapade and we greet in the pre-dawn chill and chat about our hauls, as any two colleagues might exchange pleasantries on a street corner, but this is four a.m. and we are far above the skein of dark streets and the firelit scallop of the bay.

Then back to the Pension Scheherazade. I swing onto my balcony from the crenelated eaves. Inside, I lay out my loot, read a few pages in each book, note torn endpapers, slipped bindings, slack stitching that will have to be mended. I take a bath, soaking away the thrill in jasmine foam. As the first call to prayer shimmers into the darkness, dragging a swelling cacophony in its wake, I don cotton pajamas and carry a glass of wine to the balcony, waiting for the sea's slow rupture, the blister of flame. And then to bed.

II

Communion of Thieves

MIDSUMMER. In the day, men slept in the shade, melting into their shadows, a little smoke trickling from their forms. The light fused objects. Palm leaves flimsy as seaweed. Nothing moved between the hours of two and four, even the waves glutinous. In the gulch of my mattress I tried to sleep, the sheet a mashed python I wrestled, the pillow a drowned and fetid rodent. I splashed my face at the sink, but the taps were warm, the water scalding. Somewhere a radio was playing Oum Koulsoum, the heat thickening the words, her voice struggling through honey.

ذات يوم بعد ما عز اللقاء   فإذا أنكر خل خله
ومضى كل إلى غايته   وتلاقينا لقاء الغرباء
لا تقل شئنا فإن الحظَّ شاء

Light lay on the tiles in thick solid panes. Dreams came,
though it seemed they bypassed sleep. Dreams of empty
glasses, dunes, bones. The afternoon mosque call was
swallowed by the haze. And then, as the sun dropped, a cat
stirred, a horse flicked its ears. A shopkeeper, face crumpled as
a paper bag, began sprinkling water in front of his doorway.
Bay leaf and barley perfume of damp dust. Brushing the
dreams away, I ordered coffee, which soaked instantly through
my skin.

The nights brought no respite. Midsummer nights in
Alexandria, the fairies grounded with sodden wings, or slain by
heatstroke. Addicted to my profession, I stumbled into the
sweltering night, among the listless bodies.

But this night I could not shake the sensation that eyes
watched from every crevice, from mashrabiyya interstices and
perforations in lace curtains, from the crystal teardrops of
chandeliers. Like you, I'm always on the lookout for the
beautiful book: intricately textured, with music to break your
heart, a typeface to sink your teeth into, a story that grips your
throat. On this night I had the notion that the book I craved
was just out of reach, that I'd walked unwittingly past the
chamber where it stood or that another, more talented thief
had rifled the shelves moments before. Prying the books apart,
I peered behind them. Shadows. The heat had addled my
mind, I guessed. It was so hot; my hands moved within the
darkness as though within liquid.

Wallowing in the melancholy of a barren break-in, I walked

back along the corniche. The minarets were melting like
tapers, alabaster pooling about their bases. The moon still lay
beyond the curve. The reflection of the lighthouse beacon
quivered like oil on the waves.

I entered my rooms. Too hot to read. On sopping sheets, I
longed for dreams. Whether sleep arrived I do not know, but
during the night I had a dream. In my dream, the moon was
low over the eastern horizon. My waterpipe with its bowl of
curdled glass stood on the table, its shapely shadow, smudged
with blue lights, smeared across the tiles. And as I watched,
that shadow peeled itself free, curling upright, then took a
step. Mute and lissome, it moved through the room. Cords of
horror bound me to the bed, a horror heightened by the
silence of the figure and the absence of a face. In the distance, a
tram gnashed, the sea lisped. The shadow—baroque hourglass,
goblet of ultramarine—slipped into every corner, bent over
my seachests, then moved to my bed.

"What do you want?" I whispered, and a parched voice
named a title. The night of my arrival I had been able to resist
her, but this night I knew I would succumb. I was afraid, of
course, but I desired to lift that veil. And I had the notion that
my currency might buy something more than her body; lifting
her blue cover would, I hoped, allow me not only into her
body, but beneath the skin of the city. So I entered the
wardrobe and pulled the book she desired from the shelf and
returned to my bed. But the shadow was gone.

Laying the book on the bedside table, I stood in the puddle
of moonlight, resting my gaze on the sea, which the huge soft
winds ruffled and stroked, uncertain whether I slept or woke.

Then, like a deadly minnow, a blade emerged from the dark
and shivered across my shirt. Buttons popped around the
room, rattling like shaven dice to repose. Whether she led me

to the bed, or I walked there of my own volition, I could not say.

She was clotted kohl, veil, blade: all exterior, except for her cunt, like sticking a finger into the guts of a slit ferret, like fucking a wounded ferret. Her garment contained her reek, harsh as a laborer's—aniseed and ammonia, vanilla, dunghill, alley cat: odors particular to her but also to the city. The odors of Alexandria, as if she had borrowed her perfume from the bell towers and alleyways and littorals. She blasphemed in her orgasm, and we lay panting in unison.

I could not remember having woken, and could not remember returning to sleep. The memory of her voice, the fringe of bells, her curses, had the texture of a dream. But, waking at last into daylight, I clutched in one fist, like my own rumpled shadow, an indigo niqab. The sheets were stained with semen and blood. My blood. Standing before the mirror I traced the red spider web across my chest. The book was gone, and within my ribcage was a book-shaped hollow. I hung the niqab in my wardrobe. Gathering the buttons from the tiles, I sat on the balcony and sewed them back onto my shirt. I knew the wounds were a warning, a redprint for future catastrophe. And maybe these scabs will heal to the vaguest chart lines. Or maybe this story will end with your narrator prettily polygoned.

Sitting on my balcony that evening I picked up, through the crowding scents of Alexandria, a whiff of burning paper, and knew at once it was no ordinary notebook or newspaper, but the finest laid linen weave. Looking down, I spied a girl on the corniche wall, a book in her lap, a light in her hand. She sat with her legs dangling to seaward, breeze toying with the hem of her niqab. I cannot look away from a reading girl, so I leaned my elbows on the balustrade and watched. But in turning the page, as an extension of that motion, she tore it free. Then, with a gesture like that of a dancer or a priest, she lifted her other hand to the paper. Entranced and aghast, I watched the flame trickle along the edges, then blossom. She released it. Borne aloft on a feather of fire, the page spun and swam to my balcony, eased over the balustrade, and lay fuming and twitching on the floor. I stamped it to death and picked up the shard: five words, trimmed by a charred margin. But, reading those words, my mind's tongue spoke on, and I knew precisely the place she'd reached. In an instant I was running down the stairs, through the midan, carriage horses rearing as I dashed across the street. I vaulted onto the corniche wall beside her and she turned to me, eyes shadowed within their slots: "I wondered if this would call you out."

"What are you doing?" I shouted. "I gave you that on the understanding it would be preserved for eternity!" I tried to snatch the book, but she held it at arm's length, plucking the knife from her garments. The passersby glanced at us mildly: another couple quarreling over a book.

She twinkled the blade at me. "You gave me this book in exchange for my services."

"But now it's gone. No one else will read it."

"The fish can read the ashes. Maybe you'll find a fragment in the belly of a whale one day."

I could hardly light a cigarette, my fingers shook so. I have witnessed violence in my trade, certainly. My hands have marked certain pages with blood—my own and others'—but I have seldom been so shaken at the sight of destruction.

"You're distracting me," she said.

23

I realized that the book was lost. "Oh, go ahead," I told her. "Rip away, veiled fiend."

I chain-smoked a ten-pack, staring out at the bay while she finished the book. On the waves floated leaves and cobs, pistachio shells, rose petals, ash. She tossed the burning binding into the sea and brushed her gloved hands together as if she'd just eaten konafa. "Excellent," she said. "First-class read. You have a connoisseur's taste. I'm impressed."

"How selfish you are."

"Oh, there are plenty of books. Believe me, I know."

"How many books have you burned?"

"A book a day, mostly. Sometimes more, sometimes less. Who are you to whine, book thief?"

"You've been shadowing me."

"Every night."

"All right, I'm a thief. But someone will read the books I steal. I take forgotten books and post them to someone who will cherish them. The books you take are gone forever."

"No."

"I watched you burn it."

"Have you ever burned a book?"

"Of course not."

"Then you don't know what you're talking about." She caressed her gloved palm with the flat of her knife.

"But why burn a beautiful book? Burn a paperback, burn a newspaper."

"Surely you'd agree that reading a beautiful book, printed in hot-metal Bembo on handmade Limoges, is so much more satisfying than reading a mass-market paperback."

"Well . . ."

"Of course. And in the same way, burning that book is more satisfying than burning a newspaper. Ah, the pleasures of

burning incunabula, papyrus, vellum. Nothing to match it."
Her laughter sounded like bones under tram wheels.

We sat a while, watching the scurf of ash in the foam.
"These traces will not dissolve," she murmured, "for they are
woven by the north and south winds." Then she swung her
legs around and slipped off the wall. "Come. Would you like
to meet some real thieves?"

She led me westward along the corniche, then across the road,
past the memorial to the unknown author and the equestrian
bronze of the turbaned Albanian. We entered the snarl of tiny
alleys behind Ras al-Tiin, like negotiating the bases of gullies,
their sides ornately eroded.

At the end of a cul-de-sac, she whispered: "Aftah, ya
simsim," and a wooden door swung open. She stood aside to
let me enter.

Immediately the holy stench was in my nostrils—ancient
incense, apple tobacco, bat shit, candle wax. For a moment, I
glimpsed a vaulted interior of muted reds, shadowed greens,
dark gold, with a waist-high speckling of candle flames. Then
the frame filled with an enormous form, voluminously
bearded, forearms tattooed with arcana like a devout sailor.
He gathered me into his church without hesitation, curling an
arm across my shoulder. Inside, he extracted me from his
aromatic armpit and held me before him: "What's your trade,
son?"

"I . . . I deal in books."

"I see. Well, you've come to the right city for that. And the
right church. This is the Kanisa Prometheus. Come. Meet my
little flock of black sheep."

He trundled me across the mosaics to the low tables where his congregation bent over chessboards and waterpipes, under the gaze of St. Isaiah, St. Will, St. Ursula, St. Vladimir.

At the first table sat a girl in black, phosphorescent crosses and virgins strung around her neck. Her skin as well, in the spangled dusk, seemed phosphorescent, so pale, washed with lavender. A dark-skinned man was gripping her wrist and sketching on her arm in oil pastel. His face was stippled and slashed with scars, so at first I thought he'd been the victim of a terrible disease, then saw that they were carefully arranged in concentric circles, stacked stripes. His clothes were a crushed calico of smudged patterns. As I drew nearer I saw that the crook of the girl's elbow was flecked with bruises, each with a purple stigma, and that the man was engaged in joining the marks, forming an off-kilter ankh or seagull. The girl looked up, then smiled and stood. She was older than I'd thought at first, too thin, her eyes huge. She took one of my hands in both of hers, and I could feel her small bones. "Welcome," she said. "I'm Nura. Abuna Makarios will fetch you a drink. And this is Koujour. An artist, as you see." She held out the arm he'd been decorating.

"And what do you do, Nura?"

"I'm a pharmacist. I have a seaside dispensary."

Koujour had stood and was stalking around me. He shoved his face against mine and peered into each eye. Sweet gust of arak fumes. Then he picked up my hands and examined them. Iron bangles clashed on his wrists.

"You need scars," he said.

"I beg your pardon?"

"Scars, scars." He pulled my palms across the stippling on his cheeks, and a delicious shiver scampered up my backbone.

"Koujour was just showing me how my scars are

constellations," Nura told me, as if in explanation.

"Zeinab will help," said Koujour, and returned to his seat and his arak.

Baffled, I moved to the next table, where two men bent over a chessboard. The shadows of the pieces danced, multiple and complicated, in the candlelight. With a fingertip, the thief across from me nudged a knight from ebony to abalone, then looked up. The trayful of candle flames blew like leaves in the sepia lenses of his spectacles. He stood and offered his hand, murmuring his name: "Amir." His opponent growled and grimaced, still staring at the board, then ground his chair back and stood. "Who's this?" he shouted at Makarios.

"Zeinab dragged him in."

"Impossible!" He folded huge forearms across his chest and glared at me. "Where did you meet her?"

"She was . . . she wanted to borrow a book."

"Nonsense! Zeinab doesn't borrow books."

"So I learned, to the detriment of my bookshelf."

"Had you acquired the book by honest means?"

"Certainly not."

"Good answer. Well, I'm Karim, undertaker by profession." His hand in mine was solid as a statue's. "Do you play chess?"

"I do."

"Badminton?"

"Badminton?"

He pointed to a net strung across a mosaicked rectangle in the center of the apse.

"Why not?"

"Zeinab, take over here," Karim shouted, and fetched two rackets from the sacristy. But before I joined him on the court, Amir placed a hand on my shoulder and handed me a book. Glancing at it, I thanked him, then smacked my pocket.

"How—?" I started, but he just smiled and returned to the game. Zeinab was already hunched over the board, chuckling like a crow.

Karim and I tapped the shuttlecock into the gloom, where it vanished a moment before dipping like a throttled dove into the candlelight again. The other sounds were low laughter and the clink of ice, the warble of waterpipes, shuffle of chess pieces, scandalous conversations, the background black noise of batshriek. Like faced shadows the thieves reclined in their den. What stories did they tell? I wouldn't trust a word: all tales, all lies.

This city has harbored a thousand gods and is still within their sway. Hark to the prayer calls, the church bells, the gnostic groans and Sephardic moaning. Dive into the bay and glimpse in the gloaming older gods, horned and tailed, barnacle-skinned, seaweed-haired, sunk to the torso in silt. Glance to the peak of the lighthouse and witness the handsome golden deities, huge humans, posturing. You thought thieves were godless? No, we have our divinities. The true gods are thieves themselves and all thieves, of course, are gods. We come in the night, to teach you what you love.

I am perhaps the quietest member of the Kanisa, often curled in a corner with my nose in a book. The other thieves are readers, of course, as are all the citizens of this city. Makarios reads his gnostic gospels, and Nura pulp paperbacks. Amir reads love letters and suicide notes, and Karim reads epitaphs chiseled into stone. Koujour inhales poetry in half a dozen languages, then spews it out, mangled and marvelous. But they lack my addiction, my aficion. Only Zeinab reads as a matter of life or death, but she won't talk about the contents of the books, only about the pleasures of burning them.

Some nights she'll sit back in her armchair, glass of karkadeh in one hand, dagger in the other, and describe wounds she's made. "Wounds are not all the same," she says, slicing bright segments out of the candlelight. "We must strive for beauty in this, as in all things. Your blade must be impeccably honed, sharp enough to cut a window in a wall, sharp enough to whittle glass. The line of the wound must harmonize with the position of the limbs. You're a painter, the blade's your brush, the skin's your canvas. Mark it with scarlet ribbons and gestural spatters. Use the blood sparingly. A single pretty cut is more charming than a dozen reckless gashes. The first painters were hunters. They fell in love with the marks on the hide, and painted to replicate that emotion. Are you listening, Koujour?"

Of the denizens of the Kanisa she seems to get along best with Makarios. She mocks Amir and Karim (both in love with her, though Amir insists she's a boy), she ignores Nura, she's cordial to Koujour, sassy with me, but she and Makarios have bawdy, rollicking conversations.

"Back from your sacrifices, Nephthys?" he'll say, tearing into a loaf.

"At least I don't eat them, you cannibal."

"Ah yes, if I'm drunk enough I can sometimes feel the transubstantiation taking place on my tongue. Wheat to meat. Try some."

"I don't drink."

"Just the body, not the blood."

She took a bite. "It's bread."

He guffawed. "Listen, sweetheart: 'To any vision must be brought an eye adapted to what is to be seen.'"

"Don't call me sweetheart."

"Virago."

"That's better."

After midnight, Zeinab and I sometimes went strolling like a courting couple along the corniche, through the alleys of al-Atariin, beneath the art nouveau lions and angels. I never ate out with Zeinab, never went with her to a nightclub, but there were a couple coffee shops in the old quarter where men and women could sit in a back corner unharassed, and it was in these places that we ended up in the hours before dawn.

One night, the east was already glowing by the time we entered the café. We ordered an apple-tobacco waterpipe and tea steeped with mint, extra sugar in hers. The coffee shop boy adjusted the ember of the waterpipe and puffed through the mouthpiece to clear it. Zeinab slipped the velvet hose under her veil and the water churned and clouded. Smoke seeped through the blue gauze. She handed the mouthpiece to me. I loved the first rush of cool, sweet smoke, but even more I loved the imagined taste of her saliva on the glass nozzle. I know why the desert poets extolled above kisses and caresses the saliva of their lovers. Outside, the tram screamed and gasped and sparks rained across the doorway. Oum Koulsoum's rough, lovely voice, singing "al-Atlal," was nearly submerged in radio static.

كان صرحاً من خيالٍ فهوى يا فؤادي لا تسل أين الهوى
وارو عني طالما الدمع روى اسقني واشرب على أطلاله

"Why am I still alive?" I asked.

"I have hope for you, book thief. I'm taking you under my blue wing."

"Are you going to burn more of my books?"

"You'll have to give them all up for what you desire."

"And then what?"

"Then you'll be free."

I sipped the tea, the furry mint leaves like a woman's downy upper lip against my own. "How did you know I had the book? The one you burned."

"By the look in your eye."

"And what look is that?"

"The look of someone who's just eaten a baby. And found it delicious."

"You have no way of knowing what that book meant to me, what I had to go through to acquire it."

"You have your wardrobe, book thief. And I have my wardrobe. Which contains the greater treasure?"

"Let me into your wardrobe, Zeinab. Tell me your tale."

"Like all tales, it comes at a price."

"Name your price."

But the mosque call sounded and she was gone. The ember on the waterpipe was cold. The coffee shop was empty. The boy began to sweep the sawdust into dingy heaps.

To pass the time before two a.m. I sometimes stroll up Sharia Nebi Daniel to the street of booksellers, between the quarter of antiques and the ruined amphitheater. The bookstores of Alexandria cater to every taste. Here is the manically organized bookstore, every volume cased in cellophane, here the cavernous dustbin, the books seemingly tipped in by a bulldozer along with half the Sahara, the proprietor snoring in a corner with his waterpipe. Bookstores that are fronts for seedier operations, so if the owner's palm is lightly greased, a row of shelves swivels to reveal a bank of ancient pornography or gnosticism. Here is the café-bookstore, of course, but also the bar-bookstore, popular in the evenings, and the stripper-bookstore, in which the patrons are torn between the novel in their hands and the dancer on the stage ripping off her dust jacket. Here are the themed bookstores—bookstores for women, children, missionaries, mercenaries, Martians, cannibals, the dead.

The proprietors all know me, because I buy my paperbacks here, bargaining ardently over a couple piasters, while keeping an eye out for the leather-bound volumes or jacketed hardbacks that trickle in from the old houses, brought by young philistines trying to salvage a guinea or two by frittering away their grandparents' hoarded obsessions. Though I enter the bookstalls nearly every evening, could recite like poetry the titles of the teetering stacks, I never fail to feel the tickle in my liver when I come again among the books, sniff their dust. This is the true heart of the city, this street of cubbyholes of stacked paper. The library is of course its soul, but it is hidden. Here, the books circulate like garrulous blood through the city's veins. They are bought and reappear, in another bookstore, with fresh coffee stains, more pages missing.

I begin to know the readers of the city. The one who tears corners off pages to chew on while he reads, so the books look as if they've been nibbled by rats. The one who marks up the books in purple pencil. The one who writes inane poems on the endpapers. The one who dog-ears the bottom corners instead of the top. The one who reads on the beach, so the ditches hold grains of sand and ribbons of seaweed, and the one who reads in the bath, leaving the pages buckled and scented with lavender. And what traces do I leave? I am a thief,

I leave no traces.

This is the city of books, where children are admonished if they don't bring a book to the breakfast table, where they're ordered by their mothers to drop their books and go play on the street, where bedtime tales sometimes continue, chapter after chapter, till well after midnight, parents pinching their children to keep them awake. This is a city where men beat their wives with books, the women shielding their heads with books. A city of book-whores, who fuck for books, and their bibliogigolos. A city of book-beggars, who spit on your money, gesturing with their stumps to the paperback in your hand. I usually carry an extra volume or two to hand out along the corniche. If I can't spare a book I'll give money, but I never admonish, as some well-meaning citizens do: "Now be sure you spend that on food, not on books and cigarettes." I know that books and cigarettes are as crucial to wellbeing as food. If not more so.

City of bookstores and steeples, libraries and minarets. Where books and religions mingle, there will always be strife, because books, though they spawn religions, are also tinder for religious flames. There are those who claim to have discovered the book St. Peter admires, and maintain that only those who've reread, say, *Alice in Wonderland*, or the Bible, or *Anna Karenina* a thousand times will inspire the Bookkeeper to jangle his keys. Certain priests and imams claim to have developed the ultimate booklists, and their followers tattoo the lists on their torsos, chanting the titles as mantras. There are sects that dress in paper torn from their religious texts; sects that forbid silent reading; sects that allow only undyed linen bookmarks; sects that advocate holding a book with the right hand only; sects that abjure dog-earing; sects whose members wed their favorite books in arcane ceremonies.

33

Books are smuggled into the city. Alexandria is bordered to the south by apple orchards and orange groves, and to east and west by desert. From these directions book smugglers arrive, with their camels trained to walk in alphabetical order. The clandestine tomes are slipped into the city in the dead of night by enterprising urchins, who flicker among apple boughs and fallen fruit, fording canals, parting barbed wire, evading the muskets of book sentries, to pass their treasures to middlemen on street corners. I have seen these nighttime rendezvous, from rooftops and upper windows—the approach of a slim shadow to a bulky one, and the node passing from one to another—as if I witnessed the transference of a soul or a disease, manifest as a dark rectangle.

The coastline of this long city contains a hundred secluded coves where oarlocks creak at two a.m. and crates are tumbled, with stifled oaths, onto the sand. Sometimes, following a tip, the smugglers are apprehended. We see their photos in the papers: blue-jawed, scar-faced, bespectacled ruffians, eyeing the camera sidelong or defiantly brazen, beside heaps of leather-bound loot.

And on the western fringe of the city, where it tapers into dunes, are the angular orchards from whose leafless boughs hang rotting fruit: the negligent book-borrowers of Alexandria. Yes, fail to return a borrowed book in this city and the booksquad, the bibliocommandos, will swing through your windows at dawn and haul you off to be hanged by the neck until dead.

Five a.m. tramcar. After a barren break-in, I was half asleep in the empty carriage. The tram howled and lumbered, sparks drenching the glass. At empty stations, lamps smeared oblongs of greasy light across torn, overlapping posters advertising religious services, bookstores, belly dancers. The doors folded open with an ungainly clatter, folded shut, and the tram bucked forward. Slow rocking meter of tram stops: Zizinia, Gianacles, Shutz, Safar. . . . At Qasr al-Safaa I closed my eyes a moment, opened them, and she was beside me, without a rustle or a breath.

"I thought you always rode the women's car," I said.

"I ride wherever I like."

"How was your luck tonight?"

"Yours was off, I take it."

I shrugged.

"No books?"

"Plenty of books. Plenty of paper, at any rate. And how was your luck?"

She drew from within her garments a lovely *Alice*. I touched it tenderly.

"What did you give?"

"The usual."

"You'll burn it tonight?"

"Of course."

We were approaching Ramleh and she looked out across the bay. Broken lights scurried on the darkness. "Imagine the tracks were laid over the sea," she said. "You could take the number 99 tram, out over the Mediterranean."

"Where to?"

"East. North. Somewhere with mountains. Yes. Mountains, pine trees. Snow. A little mountain town. Children are flying kites on the promenade. It's the festival of lights. You drink hot chocolate on the terrace of the hotel."

"You sound like you've taken that tram."

I couldn't tell whether the motion of her veil was a nod or the rocking of the tram carriage.

"This is my stop," I said.

She was silent, still looking out at the horizon.

"Where are you going?"

"End of the line."

I'm not a religious man, but even thieves need a confessor from time to time. I went to Abuna Makarios one evening, early, before the others arrived. He was sitting in the belfry, eating konafa and drinking coffee and going over the catechism with an adolescent boy. Sticky strands of konafa had become tangled in his beard.

He set his plate aside and sent the boy home to his mother with an affectionate slap on the bottom. I sat beside him on the stained mattress. He poured me coffee, then slid half a dozen nests of konafa onto a saucer and passed it to me.

"How did Zeinab join your congregation?"

"The others came by invitation. Nura met Amir in the hospital. Amir found Karim on a tram and was intrigued by the contents of his pockets. Karim discovered Koujour taking rubbings from gravestones. But Zeinab just showed up one evening. I was cleansing the church, casting smoke into the corners. When the smoke cleared, there she was, in front of the altar, as if I'd summoned her. "

"What did she want?"

"She wanted to see my books."

"Did she burn any?"

"She told me they were already on fire. We had an interesting little discussion. You know, she's very well read.

You'd never guess it, the way she talks. She's the least constant member of our congregation, sometimes disappearing for a month or more. And she's the only one who's famous. Even when she doesn't show up, we read about her in the papers. Look."

Makarios pried from among his gnostic gospels a folder of newspaper clippings, the black-and-white photographs of books on fire. And, peeling through them, I began to see them as works of art. Books like flowers blooming in darkness, lit pages scattered like rectangular lily pads across sidewalks. Books burning in archways and minarets, bookcases on fire, burning books like stepping stones, a trail across rooftops, into the night. Leafing through the stack, the paper yellowing as I descended, I felt, mingled with the horror, a swelling wonder.

"Who is she?" I asked.

Makarios plunged a hand into his beard and rummaged there. "Yes, the question we've all been asking. There are goddesses of the sun and goddesses of the earth, the many-breasted, the six-armed. Goddesses of the floodwaters, kissing crocodiles; goddesses of the night sky, bellies full of stars: these are the revealed goddesses. You can find them in any church or temple. But most potent of all is the unrevealed goddess. We don't know where she lives, we don't know her powers. She has no shrine. And yet she's the goddess we pray to, the faceless one. She's the goddess we dream of, sphinx buried to the eyes. Her eyes are all we see, but they are not her most important aspect. Crucial to the goddess is what lies beneath the sand."

"Can I trust you with my secrets?"

"Secrets are my job."

"In my rooms I have a shelf of books. Hidden from every eye, from every hand. Yet she knew the contents of that shelf, and . . . well, she acquired one."

"And then burned it."

"Yes. But I don't understand why she couldn't enter my hiding place and take the book herself. She wants to burn them—why doesn't she just go and burn them?"

"She needs your hands, you see. The gods are nothing but shadows without our hands, our breaths. They require our offerings, our sacrifices, to do their work."

I bought a phial of kohl. Closing the balcony doors, I overlapped the curtains. Then, standing before the mirror, I slid the brass peg along my eyelashes, extending the outer corners of my eyelids with long serifs. Zeinab's niqab had hung in my wardrobe since our midsummer liaison. I put it on, adjusted the eye holes, and stared at myself. I inhaled my breath, warm inside the veil. I could not look away from my eyes, the eyes of a ghost. Suddenly I was vertiginous, uncertain who I was looking at. Ripping away the veil, I poured myself a glass of wine.

So, trailing me like a tethered cat, you've gathered my life a little, my nights and desires. You've begun to hear my song, the rough voice I use when I sing in the bath, hoping for a tune. And you've sampled a little of my Alexandria. Not, as you see, the city of memory, but the city of imagination, eternally created, eternally abundant. And the city of books, of course. What's a book made of? All the rhymes and jangles in my ears, all the fears and faces, a fan's clatter, radio static, the tune in a turning grindstone (miller's music). Hours at windows and afternoon dreams, moments just after waking, cities conjured from street names on obsolete maps, the shapes of unknown scripts, my own illegible handwriting, the urge to plunder a virgin page. Also the notion of the book, the grail of the book on the shelf. The book exists, as surely as if I hold it.

Alexandria, Alexandria. It took me a while to fall in love with her; she's harsh, raucous, she stinks. Moving through the streets the first day I couldn't see a pattern; each doorway and window frame a different color, the sidewalks a plowed pasture of broken tiles, the rooftops flat or gabled, towered or crenellated, skyline sketched by an alcoholic epileptic. A mosque bore seven minarets in clashing styles, each decreed by a different pasha, and in churches posters were pasted on ancient icons, marble Virgins cradled plaster Saviors. So I walked the streets bewildered for a while, and then one day glanced at a facade and saw that the parti-colored shutters shimmered like a Klee or an Abushariaa and I thought the disheveled skyline formed a nice counterpoint to the ruled horizon of the sea. I began to notice the corners of prettiness: red peppers among platters of sardines, tomatoes on watermelons, narcissi in hillocks of strawberries. Parakeets against brown walls. Painted cartwheels. Silk roses in horse harnesses. And this daubing soon seemed necessary and my eye began to crave roughness and clash, longing for the abrasive textures of Alexandria, mellowed and melded in the Mediterranean sunlight, the glow of the night city.

. . .

In winter, Alexandrians long for summer, and in the furnace of August they crave the chill, but for a few days in spring they're content. In spring, the streets are filled with carts of apricots and little delta peaches. Days of breezes, shoals of lights skimming across the bay, the air sprinkled with sugar. A few weeks like gifts before the khamsiin blows in from the desert, fifty days of yellow skies and scraped nerves, the shutters of every room bulging with pent quarrels. And then, as the dust storms subside, on one day a year Alexandrians dye eggs and buy green onions and salt fish and brown bread and venture out to sniff the breeze. The sun always shines on Sham al-Nasiim, the air is always polished.

The denizens of the Kanisa Prometheus did not ordinarily circulate as a group. We met outside the church walls in duets or trios, but on Sham al-Nasiim our congregation shucked stone and stained glass and strolled together down to the beach at Chatby. In the lee of the seaside dance hall, whose barnacled pillars shredded the waves, we spread a kilim on the filthy sand and laid out, on nests of green onions, eggs dyed with turmeric and karkadeh. We opened reeking boxes of half-cured fish, uncorked communion wine, and ate in silence as the sun rose. The fish was so salty, the onions so pungent, the wine so sour, I felt I was munching the sun itself, sipping the sea. That first morsel of fish at dawn on Sham al-Nasiim was the most delicious thing I'd ever eaten, but then I found myself hoarding the wine bottle, the roof of my mouth flayed, my tongue rough as a cat's.

After breakfast we swam, Karim and I in our boxers, Amir in his lavender panties, Makarios in an extraordinary pair of hierophantic undergarments, black, with suspenders and crocheted crosses, Nura in a lace monokini, Koujour in the ebony, and Zeinab fully dressed. Amir and Nura dabbled in the shallows, but Karim stroked out powerfully to an anchored fishing boat, hauled himself into it, and dove off the prow. Makarios ducked his head, then stood, arms crossed, water sluicing from his form as though from a breaching orca. The water beaded as the pelt across his chest and shoulders freed itself, the cotton at his groin sucked about his bunched beasthood. Zeinab remained motionless, eyes turned to the horizon. Her niqab floated about her in the swells. I imagined the sea bream nosing her bellybutton.

By the time we emerged, the beach was crammed and we had to hopscotch picnickers to the corniche. Their day was beginning, but we silently parted and walked back to our chambers, our churches, our culverts, to sleep the holiday away.

III

Minarets

A YEAR AFTER my arrival in Alexandria, I finally turned my attentions to the library at its center. This delay was not from cowardice or lack of interest. The library is famously impregnable and I wanted to be certain in my surroundings, to acquire all the information I could, before attempting to breach its stone carapace. Though I will not disown a certain unwillingness to rattle the life I'd built here: my friends at the Kanisa Prometheus, dawn wine, afternoon coffee, the occasional late-night rendezvous with a book-whore. Alexandria had seduced me, but, like all lovers, I had to pry beneath the surface.

No one knows when the library was built, and the stone betrays no secrets, but all agree it is more ancient by far than the lighthouse, more ancient than any structure in existence. The librarians are all women, this is known, and occasionally a girl will arrive from a distant land to stand empty-handed outside the gate until it is opened and she is ushered in.

Mentioning the library in the Kanisa Prometheus elicited guffaws. Easier to snatch the earrings off the Empress of China, they said, easier to nab the pharaoh's testicles, easier to carry off the Eiffel Tower. Why not steal Halley's Comet? The Persian Gulf? The island of Zanzibar? And they told tales of foolhardy bibliomaniacs who'd attempted to enter the library in past millennia. The adventurer who'd tattooed the open book on his wrist and donned a gray gown and tried to pass himself off as one of the librarians. His quartered carcass had hung from the gates for a month till it was picked clean by crows. The billionaire who'd tried to bribe his way in. He'd been cremated in a bonfire of his own cash. The sultan who'd arrived with an army of two thousand men, determined to assault the fortress, liberate the books. Though they bore scimitars and lances, they were eviscerated by the barehanded librarians and the sultan's head adorned a gatepost for a week, eyes cast down and swiveled slightly inward, as though bewildered by the loss of his body. Mild as the shaven-headed women looked, they were fearsome warriors and were rumored to undergo secret training that enabled them to sever a spine with a flick of the heel, crush a windpipe with a finger-snap.

Alexandria portions out its seasons by winds: the dozen named winds, each with its allotted days. From the first wet kiss of Kassem through the yellow gasps of al-Awwa I spent

many hours unobtrusively observing the library and its
grounds, examining the structure for hidden apertures,
marking the rotation of the sentries. I lay sleepless a night and
a day, sipping coffee in a rented room above the library gate,
watching for gaps in the vigilance of the librarians, but there
were never less than ten pairs of eyes on the doorway. Boxes of
books sometimes arrived at the gates from overseas, and I
wondered if I might insinuate myself into one of these, but
they were carefully inspected even before they were let into the
grounds, as were the crates of fruit delivered to the entrance
every morning. The taunting of my fellow thieves began to
chamfer my resolve, and I wondered if perhaps they were right,
that the library was impregnable, a closed book, that I would
live my life unrequited.

The library was not always fenced away from the world. In
times past, scholars and emperors had arrived across seas and
deserts and been allowed past the door. From their accounts I
knew that once within the library they were forced to strip
naked, even the most exalted suzerain, the most sagacious
professor, and, leaving their garments folded on a shelf, don
spotless silk gloves and shifts of rough cotton and barefoot
enter the great reading room at the heart of the library.
Among spears of sunlight or beneath the waver of candle
flames, they sat at stone benches, in depressions worn by
centuries of restless buttocks, and ordered by name the
manuscripts of their dreams. And they were seldom
disappointed, for the Library of Alexandria contained books
like sand, like stars.

When they scribbled the title of the book they pined for,
which perhaps had not been written for a thousand years, one
librarian among those standing at attention around the
perimeter of the room would turn and enter one of the dozen

passageways branching from the center of the library. Often the book would arrive within the hour, but sometimes the patron might sit for half a day waiting for the librarian to retrieve the volume from the dark web beneath the city. Among the readers strode shaven-headed attendants bearing limber rods with which they would lash any who dared utter a word to his neighbor, or even mutter over a difficult passage. A hierarchy may have existed among the librarians, but there was no way of telling who served in what role: their heads were all shaven, their wrists tattooed, they wore identical gray smocks. Some were tall, some short, some had green eyes or pale skins or moles on their necks, but all wore the same expression, at once impassioned and impassive, the expression of a meditating swami or an addict after the first rush. They responded to questions with a swipe of the rod.

The only sounds in the reading room were the clawing of pen nibs, shifting of buttocks, stifled sighs. Those who sat on the benches sometimes raised their eyes to peer into the hallways, though they could report nothing save gloom and the flutter of footsteps. But each mind strained into those shafts, imagining the ore that glimmered there. And they wrote of the remarkable volumes they fondled with silk-clad fingers: great jewel-encrusted tomes fabulously illuminated; tiny duodecimos with paper fine as peeling skin after a nasty sunburn; ochre paperbacks shorn of their covers, the only surviving copy of their print run; books so fragile each page was sheathed in transparent horn, the sheets stored in cedar chests.

But eventually those chaperoned admittances had been curtailed and only once in a great while were scholars allowed within the walls, and those only if they could present impeccable credentials and precise purposes. And then even they were banned and the library closed itself off, still inhaling books but never exhaling.

As I wandered through Anfushi one night, ostensibly scouting likely houses to rob, but my mind in reality consumed with the library beneath my feet, I met Karim skulking through the streets behind al-Khedewi al-Awal.

"How now, spirit?" he said.

"Whither wander you?"

"Come along."

We walked up hammocked steps to Pompey's Pillar. White flowers glimmered beside the path like droplets of molten moon. A ferret paused above us, then like a shaken ribbon vanished among the blossoms. We swarmed the column, fingers and shoe-toes seeking crevices. Gripping the tendrils of the capital, we swung our legs up and over, hauled ourselves onto the plinth. It was as broad as a badminton court, frosted with bird shit, sprinkled with melon-seed shells. "Who eats melon seeds up here?" I wondered.

"This is my perch," Karim said, sitting on the edge of the capital, kicking his legs. He pulled a paper cone from a shirt pocket, poured a heap into my palm, and began slipping the seeds into the left corner of his mouth, cracking them, ferrying the shells out the other corner, where they stuck to his lips and chin.

Karim is as solid as a coffin, head set like a baroque pearl into his great neck. He moves with deliberation, is always laying a hand on my thigh or forearm as he talks, fingers heavy as ingots, as if working among djinns has made him more substantial than other men.

"Where were you coming from?" I asked.

"Catacombs."

"Any luck?"

"Look." He loosened the drawstring of his swag, lifted out ancient trinkets: a silver mirror, carious as old iron, a lapis lazuli hand to ward off the evil eye, gold coins stamped off-center with a stylized lighthouse, a few beads.

I rolled the beads in my palm. "What are these?"

He sorted among them, plucked out two. "This is glass, this is emerald." He held them to the moon. "What's an emerald worth?"

"A stroll on the corniche."

"A game of backgammon."

"Stuffed grape leaves."

"A handjob."

"But not a book."

"Really? How's that?" He turned to me.

"An emerald's just a pretty stone, but a book is a world."

"So I've heard. But books don't last. Paper burns."

"Books are alive, so they die."

We sat for a while looking down over the city. Bats tinkled by. At night, the zones of the city revealed themselves as textures of light. The close mesh of Anfushi, windows skewed, crushed together, the shapes of the light contorted by figures at windows, smoking, reading. The looser elegance of al-Atariin. In the distance, the Gothic wafers in Mahmoudiyya and the stately arches of the Cecil. We could hear a late-night quarrel from some window, a weary lovesong from another, accompanied by a semiquavering violin, the voices and music eroded and meshed by the wind.

طائر الشوق أغني ألمي   يا حبيباً زرت يوماً أيكه
وتجني القادر المحتكم   لك إبطاء المدل المنعم
والتواني جمرات في دمي   وحنيني لك يكوي أضلعي

"How did you get into your line of work?" I asked.

"Graverobbing's an ancient profession in these parts. Like most professions in this city, it runs in families, and there are hierarchies. Common graves are raided by commoners, the middle class by the bourgeoisie. But I'm of the royal line. My paternal great-grandfather raided the tombs of Ramses and Akhenaten. My great-aunt on my mother's side made off with Hatshepsut's jewels. Took her a year of planning. She burrowed through the desert, drilled a hole in the burial chamber, and hooked out the gemstones like a mummifier hooking brains through a nostril. My second cousin on my father's side tried to give it up: some moral crisis. Decided to become a farmer. So he sold his inheritance and bought a plot in the south and planted date palms. But while he was digging phosphorus in a bluff near Nag Hammadi, he bashed open an old pot filled with books. They're underground again," he gestured with his chin to the library, whose spangled hump we could see from our perch, "and my cousin lives in a twenty-room house with four wives.

"I'm a little different, though. Or so I like to think. I have the calling, sure, but there's something deeper. Even when I was a boy I used to go to cemeteries. It was quiet. I liked the little houses. The stone people, almost kissing, almost touching, forever. Or till their heads fell off. I loved the day when families took picnics to graves, eating red dates and guavas. I wanted that holiday every week." He slapped the stone between us: "This city is built of broken tombs. Every wall has stones ripped from pyramids and mausoleums. We sleep on gravestones. That's where I'm happy—among the dead. Well, you're good company, Balthazar, but all those . . ." he waved a hand at the windows and shook his head.

"What does that say about me?"

"Thieves have one foot in the other world already. Don't you love the dark? Bones, the clean polish of bone, is so much more erotic than flesh. And the whisper of a ghost is more of a turn-on than that of a mortal, don't you think?"

"You've met ghosts?"

"Of course. A graverobber in this land must be half magician. I know the spells to lull them. Libations have to be poured out at certain doorways. In my family, we learn these things as soon as we can talk."

"Can they go where they want, the ghosts? Are they free?"

"Less free than we are, strangely. They can't go underground again, but also they can't stray too far from their bones. They can't move from city to city. They can't cross water."

"What do they look like? Describe a ghost for me."

"Some like you or me. Some like smoke or mist; you could mistake them for the damp. Some are just a feather along your spine; you know they're passing, you wait."

"Why don't I see them?"

"Maybe you do. What we think we see is just a fraction of what we see. Everything that's out of focus, at the edge of vision, all the afterimages, the speckles on our eyeballs—our minds sift them out. And what about the blinks? Our minds step over them, but how much of our days are spent in those moments of darkness? We could make another story from darkness and afterimages. And you see Zeinab, don't you?"

"Who is she? What does she want?"

"She's nothing more than a ghost, I suspect. What does she

want? What all ghosts want: rest. Sleep. She wants to go back underground."

"So what's keeping her up here?"

"Unfinished business." He tipped more melon seeds into my palm.

"How deep do you go, Karim?"

"Only the catacombs."

"Is there nothing lower?"

"Chambers and caverns, fabulous wealth. Or so I've heard. I don't go there."

"Scared?"

"I know too much. Too many tales, they can't all be false."

"Tell me one."

He shook his head, munching. Then he laid his heavy hand on my thigh. "Don't try, Balthazar. Don't go down there. I need someone to eat melon seeds with. I need someone to beat at badminton."

When I queried at the Kanisa Prometheus about what lay beneath the mosaicked church floor they cast their gazes into their tumblers, fiddled with captured pawns. "Let the dead walk with the dead," they muttered, and Abuna Makarios held a finger an inch from my nose. "Let the bones lie," he said. So I dropped the subject, guessing this was Alexandrian bugaboo. Thieves, though they work in the dark, were children once, and were not immune to the specters summoned by nursemaids to keep them indoors, in bed.

Later that evening, I was engrossed in a chess game with Koujour when Zeinab whispered in my ear: "Scared of heights?"

I shook my head.

"Come," she said.

I toppled my queen and left with her, shrugging off the dirty glances of Karim and Amir.

She led me that night to the clustered minarets of the Jamiat Abu al-Abbas al-Mursi. The mosque was empty. A breeze riffled the pages of a Quran on a lectern near the minbar. We removed our shoes, placed them in an alcove, and walked into carpeted darkness. She was ahead of me, but vanished once we entered the mosque. Footsteps mute on the carpet, niqab precisely the blue of the nighttime interior, so from behind, without glitter on her eyes, she was no longer there. I only glimpsed her when she entered the spiral stairwell of the minaret, and hurried after her.

"Not this one." She pointed to the far wall, and I threaded the stairwell of the eastern minaret, a child caught in another's game. From our slotted cages we eyed each other, but she was already slipping out, over the marble bulb, to the copper moon at its peak. She passed over the stone as smoothly as a blue shadow, but I slipped on my ascent, caught myself on an arabesque. Lunging, I reached the metal sickle and hauled myself into its curve. It was comfortable as a bathtub, a bath of Mediterranean night, breezes sloshing against my torso.

Zeinab lay in the facing crescent, soles against the copper above her head. She pulled a flask from her garments, took a swig, and slung it across to me: tin asteroid wobbling between moons. Warm karkadeh.

"Got a light?" she asked. I flicked her my matches, saw the flare, caught them back. Snug in our copper hammocks, we

51

smoked. If I reached up I could pluck that star, that one just there. The corniche was deserted except for a single carriage that ticktocked down the cobbles. I counted out the minutes as it entered the knotted alleys of Anfushi.

"Do you bring all your dates up here?" I asked.

"I've never been here before."

"Why did you bring me?"

"You don't like it?"

"It's lovely."

Suddenly the towers shivered and swayed. Heart walloping, I gripped the copper. Crockery smashed in a nearby house. A woman began screaming.

"Earthquake," Zeinab said. "A big one might bring down the lighthouse. Its foundations are riddled with caverns."

I imagined that sight, watching the tower, great-grandfather of the minarets we perched on, crumble and spill sideways into the bay, the colossal hiss as the seawater doused the flames, the wave surging across the corniche wall.

She raised a hand. I heard faint footsteps, echoing louder, then a rustle beneath me. The muezzin's breath plumed into the damp air, exhaled to the east, scattered to the south. He muttered, cleared his throat. Light dusted the east silver and apricot. I closed my eyes, feeling the sun welling against the brim of the world, dragging in its wake a tide of prayer calls. The devout, on carpets, on sand, tumbled after the sun, around the world, aligned like iron filings to the magnet of the Kaaba. I heard the drawn breath, then the first alif, shaking my throne. "La ilaha ila Allah," he yelled. "Haya ala al-salah. Come to prayer. Prayer is better than sleep."

In the interval between the muezzin's descent and the arrival of the dawn worshipers, we slipped out of the mosque, put our shoes back on.

"Breakfast," she said.

"Thief's supper."

We could hear the cries of an early bread-seller along the corniche and walked to where fishermen and street-sweepers and whores stood around a painted cart. We ordered bowls of ful drenched in sesame oil, verdigrised with cumin; a salad of cucumbers, tomatoes, and cilantro; olives with coriander; fried aubergine; falafel; and fresh brown country bread, and ate on the corniche wall. The sea nodded drowsily at our toes. Our fingers touched as we reached for olives and I crossed my legs to conceal my arousal. She slipped the food decorously under her veil, gloves unsoiled. Then the glasses of cardamom coffee, viscous and salubrious as molasses.

Setting her glass on the wall, she pulled out her knife and ran a thumb tenderly along it. Then she took my ink-stained hand in her gloved one and slowly pressed the knife through the flesh at my wrist, between ulna and radius, easing it among veins and tendons till a silver triangle lifted like a canine from the underside. I felt no pain, just the queer shock of seeing my flesh violated. Shifting my wrist slightly, I could feel the metal inside me. She closed her eyes and gently withdrew the blade, wiped it clean, whisked it back into her garments. The cut was so precise, the knife so slender, that the wound closed instantly, just a line, slightly burred like a misprinted I, serifed by beads of blood.

"Why did you do that?"

"Wanted to check the color of your blood."

My wrist had begun to throb. The sun was a hand span above the breakwater, the sea a meadow of drifting shadows.

"What would it cost to see your face?"

"Hush."

"What would it cost?"

"You know what it would cost. Can you sing?" she asked.

"Sorry?"

"Can you sing?"

"No."

"Neither can I. But it would be a good time for a song." She asked a passing boy if he could sing. He shrugged. "Something for the morning," she urged, and he sang the sunrise quatrain of the *Rubáiyát*, in an accent colored by the south:

> *"Wake! For the Sun, who scattered into flight*
> *The Stars before him from the Field of Night,*
> *Drives Night along with them from Heav'n and strikes*
> *The Sultán's Turret with a Shaft of Light."*

When that afternoon I walked sleepily onto my balcony, the words of the song were still in my mind: "*The Sultán's Turret . . . a Shaft of Light . . .*" Zeinab had told me that the foundations of the lighthouse were riddled with caverns, and as I looked across the bay to the lighthouse I realized she had handed me the key.

IV
Under Alexandria

BENEATH EVERY CITY is a shadow city, a city of dank hallways, decaying passages, thick reeking rivers, the filthy highways of rats and roaches, which are nevertheless at times the haunt of thieves, for that city is tethered to the one above by clotted umbilical cords. And the earth beneath a city as ancient as Alexandria is rotten with the subterranean anthills of the dead, plantations of bones from which, one presumes, souls spring on fantastically long stems like potato shoots from shriveling tubers. And also, of course, this city floats upon a sea of books.

Still, I could not shake the gravity of Karim's look, Makarios' admonitory finger. As I walked along the corniche to Pharos at two a.m., my satchel crammed with candles, matches, a couple of sandwiches, a compass, and a paperback, I wondered what arcane honeycomb lay beneath my tread.

As I neared the corner of bobbing caiques, I heard a whisper like a whetted knife, and turned. She was sitting with her back to the city. I stood beside her, thighs against the coral.

The masts tipped like a grove of bones, trammeled water sloshing among the hulls.

"Listen," she said. "After you cross the dark river, close your eyes."

"What?"

"Close your eyes, Balthazar. After you cross the river, close your eyes. You'll only be able to see in the dark."

"How do you—?"

"Give me your hand."

I expected to receive her blade in my wrist once more, but she pressed something cool and round into my palm. "Put it in your pocket."

"What is it?"

"Your fare. The dark ferrybeast waits for you. Pay him, and he will do you no harm. Fail to pay at your peril."

Though the night was balmy, I shivered as I walked on. What did she see from beneath her veil? How much did she know?

The lighthouse is the bastion of tourists and lovers and suicides, open to all, and in my first weeks in the city I had climbed it more than once, skipping up the countless flights, to pace around the giant flame and the mirrors that bounced its light to sea. I fingered the hieroglyphs, the cuneiform carved into the balustrade, graffiti so dense the stone banisters might have been munched by literate termites. With my bodkin I added my mark—stylized silverfish—then leaned over the edge, peering north to Knossos, south to Cairo, west to Carthage, east to Jerusalem.

But this night I did not mount the stairs. Instead, I

crouched under the stairwell in the detritus of millennia: orange peels, false teeth, fish bones, walnut shells, condoms, corncobs, rat hides. I hauled up rank handfuls, plunging like a careless archaeologist till my nails scraped on stone. In a minute I uncovered an octagonal tile with an iron ring in its center and, after rearranging the rubbish around me, lowered myself into the shaft it revealed.

Are you still there? Do you have the courage to make this descent? Here the adventure begins. Dare to take the first step downward, into the dark.

A stairwell, echo of the one above, augured the rock. I pulled the tile into place over my head and, clutching a candle, shuffled my way in, winding so long I felt I must be nearing the earth's core. Somewhere far above, the sea shifted in its bed. Though the city had seemed silent, there was the racket of whispers and the clatter of moth wings and the pale shriek of stars. In this space, if I stopped and held my breath, I could hear only the surf of my blood. When I moved again a thousand footsteps rippled from my own. At the base of the stairwell a passage foundered in darkness, aiming southeast by my compass.

I entered a cavern glittering with mineral candelabra, through which a great slow river ran; a river of shit and semen and menses, rich and rank, the current unraveling my flame to filaments. This is the true democracy. Here, in gentle reeking wavelets, mingled the shit of pharaohs and bugle boys, whores and nuns, writers and readers, the lame, the whole, the dying.

A boat rocked in the waves near the shore, a black jackal seated in the prow. A figure that I had met before, at the farthest boundaries of my dreams, and had seen in certain illustrations, and among certain hieroglyphs on temple walls. Trembling slightly, I paid the obol provided by my veiled

shadow and anchored the candle in the bow bench. Freeing
the craft, I rowed it to the far side, the sluggish splash of the
oars startling a thousand bats from the ceiling. They twittered
about me like blind swallows on black suede wings. The dark
ferrybeast watched me with pupils that drank light and image
and returned nothing.

Beneath the city, time is dead, and I abominate watches,
refusing to be trapped beneath curved glass, tormented by
needles. So the sun might have sped a dozen times over my
head for all I knew, as I drifted through the dark matrix; a
subterranean firefly.

Under Alexandria, the dead slumber; parched cadavers and
scoured bones and the freshly decayed, palaces of maggots,
slouch in a welter of possessions they cannot finger. I
wandered through the burial chambers of scribes and poets;
the walls illustrated books of their lives. Here the shaven-
headed scribe handed a manuscript to the king, here speared
his enemy with an outsized pen, here accepted a goblet of ink
from a pert-breasted priestess. Prying open the lid of a poet's
sarcophagus, I peered into his wrecked face, trying to know
from the shape of his skull what words he might have written.
Other poets sat cross-legged, finger bones still clutching
styluses, eye sockets bent to stone tablets where their last or
greatest poems were written. And I could not resist reading
them, and reading the walls, trying to decipher the archaic
scripts. Gods crouched in corners; winged, beaked, clawed.
Overhead were stone fronds, frescoed sky, so, squinting, I
could almost imagine myself in the open air, strolling along
the shore of Lake Mareotis or beside one of the canals where

the Nile frayed into the delta.

I moved on, among caskets of gold and gemstones enough to keep the entire Kanisa Prometheus ecstatic for a dozen lifetimes, if they'd had the courage to enter the dark, but I remained unmoved. Books are the only true wealth. What lasting pleasure is there in fingering clammy metal or wads of grimy cash or even a sackful of cowries? But a bookshelf is a stash forever opening new eyes, sprouting new limbs, shouting in new voices.

Several times, in passages or caves or within the graves themselves, my candlelight snagged a moon, full or half, and I bent to a skull from whose raw cheekbones spectacles dangled. My twinned splinter of flame and tiny shadowed face stirred in the lenses. Sometimes, ancient puddles of wax lay beside the bones of these bespectacled skeletons, sometimes rusted paper knives and pen-nibs. The mysteries of the underground seemed impenetrable.

I passed cataracts of urine like shaken golden tresses and fetid pools about which rats crouched on cocked forelimbs like squalid diminutive lions at water holes.

There was no telling how far I had walked. Though I tried to keep southeast by the compass, the fickle maze constantly forced me off course, so I had no idea if I was nearing my goal. For all I knew I was deep under the sea or halfway to Cairo. In a queen's crypt, I ate my sandwiches on a dusty throne and smoked a cigarette as I read the story of her life. Then I evicted the mummy—light as papier mâché within her linen shroud—and napped in her granite cot, beneath the painted gaze of vultures.

When I woke, I lit the candle again and counted those remaining. Though I had filled the satchel, I'd used more than half my store and still saw no signs of the library. Also, though

I tried to keep to passages that slanted upward, I suspected I was being shunted deeper, fathoms of rock between me and the forgotten sun, the mythic moon. I began to retrace my steps, but soon found myself in chambers I had not seen before and understood suddenly how desperate was my situation, how foolish I had been. I had no food save dust; no one knew of my plight. In a few days I'd curl up in a gold coffin, unable even to read myself into endless sleep.

For an hour, I charged recklessly through the tunnels, hoping fortune would chaperone my choices, then realized I was only exhausting myself. I sat where I was, my back against a wall, and stared at the dwindling flame. Finally I recalled Zeinab's advice: "You'll only be able to see in the dark." What could she have meant? Though it was terrifying, like cutting away a lifeline, I blew out the candle, and let the darkness close around me. Winding through the stone web, among baubles and bones, my eyes had swallowed my body. Heart deafening me, I'd inhaled images. Now I let the glitter fade.

I'd been in dire situations before, in open boats on stormy seas, bookless in the Sahara, but had never felt more certain of my impending demise. At last I recognized the bespectacled skeletons that scattered these dark hallways. They were the book thieves of past millennia, who'd wandered into this labyrinth, as I had, and had failed to find the library or their way out. No wonder the thieves had a taboo against entering the subterranean ways, if none who entered them ever returned. My chuckle was joined by a consumptive choir, sniggering away into the tunnel.

And as I sat thus, my thoughts wafted to books, as always when I sit alone or lie in bed waiting for slippery sleep. I dreamed of bookshelves wealthy with tooled leather bindings. I could almost make out the titles, almost feel the grain of the fine oasis morocco under my fingers, almost hear the poems chanting within their covers, sense the tales unraveling through the pages. Leaning toward the phantom books, I breathed their odor, that frankincense, myrrh, golden dust. Scent is the most fragile of the senses, so easily lost or confounded, but also the most tenacious, twining its tendrils about our memories. For the blind, and for those who work in the dark—sentries, whores, thieves—the sense of smell is sharpened. When I opened my eyes, the marbled endpapers and linen wove pages vanished, as did the slither of turning leaves and the murmur of poems, but the scent lingered, as if the residue of my reverie had soaked into these tunnels. I smiled, then sat up and ran my palm over the rough rock to bring myself back to reality. I sniffed. The scent remained; elusive, oscillating, but present. And I realized I had known for many hours that I was near books, but in my haste and terror had neglected to sit quietly and use my thief's talent.

Still in the dark, I stood up and, fingers antennae on the wall, stepped in the direction of the scent. At branching tunnels, I shoved my nose down each possibility before choosing. Mind in my nostrils, bibliophilic mole, I wound the thread of that incense through those dark halls till I arrived at a doorway I was certain contained books. I lit a candle and found myself at the threshold of a small chamber, flanked on either side by knotted serpents, the lintel adorned with spread wings. The room was empty except for a single lidded sarcophagus carven with the likeness of a woman. I paced the perimeter of the room before I realized the scent rose from the sarcophagus itself. Lifting the lid I saw no mummy, no chiseled stone bed, but steps leading into more darkness. A darkness spicy with the odors of brittle paper and crumbling leather and ancient ink.

The eroticism of thievery is seldom discussed, but any thief will be able to name that titillation. The nearness of the prize, coupled with the aphrodisiac scent of books, gave me an indelible erection as I descended the stairs. At the base of the steps, I picked the lock of a wooden door, then blew out the candle. Reaching out in darkness, I touched the edges of sliced pages. I stood motionless a minute, fingers against the book, listening for a breath or the sigh of a turned page, but only my heartbeat rumbled. I relit the candle and immediately achieved orgasm. The first sight of that underground treasure tipped me over the brink and I soaked my pants. I was standing behind a bookshelf, peering between shelves. For a long time I stood there with my candle, besotted by my first glimpse of the Library of Alexandria, then moved out from behind the bookcase.

I was in an irregular cavern, a grotto with several apertures through which I could see other caverns like the chambers of a honeycomb. Around the walls, set in nooks cut into the stone, wooden bookcases stood, each uniquely shaped; some with glassed doors, some inlaid with mother-of-pearl and exotic woods. Framed engravings and poems and manuscript pages hung on the walls. Within the cases books stood, slightly disheveled, some leaning together, some placed sideways upon the others. There were brackets for candle holders on the walls and carpets on the floor and dilapidated sofas and armchairs, all piled with worn, embroidered cushions. Beside one sofa, on a linen-covered end table, lay two thermoses and a battered silver pitcher of milk and a bowl of brown sugar and several stoneware mugs and a jar of cookies dusted with powdered sugar and another of salted almonds and a blue bowl of apricots. Well, you can imagine my transport. Without further ado, I returned to the bookcase that hid the door and pulled out the book I'd first touched. I settled myself into a sofa, the cushions about me like a plump embrace, and poured myself a mug of cocoa. Eating cookies and almonds and apricots, I read the book from beginning to end, while the semen dried to a new-found islet on my crotch. And if some savage librarian had chanced upon me during that read, I'd have opened my arms to her and smiled and said, "Strangle me with your ink-stained fingers, miss, for I have achieved nirvana."

The finest books are at once completely ordinary and completely strange. You feel you've read them before, or something like them, but the more you struggle to pinpoint the references, the more you realize that the books create their own references: they are their own histories. The first book I read in the Library of Alexandria was such a book. It had, I felt, been formed in my shape, and was waiting for my arrival. Completing it, I blew out my candle, curled on the sofa, and slept like a newborn.

My thief's sense woke me. Opening my eyes, I saw a grain of light, heard a footfall. I gathered my satchel and candle and retreated behind the door through which I had entered, closed it softly, then peered through the keyhole. My initial reckless euphoria had been replaced by the need to explore further and I did not wish to be apprehended. A woman in gray, bearing a candle in one hand and an ostrich-plume duster in the other, emerged through one of the apertures. She sniffed the air a moment, then spotted the spread-eagled book and dirty mug and apricot pits beside the sofa and pursed her lips. She replaced the book on the shelf, picked up the mug and pits, tidied the books a little and swatted them with her duster, then passed out of the room.

I stayed motionless for a time before venturing out once more. Replenishing my stock of candles from a stash on an upper shelf, I started through the library, going in the direction from which the librarian had come. For hours I wandered, from node to node of that vast net, utterly lost, as I had been in the catacombs, but lost in paradise.

In tremendous caverns, bookshelves lifted tier upon tier into the gloom; long ladders were affixed to the shelves, which I climbed, up to the ceiling. I perched there at the edge of a cliff of books, and looked across the canyon; it was as if a river, in carving its valley, had exposed strata of titles. Other rooms were mere nooks, no bigger than a cupboard, with space enough for a single bookcase.

I read impossibly gorgeous scripts. Scripts in which each hieroglyph filled a page and took a day to write, but could express an entire philosophy. Scripts in which each letter stood for a notion, so the writing dictated thought patterns rather than words. Scripts that had no meaning at all, or that started out meaningfully but then, as the author was caught up in the physical act of writing, became relationships of lines and shapes on paper, beautiful and abstract. Private scripts, the authors long dead, so the script stood isolated, unreadable, precious nonetheless. Rainforest scripts of samara and turaco crest. Marine scripts of shark tooth and sand dollar. I passed through rooms of books the size of doors, each cover the death of an eland, and rooms of books dainty as ladybirds. Books written on communion wafers, grains of rice, sheets of ice.

Books are hiding places. I found books grangerized to twice their normal thickness by pressed flowers, letters, panties, snapshots. And of course books are palimpsests. Some books had been read by so many scholars they were entirely underlined, in blue pencil, ballpoint, fountain pen. Some ancient pages were black with notes scribbled in a hundred hands around the margins, between the lines, across the print itself, the text subsumed beneath a lichen of commentary.

I passed through caverns of drifting paper that fell like rectangular snowflakes. Caverns of dark pools, where books swam like fish, all gills and fins. Empty caverns of dream books, the beautiful books imagined by authors who died too young to write them. Many rooms had sofas or plump chairs or cushions piled on carpets, many were provided with thermoses of coffee and cocoa, bottles of wine, bowls of fruit and nuts and baked goods. It was the most wonderful place in the world.

In the Library of Alexandria, time lay between leather bindings. Drinking cocoa, eating fruit and cookies, I wandered through the fabulous chambers. Several times, I saw a librarian's candle and swiftly snuffed my own and moved farther in. Though occasionally I was forced to plunge into a book, I struggled to remain on the surface, skimming titles, trying to gather the layout of the place. When I first entered it, saw the books scattered around the room and read the titles ranged in no alphabetical order, I thought there was no pattern, that the library was just a big dustbin for books, and this both pleased and alarmed me, but as I moved deeper, I began to sense a different paradigm at work. The library was vast, and in those initial days I entered only a smattering of the rooms, but even so I began to feel my way into its order.

When you are unable to remember a name, some character in a book, say, you can nevertheless smell it, taste it, as if words have auras. So you know it begins with an S or a Z, is scented like cinnamon, colored like lapis lazuli, chimes with sheen or serene. You know how long the word is, its curly shape, whether it was recto or verso, and its placement on the page, but the sound will not trip off the tongue. Just so, slipping through those rooms, I began to sense the books I might discover next, as if the halos about them were other books. I could not have stated precisely my reasons, but holding a volume in a chamber I could have said that the surrounding books had to do with dreams of flying, and that if I entered the chamber ahead of me I might find books on angels, and the chamber to my right might contain books on the phoenix and quetzalcoatl.

Thus, as I moved through the library, I had the sensation that I was encountering the books of my childhood, books forgotten for decades, titles on the tip of my tongue. And indeed I did encounter, from time to time, books I'd read so long ago they seemed myths, and books I'd been searching for my whole life, upon which I pounced like an urchin upon coconut candy, and books that had been rumors in other books, their very existence putative, like sightings of basilisks or unicorns. But most of the books were strange and new. When I moved through the libraries and collections and bookstores of the world above, I seldom encountered books unfamiliar to me, and most I had seen dozens or hundreds of times, but here were rooms filled with volumes that might have been written on another planet, so odd were they.

And slowly I arrived at a realization so startling I was almost afraid to believe it. I found, as I moved through this subterranean forest, that I could imagine a book, known or unknown, read or unread, and be certain of the path I would have to take to find it. I tested it, over and over, and could not fail, as if my mind had been somehow prepared for this library, or as if the library had been modeled on the patterns of my

THE BOOK ON FIRE

mind. And when I realized this, I knew I could follow the patterns back through the caverns to the room where I had entered the library, to the book I'd read when I'd first arrived. I could not be lost, and this seemed right. Was Adam lost in Eden? Only cast into the eastern thorns did he lose himself, but in the garden of the tree of life and the tree of the knowledge of good and evil, where God strolled in the afternoon, he could name every flower, every bird and beast. There was something so heady about this, I felt I was under the influence of a drug. We all have titles, questions swept like sodden leaves into the corners of our minds, that we have little hope will ever be answered or solved, but that we cannot get rid of. Suddenly, I found myself in the orchard of answers. Any title, any question I could think of, was waiting to be plucked. Greedily, I dashed through the library, finding this volume and that, seizing on ideas, and what I encountered of course engendered new branches.

But with this realization came the knowledge of the precarious nature of the library. In the aboveground collections, a book here or there might never be missed, but this library, so carefully tended, was in a delicate balance. A theft, I thought, might create havoc.

For a time, I wondered if I would simply stay here forever, reading, sampling the delicacies, hiding from the librarians— the ghost of the Library of Alexandria, a reformed thief in paradise. And I wondered what would become of my soul if I chose that path. Even in the world above I was reclusive and solitary, often sunk in a book or in my thoughts. But if I eschewed human contact altogether, my only companions fictional characters, my only landscapes those manufactured of ink and imagination, what would I become? Would I start to resemble a book myself? I imagined the process: a male

Daphne, spine curing to leather, ribs ironed to leaves, fingers and toes and tongue flattening, elongating, blood darkened to ink, veins strung like boustrophedon across the pages. My pressed heart would beat out iambic pentameter, hendecasyllabics, and some day I'd simply lean in a corner with my companions, waiting for a female hand to pick me up, lift my cover. And what book would she read then? Ah, that is the book we step toward, you and I. Can you see it? Can you feel the texture of those pages?

Before I entered the Library of Alexandria, my dreams had been of the books I would discover there, but I found, once I had penetrated the labyrinth, that I had to know who the caretakers of these volumes were, who had ordered the pretty cabinets and who had chosen the framed engravings and who had baked the cookies and plumped the cushions on the comfy sofas.

So, rather than fleeing the librarians, I began to stalk them. The rooms of the library were so cluttered it was not difficult for one accustomed to stealth to find places of secret vantage from which to spy on the librarians. Like a child in a vast game of hide and seek, I edged closer to the gray-garbed women; a dark asteroid passing through their system, intent on piecing together a little of their lives and days.

At the heart of the library was the great reading room. Here, as dawn poked rosy fingers through the skylights, I peered through a keyhole at the librarians ranked beside the benches. In the swelling light, they performed, with taut grace, a curious dance, in unison, paperknives slicing slowly through the dusk, ankles arcing in legato arabesques. At the conclusion of each sequence of movements, as their hands reached the end of a swing or their feet the apex of a kick, they snapped them into a pose with sudden power, and a choral yell that startled me even when I was prepared for it, and I realized I was watching the rehearsal of a martial art, though one so finely choreographed it seemed more than half ballet. Birds, of the silent, long-tailed species unique to the library grounds, dropped through the apertures and looped about the room before flicking back into the day. The movements of the librarians in the lessening twilight, the birds pulsing silently over them, were chilling and beautiful. I imagined receiving a blow from a librarian's hand, and desired and feared that touch.

When they dispersed, I followed some as they moved through the caverns of books. They dusted and straightened the volumes and swept and mopped the floors. They filled jars of cookies and fruit and replaced thermoses of coffee and cocoa. But they were continually distracted by the books. I saw the guilty expressions on their faces as they pulled down volumes and leafed greedily through them, the look of a dieter succumbing to apple pie, and I realized that even the denizens of paradise were not entirely at liberty to enjoy the fruits therein. Though there were hundreds of librarians, the library was enormous, and the tasks of dusting, tidying, cataloging, and binding were such that they could not read to their hearts' content.

What turns you on? Ligotage, rectal mucus, watersports, fisting? Chains, children, sheep? The sexiest sight in the world is a woman reading. A stroll along the strand at Biarritz, past oiled breasts and roasting loins, can leave me cold. Page through those clandestine glossies, every orifice filled, no permutation unexplored, and watch me yawn. But it's night, a tram passes, and I glimpse, in a pocket of light, a woman in a blue dress, auburn hair tousled, lost in a book, and that image can sustain weeks of wanking. I've long imagined an illicit literature tailored to my perversion, reader's porn, with paintings in the style of Sargent or Lord Leighton: Marilyn Monroe nude on a divan, reading *Ariel*. Audrey Hepburn in a Spanish café, miniskirted thighs converging on darkness, immersed in *Fiesta*. Josephine Baker in her dressing room, fondling a gilded nipple, sunk in *Les Illuminations*. Madhubala reading the *Thousand Nights and a Night*. These are the images that would turn me on. Let me paint you the most erotic picture in my gallery, spied upon while crouching behind a bookcase, peering through a gap between two leaning volumes.

The youngest librarian sat cocooned in candlelight, on an owl-colored armchair, legs drawn up beneath her so just her toes peeked from beneath her gown. A book lay open on her lap. One hand rested along the top right corner of the pages, caressing them as if she cuddled a cat, a finger moving down along the pages, brushing slowly back up the edges. When her eyes reached the end of a spread she flipped the page greedily, then continued her fondling of the book. The rest of her body was still, the other hand supporting her cheekbone, her head angled down and to the left. Her robe was too big for her and tumbled in thick folds, concealing the shapes of her breasts and thighs. She had not shaved her head for a few days, so it was shrouded by a downy aura that glittered slightly if she stirred. She wore round wire-rimmed glasses. I obsessed over the shape of her ears, delicate as halved nautili, the crescents of her nostrils, her slightly parted lips. Once a strand of spittle shone between them before she turned a page and her tongue severed it. Her eyelashes beat like slow moths. She had a tiny mole on her neck, like a clove embedded in her flesh.

There was a glass of wine on the floor beside her, which she forgot about for long stretches of time. Then she'd sigh and shift on her chair, lift her eyes, and discover the wine. She'd sip slowly for a minute, the reflection off the liquid rouging her cheeks, then set the glass beside her and sink once more within the book.

For an hour I watched her reading, till she reached the last page and slowly closed the cover and placed a palm upon the leather. Now I saw her eyes, as she glanced unseeing at the wall above my hiding place. They were dark and soft, magnified by her glasses. There was something strange about them, but before I could make out what it was, she looked away. With a rustle, she stood and placed the book on a shelf. She slipped on her sandals and picked up her wineglass and candle and was gone. I went to the armchair and knelt, placing my cheek against the warmth her body had bequeathed. I tried to catch, beneath the must of the baize and the odor of the books, her scent, but there was nothing.

Walking away from that image, cradling it like a nestling, I realized I had learned something new about myself. In the world above, I'd assumed I could spend all day, every day immersed in literature, but I now discovered a submerged yearning for afternoon sunlight on the bay, curtains belling in a sea breeze, the swat of Abdallah's bare feet on the tiles as he brought me coffee, for ragged flower sellers on the corniche at dusk and the darting of swallows among minarets, for mosque calls and sandalwood, for grilled sea bream with red pepper and garlic and lime.

71

Drifting through the caverns, I pondered the possibilities for exiting this place. Though I could find my way back to the door that led to the tombs and sewers under Alexandria, I would still be lost once I entered that labyrinth. I imagined making forays through those tunnels, returning to the library when I needed food, till I chanced upon the stairwell that led to the light. But even as I mulled these options, my feet were guiding me toward the answer. I found myself eventually in a room that, had I thought about it, I would have known existed: a room of books about the dark labyrinths beneath Alexandria, cataloging the tombs and their treasures, mapping the caves and tunnels. And I found among the maps one that spun a red line from the underground doorway of the library to the stairwell of the tower. Not daring to steal from this place until I knew more about it, I copied the map onto the inside cover of the paperback I carried.

So I wound back through the caverns of the Library of Alexandria till I arrived at the room with the hidden door and exited Eden. With the map to guide me, it was a short walk to the tower entrance, passing tombs I'd read my way through, and the skeletons of ancient book thieves who'd lacked my sense of smell. I taunted their bones, ground their glasses beneath my heels. I crossed the dark river, retrieving my obol from the impassive jackal, and arrived at last beneath the lighthouse. Then the long spiral up to the sudden salt breath of the sea.

The season had shifted while I was underground and I emerged into a rainy Ramadhan, festival of fasting and feasting. Colored lanterns swung above every alley. Strings of semaphores cut from old notebooks and dyed in washing blue and karkadeh fluttered above my head and, darkly, in the puddles below. Children sent tiny rockets into the slots of sky between the buildings and ran through the rain with sparklers pouring fire from their fists. The shop fronts were embankments of hazelnuts, figs, dried apricots. As the sun set, I walked along the corniche, slowly, like one who has risen from momentous dreams or a long illness. The world underground was still more vivid than that I walked through. I bought a rose from every flower-urchin till I clutched a great bouquet. At the sound of the mosque call, I bought a paper bag of nuts and dried fruit and walked through the alleys munching, clothes stuck to my skin, feet sloshing in my shoes, glasses speckled so the scene fragmented into kaleidoscopes. I handed my paperback to a beggar.

Back in my rooms, I ran a hot bath and soaked a long time. When I got out, the rain had stopped. The streets were a dewy spider web. I sat on the balcony sipping wine, watching the crowds on the corniche and listening to the Ramadhan carols.

I woke into an afternoon quieter than usual, as the fasting households slept away the hours till sundown and the recitations of the holy book coiled like smoke from the minarets. I fasted as well, watching the preparations for the iftar, the great pallets of bread on the heads of bicyclists, the basins of kosa and mahshi, the saucers of dates. For an hour, the streets bubbled with quarrels as citizens rushed homeward and then, as the sun dipped to the water, miraculously emptied, as if all the people had been poured out. There were several minutes of hush, the whole city suspended. I could see the diners sitting on mats outdoors, hands poised over dates, and then the sea swallowed the last droplet of sun, igniting the prayer calls, and hands went to mouths. The hawkers of tamarind juice, trundling tuns of sloshing mahogany liquid, began to clash their plates together. I ordered coffee.

That evening, when I finally returned to the thieves' church, there was a moment of silence after Abuna Makarios opened the door, then cacophony as the thieves rose from their chairs and crowded round. "We thought you'd drowned!" they cried. "We searched the hospitals and prisons and the morgue. You're so pale, so thin. Where have you been?"

"Might there be an arak on offer for someone returned from the dead?" I inquired, and they scrambled to fetch me a glass, but I realized, as I settled into an armchair and looked around at their eager faces, that I could not reveal my adventure, imagining a sudden dash for the lighthouse and the plundering of those silent graves.

"Did you leave Alexandria?" Karim asked.

"I did and I did not. I was farther than a world away, yet we probably passed within a stone's throw of each other at times. Would anyone care for a game of chess?"

Though they whined, I would not release my secret. That evening, Makarios tried to get me drunk and Koujour sulked. Nura tried to bribe me with a syringe and Karim took me aside and feigned distress at the termination of our friendship, but I smiled and nodded and would not talk. Only Zeinab said nothing. She watched me, but I could not read her eyes. She was fasting a whore's fast, thief's fast, all night, waiting to sip her karkadeh and eat a date at dawn.

We went out walking, in the gorgeous night, with the revelers. She gestured to the minarets. "Do you see the angels dancing? All night long."

I saw nothing but passing clouds and shadows, but didn't wish to tamper with her visions. "Where do they sleep in the day?" I asked.

"There are secret pockets in this city, where they read the burning books."

"What are you reading?"

"It's the month of the angel's book. You've read it, or pieces of it, or you've heard pieces of it, from minarets, on the radio, but I have swallowed it whole. To have swallowed the book and sung it out on a winter's night in Alexandria is to be burned alive. I weep as I sing, and it seems I'm not singing but being sung by the angel's song."

"And then you burn it?"

"No need."

As we walked through the festive streets, I pondered holy books, the books delivered to us by angels. In deserts. Why do angels love deserts so? Is it the spareness that attracts them, the horizons? The loneliness? In how many caves, on how many rocks are angels waiting, their voices full of poetry as the wind is full of light. All we have to do is encounter them, it would seem, and their voices are released into our ears. If our ears are unstopped.

And perhaps this is the crux: perhaps we're constantly banging into angels, on street corners, entering tramcars. We sever them slamming doors and topple them off windowsills and trample them underfoot in theaters. And they are shouting at us, seizing our shoulders, crouched on our shoulders and seizing our heads, bawling in our ears, but we're closed vessels, and from our pencils dribbles this spillage, fragments glittering in the jam. Perhaps only in deserts, or fasting, or underground, can we pop our corks and hear the angels whole.

It was wonderful, over the following days, to spend time in the sun, under the sky, to read on my balcony and watch the crowds on the corniche, but my thoughts were constantly settling, like rain, through the cracks in the cobblestones, seeping under foundations, to the vaults of books. And though I walked through the alleys of Alexandria, my mind traveled among books, for I found that, even away from the library, its patterns remained in my skull, and in my dreams I sought this book and that, imagined the marvelous rooms where they might be found, imagined the books that stood beside them, and thus could wander from book to book till I was far away, lost in subterranean groves.

But dreams are no substitute for a book in the hand. I returned to the lighthouse, paid my obol, and entered the library through the back door. I woke a thousand books over the next few months, reading for days on end, sustained by coffee and cookies and the sandwiches I carried in with me, till my mind was so full of stories and characters I felt I was constantly dreaming. Ah, the wonders of the Library of Alexandria. There are, in the world, sights to make you draw breath, clutch your forehead: Kilimanjaro from the Serengeti, the pyramids at Karima, Cape Town, Santorini Island. There are strange beasts on this planet. Have you seen the turaco's flight? Have you heard the chameleon's song? Have you seen the pygmies dancing or listened to a didgeridoo? These things are marvelous, but are not equal to a single room, a single book, in the Library of Alexandria. The things in the world are bound by the laws of nature—by gravity, three dimensions, the speed of light—but in a novel nature explodes; you somersault through the ether, glimpsing rabbits with pocket watches, hobbits and marsh-wiggles, resurrections, talking fish, lonely minotaurs.

But the pleasures of the library were not only to be found in the books. Half my time there was spent stalking the youngest librarian. I spied on her for entire nights, watched her read for hours on end. I admonished myself, telling myself I should be reading, I should use this precious season to inhale more books, but could not pull away from her, the reading girl, from her sighs, the rustle of her fingertips on pages.

As I strolled along the corniche muttering one evening, newly risen from the earth, Koujour blocked my path. I stared at him. He seized my arm and led me across the road to the Cecil. We entered through the revolving doors, into the odors of pipe smoke and wood polish, walked past dusty potted palms and huge gilt-framed mirrors, and took the paternoster to the roof. Koujour tipped the lift attendant and they exchanged a few words in Nyima Nuban. The rooftop garden was deserted save for a couple leaning together in a corner. We ordered gin and tonics and sat in the wicker chairs, smoking and watching the swallows over the water.

Koujour can paint like Lucifer himself, but he can't talk. Talking with him is like talking with a foreigner who speaks a language related to yours, but not mutually intelligible. He brushes the air with his hands as he speaks, so after our conversations I wish I could slice out a square of sky, hang it on the wall.

"I saw you walking." The smoke of his cigarette drew spirals, halos. He bent out over the sea, so I had to lean forward to hear him. "You were walking, not here. Your eyes. You saw."

"I don't know if I can talk about it, Koujour."

"Something beautiful. A girl? A painting?"

"Have you ever wished you could step into a painting? Live in it?"

"I walk in paintings, sleep in paintings."

"Imagine you'd dreamt about a painting, all your life. Then you found it. What would you do?"

"Steal."

"Why do you steal, Koujour? Why don't you make your own paintings?"

"I make my own paintings."

"Of course, but—"

He made a bowl of his palms. "Here are colors. I eat them. There's nothing new."

"But surely—"

"No. They think it's new, but no!"

"All right."

"Take me to your beautiful."

"I can't."

"Tell me sometime."

"Maybe sometime, Koujour."

"You want advice? I give advice. Nuban advice. Listen. You see the beautiful, you take it. Now. Don't wait. Take. With your hands." He was grappling with the air, ash spilling into his drink.

"Thank you, Koujour. How's Hala? How are the girls?"

"Ah, the girls. One says this, the other says this. You know."

"They're fighting?"

"No. They have their world. With Hala they fight. Girls like to kill their mothers."

"And your painting?"

"The painting." He snorted, made small circles with lifted palms.

"Not going well?"

"Like the Nile at Khartoum. You know the Nile?"

"Yes. Well . . ."

"After the rains, the Nile comes, up, up. Houses fall, everything underwater. Fish in the bed. Crocodiles in the kitchen. But when it goes down, you plant seeds. Now the Nile is up. In my painting. You understand?"

"Sure. More gin?"

"Always more gin."

I could see the fishing boats like shavings off crayons in the western curl of the bay, and the long wharf. Sunfloes broke and reformed on the sea as clouds buffed the sky, but my thoughts took the paternoster to the ground floor, and lower, beneath the cellars and foundations to where books slumbered and shaven-headed librarians wandered silently through caverns, feather dusters in their hands.

Occasionally a woman has snagged in my mind like a burr. Obsession does not make us monogamous, despite the fairy tales. Rather, it turns the world into a woman. You fall in love with palm trees, rain, your mother. There is a treatment for this disease. Come.

Two a.m. I entered the hot parlors of the Tempest: fumes, geysers of colored light. I was deaf the instant I stepped through the doors, but the beats trampled my bones, jangled my neurons, so there was no need of eardrums. The bartender lip-read my order and slid an arak through the slick on the zinc and I sat in a corner, watching the dancers boiling. Already the girls were swarming. They emerged from the murk like sharks. One brushed my leg, disappeared, returned to sit on the arm of my chair. She put her tongue in my ear, warm slug. On the dance floor she wiped her belly on my cock. She was sixteen, all in tinsel and cotton, coarse hair falling over her face. She couldn't keep her balance on her platform shoes; I had to hold her up by the ass. The music slowed and she slumped against me, nipples fingering my chest. Lights circled on the floor like small suns in a palm grove. I felt a tickle at my cheekbone. She might have been whispering. For a while we meandered around the floor, which was tilting and splintering, then ordered a tableful of alcohol and cigarettes. The girl smoked and drank like an urchin eating sausages, gulping and spluttering. When she was drunk enough, I dragged her out and into an alley, shoved her against a doorway. Her tits were soft. She smelled like charred roses, tasted of yeast and ashes. She might have said something. She pulled up her little skirt and there was her bony cunt for me to fuck, so I did. It felt good. Then I placed the book in her hand—this was Alexandria, city of book whores.

Now, as if a storm had passed, my mind was suddenly clear. I could see each cobblestone I trod, the litter in the gutter. The stars had ceased their quavering. I walked down to the corniche and sat a while watching the sea, which I could not hear, my eardrums ripped out. The sea was big and full of lights.

I went to bed, but it was a long time before I slept, the music still whacking away in my head. And I thought I'd succeeded, I thought I'd shaken that burr loose, my head would be clear again, I could drink my macchiato and read my novel, but I woke in the afternoon from dreams of a shaven head bent over a book, of slim brown fingers turning pages, and knew it was all in vain.

I read the books she read. After she set them on a shelf, her bookmark—a palm leaf from the library grounds—still within the pages, I took them down, read to where she'd stopped. There is no keener path to someone's heart. Following her through the pages, I felt I was stalking a wild beast, its spoor these inky footsteps I deciphered, in a dozen scripts. And as I stalked her, I learned that she was also stalker, huntress, seeking what all readers seek: the beautiful, the annihilating, book. Poetry and story are the unruly siblings of literature, constantly squabbling and separating. They live in different cities, will hardly deign to speak at family reunions. In the book we seek, they have broken all laws and moved in together, flagrantly incestuous, but that book does not exist. We can sense it, though, long for it, the book so beautiful it will survive even death, even fire.

She jotted notes in the margins, a dialogue with the texts, with the authors, with other readers, which sometimes spun into soliloquy. I studied her handwriting, trying to decipher her spirit from the curl of the c, the delicate e, the tail of the Q. Her prose, even in these marginalia, was careful, questing; many words struck out, thoughts stashed into each other like nesting dolls. I found myself most enamored of the small drawings tucked into corners; letters doodled into figures, the G a reading girl, the B pregnant, the S in prayer. Drawings like dreams, the effluvia of our obsessions. I wanted to kiss them but was afraid of smearing the ink. I left giddy with desire.

I could not read. Back at the hotel I sat on the balcony clutching my demitasse or wineglass, peering at pages, but they lay beneath the sea. For an hour, I'd rub paper between my fingers, while my eyes foundered in the bay. I could sometimes make out a stanza before the lines swam, and again I'd remember her face and the rhymes would clang between my ears.

I lost at chess and badminton.

"He's drinking too much," said Zeinab.

"Not enough," said Karim.

Even the head waiter at the Elite noticed my distraction and tipped into my wineglass a dollop of a tonic concocted of desiccated lion penis and curdled buffalo semen, which he claimed would invigorate my manhood. It turned the wine blue and salty but had no effect on my mood.

One midnight, as I exited the Elite, having polished off a late dinner of grilled swordfish, red rice with almonds and raisins, half a carafe of Omar Khayyam, and a couple *Gothic Tales*, I heard above the French pop from the open doors behind me, above the clatter of a late tram and squabbling lovers at Pastroudis, strains of something richer, denser. I strolled down Sharia Fuad to investigate, aware that I was moving along the

most ancient road of this ancient city, once the Canopus Way
that led from gate to gate of the old city, and which has since
borne a hundred names. I muttered those names as I walked,
treading them underfoot.

The music faded, then resurfaced as a single clarinet, faint
as an early star. The note wavered, deepened, and was joined
by a tenor crying the name of a girl: *"Aida!"* The music seemed
to shift as I walked, coming now from the south, now the east,
but finally settled north of the sidewalk, and I looked through
an archway into the stone courtyard of the opera house,
guarded by the immense bronze figure of the seated poet. Now
a soprano soared like a spark into the space:

> *"La . . . foresto virgini.*
> *Di fiori profumate,*
> *In estasi beate*
> *La terra scorderem."*

A half moon brushed the seated statue with blue, ink
soaking the bronze folds of turban and galabiyya, soaking the
bronze books beneath his chair. I longed to peel apart those
metal leaves. Though the courtyard was deserted, I stayed in
the shadows as I moved around its edge. The ticket collector
napped in his booth beneath a painted poster of a lissome
Nubian. On the roof of the theater was a certain window, long
known to thieves, beside which we kept a wicker chair and an
antique pair of gold opera glasses, and from which one
commanded an immaculate view of the stage. Many an
evening I'd brought a bottle of Chianti to this star-ceilinged
private box and reclined, feet up, immersed in *Orfeo* or *La
Bohème*, lassoing stars with my smoke rings, swigging wine

straight from the bottle.

But this night, as I sidled through the courtyard, I saw two figures dancing on the roof to the throbbing of the violins. Approaching, I recognized Karim and Amir, teetering with drawn knives among flagpoles and parapets. From their writhing silhouettes it appeared Karim would surely shred Amir into brown and lavender confetti at any moment, but the pickpocket, though flimsy as one of Karim's djinns, sucked himself away from the blade. Radamès and Aida bantered as I scaled the wall and sat between the masks of terror and tragedy, watching the dancers.

> *"Il ciel dei nostri amori*
> *Come scordar potrem?"*
> *"Sotto il mio ciel, più libero*
> *L'amor ne fia concesso;*
> *Ivi nel tempio istesso*
> *Gli stessi Numi avrem."*

After Aida's lovely, hopeless offering, I lit a cigarette. The flame snapped the skirmishers out of their deadly pas de deux and they stood apart, panting.

"And what's the fuss about, pray?" I asked. "Don't let me stop you. Do go on. I'm just curious what started it."

"Ah, fuck it," said Karim. He sliced the sweat off his brow with his blade, then wiped the knife on his trousers, leaving a dark triangle on the blue. He sat beside me, drove the knife shivering into a flagpole, pulled out cigarettes, and shook up three. I lit them.

"What's the quarrel?" I asked.

Karim shrugged. "The usual."

"Zeinab?"

"What do you think Zeinab wants, Balthazar?" Amir asked.

"Good question. Have you checked her pockets?"

"Nothing but a knife. I sliced my fingers to the bone."

"What do you think, Karim?"

"She doesn't exist. Not in this world."

"So how are you going to resolve this?"

Karim yanked his knife out of the flagpole and aimed it at Amir. "The easy way," he said.

"You'll never catch me," Amir told him, but he sounded more melancholy than usual.

I sat on the chair, and with my bodkin pried the cork from the stashed wine bottle. Amir and Karim sat on either armrest and we passed the bottle back and forth.

Now soprano and tenor joined:

> *"Vieni meco, insiem fuggiamo*
> *Questa terra di dolore.*
> *Vieni meco t'amo, t'amo!*
> *A noi duce fia l'amor."*

Through the window, like peering through a rip in reality, we watched the spotlit lovers clasp and part.

85

V

The Youngest Librarian

HOW DO YOU approach a reader? A noise or a nudge is too much, will shove her too abruptly out of the world she inhabits. No, you must seek a gentler entrance.

I began switching her bookmarks. One day I swiped the palm leaf and replaced it with a pressed rose. Then I hid, heart like timpani, while she entered and took the book from the shelf and poured a glass of wine and parted the pages. She paused a few seconds, wineglass a hand span from her lips, when she saw the rose. Setting down the glass, she lifted the stem, twirled it slowly. Her gaze bounced around the room. Then she shrugged, tapped the brittle petals against her lips, and began to read.

Next day, I left a feather from a hoopoe's crest, and this time she laughed aloud, then frowned and flipped through the pages searching for other clues. As she read that evening, every so often she'd stop and lift the feather and draw it across her cheek, then replace it within the pages.

Over the next week I left the following bookmarks: stripe of seaweed, peacock wishbone, sand dollar, moth wing, lemon peel, molted asp skin. Now she knew the game and would enter the room eagerly, rush to the bookshelf to discover her present, which she'd examine for a while before turning to the book. She began to read more slowly as she entered the final chapters, trying to prolong this enchanted story that brought her gifts.

On the day I knew she'd finish the book I returned the palm leaf, but I'd pricked a message into it. She smiled when she saw the leaf, nodded a bit sadly, then bent to it, held it to the light, and read my query. She leaned her head back against the cushion and looked up at the ceiling. "What do I desire?" she whispered. "Strawberry jam? Sea breeze? Kiss?" She smiled, then sat up and finished the book. But when she lifted the candle from its bracket and left the room she took the leaf with her.

The next evening, when she returned to her room, she found a jar of strawberry jam on her pillow. I spied on her through the keyhole as she startled. Questions struggled on her lips. She took up the jar and held it on her lap. Then she twisted off the lid and lifted out a sticky strawberry and placed it on her tongue.

I saw her hunted stare the next day as she moved through the library. Often she glanced quickly over her shoulder. But a thief walks in the second world, among djinns and angels, watching but invisible, and she saw only her shadow.

She moved through the library that afternoon, chamber to chamber, plucking books. No hesitation: she knew exactly what she wanted. When she'd gathered three, she returned to the chamber where I'd first encountered her and on a shelf built a little house of books, posts and lintel, a house or a shrine. In the alcove they made she placed a pomegranate. These were her offerings. Three books and a blood-red fruit.

Seated on her sofa, drinking her wine, I read the books, ransacked the pomegranate's ruby honeycomb, recklessly swallowing the seeds, and knew I had eaten her heart. Harboring the books and seeds in my belly, I carried them into the upper world. It was utterly changed. Those three books had bent the bay backward and dyed the sun a smoky mauve. The soles of my thief's shoes banged on the tin cobbles. Lifting a fingernail, I tapped the china sky. I twirled on palace gables, cartwheeled over the waves, and might have blown off among the stars like an escaped balloon had Nura not plucked at my arm as I skipped along the corniche wall. "Come," she said.

We took the tram to the docks at Anfushi and walked down to the waterfront. On a strip of grimy beach, between stacked crates of figs and sacks of cotton and coffee beans, under the spider-leg architecture of cranes, a man scooped mussels from boiling water with a slotted spoon. We sat on an upturned crate, side by side, by the water's edge, eating mussels and fried potatoes off newspaper, squeezing halved limes over the shells. A colorful flotsam of beer bottles and cigarette butts, syringes and mango seeds and stray buoys jostled in the surf. Mutilated cats squabbled over fish heads. While I lit a cigarette, Nura ladled a little heap of icing sugar into a corroded spoon and fried it till it sizzled brown and sticky. She handed me a scarf to knot around her skinny bicep, then sucked the caramel into a syringe and I watched as she searched for a vein in her devastated arm. A tiny poppy bloomed in the glass, withering as she pressed the plunger. Replacing the paraphernalia in her handbag, she cocked her sparrow head at me, her glossy eyes. "I didn't know you got high, librarian. What are you on?"

I held up the cigarette.

"Come on," she smiled. "I watched you along the corniche. You were flying. What's your poison?"

"You want to know my drug, Nura?" I reached into my pocket and pulled out a paperback. "Mainline this."

She touched the cover shyly. "You're so smart, Balthazar. Why do you hang out with us?"

"Books are a drug, no nobler than heroin or opium. They're the addiction I feed with my thievery."

"They don't ruin your veins."

"They can ruin your heart. And a bad trip can give you hallucinations for the rest of your life. As can a good trip. The great libraries of the world are filled with people ruined or beatified by books. They walk through the hallways twitching, a thousand voices in their ears. They have no idea whether you're real or a character from a printed page."

"But you're always reading, Balthazar. Why were you flying today?"

"That's the difference between heroin and literature." I touched the skin of her inner arm, the overlapping circles of fading bruises—plum, peach, lemon, loquat. "The drugs you take are lonely voyages. I can share your needle but I can't share your trip. Each reading is separate, to be sure, but I can come much closer to another person's experience. Yesterday I shared someone else's drug."

"Whose?"

"I don't know her name. She shaves her head, she wears glasses."

"Oh, I think I've seen her. On a tram, late at night."

"Perhaps."

Nura laid her head on my shoulder. "I wish I could take your drugs, Balthazar, but books are hard. Needles are easy."

I put my arm around her and we sat there like strung-out lovers, watching the seethe of refuse in the foam. Along the horizon, ships lay like a string of festival lights. One must have come in, because we heard the dockers bellowing beyond the crates to our right.

"Have you ever tried to quit?" I asked.

"A couple of times. But I love it too much. The drug and the life. I know I take a little death with the sweetness each time. And I'm afraid, of course, but I tell myself death's just another vision, the last vision. You look at my arms, and I can see the disgust in your lips, but"—she dabbled her fingers on the scars like a concertina player, glancing down at them fondly, ruefully—"these wounds have given me so much joy. What about you? Have you ever quit?"

"Never tried. Once in the Sahara a camel ate my book, and I learned what I become without my fix: a raving madman. I love it too much. The drug and the life."

"We don't see you as much as we used to."

"No."

"Where do you go?"

"Down."

She nodded. "You take care, Balthazar, okay?"

I kissed her cheekbone, smoothed her hair back from her temple.

"Sweetheart," I said.

I returned to my rooms that evening, to the shelf within my wardrobe, and removed a single book. Carrying this book, I walked to the lighthouse.

Once again Zeinab was waiting for me, this time at the entrance to the lighthouse. I didn't see her until I was within the archway, then heard the gnash of bells like crushed foil.

"Have you thought at all about what you're doing?" she said. "What kind of perverted book thief have you become?"

"It will be safe underground."

"Or so you think."

"Yes. So I think."

But I laughed as well as I placed the book upon a shelf in the room the youngest librarian frequented. Zeinab was right—this was absurd. Alone of the world's book thieves, I had succeeded in penetrating the Library of Alexandria, but now, inside this bibliophile's paradise, I was not stripping it of its treasures but was instead bestowing upon it one of my most treasured possessions.

I lay in wait on an upper shelf, reading, nibbling cheese, sipping from a flask of cocoa. When I heard her sandals in a distant cavern I snuffed my candle. She poured her ritual glass of wine, then reached for her book. But I had covered it with my own. She took down the new book slowly, turning it in her hands, brushing her fingers across the leather binding, the gold leaf. Still standing by the bookshelf, she opened to the first page and I saw her lose herself, instantly, within the opening paragraph. When she looked up she was thirty pages deep. She shook her head slightly, bent it again. Forgetting her glass of wine, still immersed in the book, she moved to the sofa and sat down, gingerly, so as not to jostle her eyes from the page, lay back, and continued reading. This was a book I knew more intimately than my own body. I knew the placement of every word on every page. I knew the stains, nicks, tears, folds, and their histories. I had read it one hundred and eleven times, and each reading was separate and fresh in my mind. So I could follow her reading, knew from the slight shifting of her loins or quickening of her breath or plucking of her thumbnail at the leather which part she'd come to. I had never before watched someone read an entire book. It was like watching someone live a life in three hours.

When she'd finished she lay back, staring at the ceiling. "Oh my God," she said. She stood up. She turned back to the book and placed her palm upon it as if bestowing a benediction or receiving its mana, then went to the bookshelf where her wineglass stood and drained its contents in a single gulp. She paced around the chamber muttering, touching books and walls, seeing nothing, like someone in a trance.

She lay on the sofa, placed the book on her breasts, and passed out. I could hear her soft breathing. Slipping the book from her fingers, I blew out her candle and left the library.

For three days I sat in my rooms drinking coffee and wine. I sent Abdallah for sandwiches. I tried to read, to paint, but the words made no sense, the colors would not adhere to the paper. The bustle in the midan seemed the scurrying of ants. I woke myself, talking in my sleep. Three days were all I could manage. Midnight of the third day I walked to the lighthouse.

When I next saw the youngest librarian, in a cavern so colossal her candlelight could not finger the farthest shelves, she'd gone mad. She moved around the perimeter of the chamber, dragging her hand across bindings, stammering, howling. "Incubus!" she cried. "Demon lover! Why have you forsaken me? I can't read, I can't sleep. Send me another bookmark, send me another book."

Her fingers scraped at the books, ripped some from their places, but one glance and she cast them aside, leaving a trail of broken-winged creatures on the carpets like downed grouse. I was her ghostly gundog, fetching the discarded volumes after she'd exited the chamber, smoothing the pages, replacing them on the shelves.

All that day I followed her, deep into the library, through rooms I'd not yet encountered, through rooms I'd not imagined, had not been able to imagine, through rooms she was able to enter, perhaps, only because of her madness. The room of false gospels written by fallen archangels; the room of nightmares of being devoured by one's own children; the room of books written by quadriplegics who dipped their tongues in ink. Rooms describing constellations in alternate universes. Rooms of books written by shamans who inhabited the bodies of lions. A room that contained a single book, made of the cured skins of a hundred Nuer virgins. Its leaves were black and smooth as the rinds of aubergines, its print the color of moonlight.

We met in a room of books written in blood, love lyrics written with pricked fingers on scraps of newsprint or ripped bedsheets, by those who had no other materials at hand, written in dungeons or tower-top cells, written by the condemned, by those who faced the executioner's scimitar at daybreak. There were no bowls of apricots in this room, no sofas, no carpets, only the terrible books and a stone floor.

She knelt, face in her hands, weeping.

I stood in the doorway. "I want to read you," I said.

She uncurled so slowly. Her lips quivered. Her eyes traveled up my body, met my eyes. "Tell me you're not real," she said.

"I'm not real. I'm a ghost in the Library of Alexandria. You rubbed your candle and called me up."

"You're the devil. I've conjured a djinn."

"Certainly." I knelt before her on the stone. She lifted a finger toward me. I bit it and she snatched it back, staring at the swelling bead beside her nail. Her blood was blue.

"What's your name?" she whispered.

"Call me Balthazar. And you are?"

In blue blood she wrote her name on the stone.

"Shireen," I read. "I've been stalking you for weeks."

"Who are you?"

"I'm a thief, a book thief: Balthazar the book thief."

"I'll have to kill you."

"Kill me or kiss me: do what you like with me, Shireen, I'm in your hands."

"It's my duty." She raised her right hand and drew a finger along its edge, pinkie to wrist, as if testing a blade. Slowly she brought her hand down in an arc, till it rested against my neck. "Just there," she said. We were shaking like teenage lovers. She lifted her hand. "Will you defend yourself?"

I shook my head.

"Why not?"

"I want your touch. I've desired that touch since I first saw you."

"You've been spying on me."

"I saw you reading in your armchair, drinking your glass of wine. When you went back to your room I sat where you sat, read to your palm leaf. I drank wine from your glass."

"But why?" The candlelight wavered on her hand. I could feel, like a fresh burn, the stripe where her palm had rested against my neck.

"When I first entered the library, I thought I'd pluck the tastiest books, spirit them away, package them, post them around the globe. But once inside, all I wanted to do was read and eat cookies. Oh, the first book I read here, after I crossed the dark river, after I lost my way and abandoned hope . . . it was like those dreams of reading, when the pages are turning in darkness and you know the lines are created as you read, and burn away as your eyes move on. I ate cookies and almonds and apricots and drank cocoa and read that book, and then I knew I didn't want to steal, I wanted to belong. I wanted to know who had placed the books just so and who had baked the delicious cookies and who had chosen the blue of the bowls to complement so perfectly the color of apricots. So I came seeking the librarians. I've seen your guilty expressions as you steal time to read."

Her hand had dropped as I spoke, and now rested in her lap. "Why me?" she asked. "There are hundreds of us."

"You fall deeper into a book. The others flip through the pages, their eyes are always floating up, but you drown."

"They call me the drowning girl. Sometimes they rescue me. They call it rescuing. But why am I telling you this? You're distracting me."

"Yes. Apologies. You were going to kill me."

She raised her hand. "Give me one reason I shouldn't."

"Kill me, Shireen. I'm a hunted criminal in a hundred countries. I've violated your space. I've spied on you. I've tampered with your bookmarks. You'd be doing the world a favor if you crushed my spine with your pretty fingers. But before you do so, allow me to present you with a gift."

"A book?"

"What else?" From my jacket pocket I pulled the book she'd read in a single sitting.

She put her hand to her mouth. "I was afraid it was a dream."

"It's yours."

She grabbed it, opened to the first page, plunged in, quick dip, then shivered like a kitten. "It's so delicious. I searched and searched for this book. There were no references to it. I had to tell them I'd dreamed about it. Then I almost convinced myself I had. Where did you find it?"

"I thought you were going to kill me."

"That can wait."

"Listen, then." We had been kneeling, but now I sat back and leaned against a shelf. "I've peeled through a billion pages on seven continents. I've examined by candlelight the shelves of emperors and gondoliers, butchers and barbers, fortunetellers and chimney sweeps. I've entered castles and caravans, hovels and houseboats, searching for books. And there are books, believe me. There is no shortage of books, beautiful books, costly books, on this planet. But occasionally, in my life of crime, I've come across a volume that annihilates me. You know the sensation. You lift the cover, naive, and suddenly tumble over the precipice. You look up and have no idea where you are, who you are. It's long past dawn, on a new planet. This has happened perhaps a dozen times in my life. Sometimes years have gone by without another encounter, and I'll think I've lost my touch. But then I'll be browsing through a shelf, business as usual, and I'll tip out a volume, and suddenly, the plummet, my heart in my throat, I'm drowning. Generally, if I discover a lovely book I pass it on. But these books, the books that combine in perfect quantity design and story and song, I keep. The book you read was one of those, a book from my immaculate bookshelf. As you found out."

"Do you let others read them?"

"You were the second."

"Who was the first?"

"She was a mistake."

"Who was she?"

"That's a secret."

"So why me?"

"You like to read. Also, I read the books you chose for me."

"Oh yes." She clasped her hands. "Did you love them?"

I told her how they had changed the city above our heads. "My friends thought I'd taken drugs. And of course I had. The most potent, deadly drugs."

"I read them over and over. The others can't understand. They laugh at me, they say I'm surrounded by a billion books, that I should read each book once and move on. They think I must be slow-witted, that I don't understand what I read unless I reread. They think I'm sick. They can't understand that I'm not reading the book, I'm trying to wear it. I'm trying to eat it."

"We have the same disease. First readings are like first kisses—you can't remember the taste, the shape of the other's lips, you have only a heady sensation of stained glass shattering."

"I've never been kissed."

"No. No, of course not."

Beat of silence.

"You can't be real," she said. "There's no way into the library. We patrol the gates night and day."

"I came in the back door."

"There is no back door."

"Then I must be a demon."

"Demon or not, you're the first man I've spoken to."

"I beg your pardon. What about your father? How old were you when you came here?"

"I'm special. The rest of the librarians grew up in ordinary houses outside the library. In the world. They came here to escape forced marriages or fathers who beat them, or because they were orphaned, or just because they wanted more time to read. But eighteen years ago, in a room of books about the third element, which is always a little warmer than most, one of the librarians heard a little cry. There I was, on an upper shelf, vernixed with paper dust, my cord a blue bookmark, tethering me to a book about the nature of fire. She cut my cord with her paperknife, swaddled me in pages, and carried me into the reading room. All the librarians suckled me. Yes, strange, isn't it? But this is a strange story. This is what they told me: hearing me cry, holding me, they felt the ache in their breasts and the milk leaked onto their robes. I was their communal child.

"As soon as I could sit I began to talk. And as soon as I could talk I could read, a gift of my miraculous birth. The librarians crowded round to hear me read, no faltering, the words floating out in my small voice. Some wanted to keep me caged, to confine me to a single room or to the librarians' chambers, to chaperone my reading. Certain librarians even argued that I should be put to death. Too dangerous, they said, to have a book at liberty, unshelved, uncataloged. But they were silenced. I'm the true daughter of this library, and this is my rightful domain."

"But you're also human."

"My nature—human or book—is the subject of endless argument among the librarians."

"What do you think?"

"I don't know. I can hear my heart flutter like riffled pages sometimes. I feel more at home among books than among the other girls. My blood is blue, you've seen that, blue as ink. And look at my eyes." I leaned forward and realized her pupils were not round but rectangular, the shape of pages, and within them, deep down, so distant I could not read them, words were written in burning letters. When she blinked pages turned.

"I cannot read the letters of fire," my voice quavered. "What do they say?"

"I can't read them either. They're too far away. Written on my dreams. But anyway, you believe me now. I've never spoken with a man. I hear men's voices calling to me when I patrol the fence, and in books of course. But it's strange to be speaking with you like this. I can't shake the feeling you're a dream. What would you do if I let you go?"

"What would I do if you killed me is the more pressing question. Then I'd really be a ghost. I'd haunt every page you turned. Would you rather have a demon lover you can talk to or one who's invisible?"

"But if I let you go would you promise not to enter the library again?"

I laughed. "Think about it. Having once tasted the fruit, could you relinquish it?"

"I've taken vows. We all take vows, to hold books more precious than our own bodies, to protect them with our lives, to kill any intruder. For centuries every librarian has studied and practiced the secret martial arts, in preparation for this moment. And now you're kneeling in front of me, and you won't even defend yourself, and I can't do it, I can't bring my hand down on your neck. Even though I've lived this moment over and over, imagined myself the heroine, the dragon-slayer, the giant-killer. I've imagined running into the reading room with my hands soaked in blood and my robe soaked in blood, shouting 'I've done it, I've killed him, I've killed the book thief!'"

"So do it."

"I can't."

"Why not?"

"I'm too greedy."

"For what?"

She was silent.

"Ah. What do I have to do to stay alive?"

"Keep me turning the pages."

"You want a story?" I said. "Listen." Now at last she sat back, watching me, the book clasped to her heart. "Call me Balthazar. Call me silverfish, sweet dreams, the end of the rainbow. Call me dust devil, night owl, will-o-the-wisp. Call me the man in the moon. But call me Balthazar, and place a book in my hands. And what book is that, the book I reach for ..."

I spun my story till dawn, the story you have nibbled at, the story you're partaking of. I snipped it off beneath a raised dagger, in some medieval abbey. Then I leaned back, looked at the ceiling. "I believe it's time to kill me. Soon the librarians will gather in the reading room to practice their pretty ju jitsu. Someone needs to inform them their exertions are not in vain."

"But we can't leave you standing at knifepoint forever."

"I'm afraid we'll have to."

"You ... you scoundrel!"

"I warned you."

"All right. I see you've left me no choice."

"You have a choice."

"Yes. Kill you now and go mad, or kill you when I've heard the end of the story. Meet me tomorrow night in ... meet me in the room of chameleons."

I returned the next day, bearing my candle, uncertain whether I'd encounter the edge of a hand or an open page, a shriek or a whisper. But the room of chameleons was empty, and seemed empty of books as well. The shelves at first glance were bare, dusty. Then, sniffing, I knew some magic was at work here. I knew pages dwelt in this room, and moved to the shelves, watching at each step for transformation. "Aftah," I muttered, "Aftah, ya simsim," but not until my hand was within an inch of the shelves did I see the glimmer of edges and bindings. My fingertips brushed invisible leather. Pulling the book from the shelf, I could feel its weight, and watched it shift, as if the air itself bent and bulked into the shape of a book, the golden rectangle that lies at the heart of the universe and is, surely, the shape of the soul of God. In my hands it became my hands. Opening it, I read my palm, life line and heart line in elegant Garamond, shifting and gathering, skewing as I turned a page. And suddenly, as though I peered not into pages or my palm but into a looking glass, I saw my story branching ahead of me, each twig terminating in a death. I followed, in a moment, a thousand twisting branches, and at the end of each my body lay, crushed spectacles and a book beside it.

I heard a whispered word, but before I gathered its meaning, the bookmark whipped out like a silk tongue, licked the syllables from the air, and tucked them into the spine. What word? And who had released it into the room? Peering into the corners, I finally spied her near the ceiling, seated on the topmost shelf, hugging her knees to her chest. Her form was uncertain, though whether this was due to the candlelight or the nature of the room I could not be sure. I climbed the shelves and sat across from her, tucked between stone ceiling and polished teak. Like breathing bookends we sat in the room of invisible, changing books, a shelf-load of lies between us. I could see the books like a thickness of glass or water, and her skin itself was slightly transparent in this environment.

"If you killed me in this room, would the books snap me up?" I asked. "Or would I become one of them, one of the invisible books? What would happen to my tales?"

"I've betrayed them, I'm betraying them." Her voice was sodden. She placed her face in her transparent hands, but I could see the tears trickling along her finger bones.

I leaned forward. "Who are you betraying?"

"It will end in disaster, I know. Fraternizing with demons is always a recipe for catastrophe. I've read the books. The raving women, shredding their clothes, ripping their faces, alone in a deserted valley or an empty room. Is that what you want me to become?"

"Why this room? Why did you choose this room?"

"I thought maybe you wouldn't see me. I thought you'd find it empty and leave."

"What do you read here?" I asked.

"Something different every time. Chiromancy of bones and blood. I come here to learn about myself, to try to read my future, which is always shifting, so the story changes moment by moment. I saw you once, Balthazar, long before you arrived, in an engraving under tissue paper. You were standing on a rooftop, a book in your hands. There was a shadowed figure beside you. In the next picture, the book was a leaf or a dagger, something bright, and the figure was your shadow. Did you see that image in your chameleon book? What did you read when you came into this room?"

"Such a strange poem . . ."

She was my Shahryar. She became, as I spoke, more transparent, as though my breath, the tale borne on my breaths, was blowing the atoms out of her body one by one. And I realized that this transparence was her nature, and that it was precisely this evaporation, this ability to lose herself, that had first drawn me to her. The drowning girl, the vanishing girl. I spoke more softly, trying to prolong her disappearance. She became more beautiful, as blown glass is beautiful because of its fragility. As a soap bubble or a sphere of gossamer is beautiful. All night long, I spun my lies, and snipped them off in mid-leap, between rooftops, leaving myself framed against stars like a tightrope walker teetering on a thread of blue ink.

"More," she said.

"No."

She raised her hand. "In your chameleon book, did you see your death?"

"I saw a thousand deaths. Deaths by paper cut, paperknife, falling bookshelves, eyestrain, but none in this room, I'm afraid. What about you? What have you seen?"

"Such beautiful things, Balthazar. You can't know."

"But this is the room of lies."

"Not all are lies."

"No. Not all." She was shivering, her transparent skin blue-tinged, almost opalescent. "Come. If you spend any more time here you'll vanish completely." I climbed down and held out my hand, which, I noticed, shimmered slightly. I could see, faintly, the lines of shelves and the shapes of bindings beneath my skin. "I'm disintegrating as well," I said. My voice seemed strangely flat, echoless.

Slowly, she let herself down from her perch, feet of blue glass descending teak rungs. Her hand in mine like a clasp of cool breath. She turned to me, eyes bright as goldstone. Hand in hand, we left that room, and as we crossed the threshold I felt my strength begin to return, as though my selves, my unleaved signatures, had begun to fold into a single volume once more. But we wandered through many chambers before her grip solidified. Only then did she seem to notice we were touching, and, horrified, shook her fingers free.

The next night she was not at our rendezvous. I waited a while in the cavern of asemic books, then strolled through the library, aimlessly, plucking volumes here and there. And suddenly, as I passed through an archway, cinnamon filled my nostrils, and she was before me. I could read the fury in her brow, the determination in her lips, as she brought her arm toward my neck. Motionless, I waited for her blow while the candle flame tumbled. But only the wind of her strikes reached my skin. Beneath the archway I stood before her, holding a candle in both hands, while she performed her violent ballet, snapping an ankle toward my torso, flicking stiffened fingers a hair's breadth from my neck. But, though her face betrayed the strain, she never touched me. One of her movements snuffed the candle. In the darkness I closed my eyes, not daring to stir, while the beating of her limbs continued about my body like a lover's breaths or a tempest of moth wings. Then it ceased and I heard her subside, panting. I sat across from her in the darkness, leaning against the archway.

"I can't do it," she whispered. "I can't do it."

I relit the candle. "Long ago," I said, "you wouldn't have had to kill me. The library was open to readers. The central room, where you do your deadly dancing, was filled with silent readers, and the librarians fetched the books for them. What changed? Why did the library shut itself off?"

"No one knows." She was still trying to catch her breath. "Too long ago. There are lots of theories, of course. Some say we'd become irritated by inanities written about certain books within our keeping, and wished to control all interpretations ourselves. Others say the city itself, overburdened by bespectacled visitors, ordered the library closed. Still others claim religious quarrels infiltrated the library: certain groups wanted certain books destroyed and the librarians, to protect their charges, sealed the library. One or all of these theories may be true, but I have my own theory: in the absence of male attention we became infatuated with our books and couldn't tolerate the touch of other hands, the glance of other eyes, on the skin we adored. And so we shut the doors, shut our lips, and retreated to the stone interior, to gloat, to fondle, to read."

"And there's no inclination to open the library again? Has no librarian tried to smuggle a book out?"

"We make our vows, to defend the books against any outsider." But her eyes strayed slightly, and I pressed her.

"But . . ."

"Well . . . I shouldn't be telling you all this. These are secrets."

"My entire existence is a secret."

She tapped her fingertips together, making a brown cage, then opened them. "All right." She paused. "This was before I was born. I don't know how long before. A girl came to the library who had been burned. No one knows why. So long ago her name has been forgotten. Somehow she made her way to the gates, and begged entrance. She didn't need to be shaved: her hair had been burned away. She always wore a veil, even alone in her room, because her face was gone. We harbor within our labyrinth girls who have been wounded. But this burned girl was different, as if the fire had not only scraped away her skin and scoured away her voice, but also scorched her blood. She had embers in her blood. Every conversation was a quarrel.

"She spent the first years reading. All of us love to read, that's why we're here, but she read as though books were oxygen, as though her life depended on them. She'd disappear into the library for weeks, reading her way through room after room, deep under the sea, out under the desert. She read through mealtimes, and only when sleep knocked her unconscious did she take a break, though often with a book on her face or clutched to her breast.

"Some of the damaged girls, arriving at the library, embrace the sanctuary—the protection of the walls, the power of our martial art. But the burned girl railed against the walls. She wanted the gates opened once more, and the readers let in. She said we were killing the books. By caging them we were killing them. And she wanted more than just allowing the readers in: she wanted the books released, free to leave the library—can you imagine?

"She opened the gates at one point—stole the keys and opened the gates—and began to call people to enter. After that she was locked in her room. For a month she was kept prisoner, but she bribed the librarian who was tending her with knowledge of a forgotten book, and escaped. They found her in the library grounds, passing books through the fence. She managed to release a dozen or so before she was subdued. We don't know what books the library lost, or exactly how many. A shelfload, perhaps more. I've often wondered what happened to those books, if they still exist in the world, if their provenance is known." Shireen looked at me, and a smile flickered across her lips. "Well, that's the story, at any rate."

"She was subdued?"

"We're not gentle with insubordinates. It's a cautionary tale, most likely."

"It's no tale."

"What do you mean?"

"I've met her. I've fucked her. I know her name."

"Liar!"

"Certainly. And storyteller. But this is no ordinary tale."

"She's been dead for years."

"Do you believe in ghosts?"

"Of course. I mean, I've never seen one, but they come into lots of books. Some of the girls say that I'm a ghost, and they want to exorcise me, send me back to my world. And perhaps I am. But how solid I feel. My blood may be blue, but it leaves a stain. But tell me about your ghost."

"Zeinab, the veiled book-burner, has chaperoned my sojourn in Alexandria. When I turned from the library grounds my first night in this city, she whispered to me in her scoured voice. The price of her blasphemous orgasm was one of the finest books in my collection, which she then burned. She's a book-burner, a book-whore. She moves across the city like a blue shadow, entering men's dreams, and they pay for her body. They pay with their books, though they know she will burn them. Through her I met my friends. Including you. She showed me the way into the library. She gave me the obol that allowed me to cross the dark river."

"Describe her."

"She's kohl, veil, bells: all exterior. I can't describe her face for you—it's hidden—but I can describe her knife. Her knife is one of the loveliest objects I've seen. It's perfectly weighted, the handle and guard and blade in balance. Perhaps it was decorated once, but incessant use has rubbed it as smooth as the skin of the inner thigh. The wood is perhaps ebony or rosewood, pouched and rippled into her grip, the blade thin as if snipped from tinfoil, sturdy as a healed bone. Once she pressed it through my wrist. We were sitting by the sea. This was following a thief's supper. Soon after dawn."

"You're in love, aren't you? You're in love with this, with a book . . . a book burner."

"In love? No, love is the wrong word. Unless you could say Cleopatra loved her asp or Imru al-Qais his poisoned robe. I'm seduced, horrified. I don't want to look any more, but I can't look away. Is it possible to fall in love with someone whose face is hidden? Could you fall in love with a book you hadn't read? If it was forbidden?"

"So the burned librarian is still awake." Her eyes darted, she gnawed at a hangnail. "How terrifying. And delicious." She shivered slightly, as if a silverfish tiptoed up her spine. "What would it be like to burn a book?" she whispered.

"Hush."

"There are girls who cut themselves. They can't stop. They say it hurts, and it feels so good. They say they feel the same revulsion we do, the blood is just as horrifying to them, but they can't stop. We hide the knives and razorblades, but they use paper, splinters, their teeth. I love cutting open fresh pages. And sometimes, slicing my way through a book, I feel I could just keep cutting, deeper. Imagine burning a book. To read it, then burn it. Imagine!"

"Don't."

"You've thought about it though, haven't you?"

"Let's talk about something else."

"Like what?"

"Anything. Apples. Lions. Roses."

"Roses. . . . What do they smell like? Do the different colors have different scents?"

She had been to Gormenghast and Xanadu, Byzantium and Macondo, could describe an ent and an ansible, but she'd never smelled a rose or heard the sea. Talking with her, I'd suddenly realize she was still less than an infant; she'd never emerged from her book-lined womb.

She made me describe the buttery, flaky texture of a croissant at the Trianon, the crackle as you bit into a corner, the soft warm core. I described the lights on the dance floors at the Tempest and the Sound and the Fury, like a galaxy gone haywire, and the flavor of the mingled smokes—apple tobacco, clove and menthol, opium, hashish. I mimicked the expressions of the icons in the Kanisa Prometheus. I evoked, with splayed, flickering fingers, the effect of sunlight on the water of the bay. I described nights after thievery, walking across the rooftops, sidestepping dead gulls and sleeping asps, dreaming poets and fallen kites.

"Oh, how I'd love to come!" she exclaimed.

"If you ever escape your paradise, I'll take you thieving some night."

"Is that a promise?"

"Yes."

We met the next night, and the next and the next, a different room every time. I populated the caverns with my devilish deeds and seedy characters, and as dawn approached broke the story off on a threshold or a rooftop, or at knifepoint, and sent the youngest librarian to sleepwalk to the reading room. I spun my story with fleece combed from all the books I'd read, carding it, braiding it into a flying carpet of many colors. But why am I describing it to you? Read on. You out there, up there, eavesdropper, fellow weaver.

We were utter strangers who shared a heart, Siamese twins separated at birth, and we were enemies. Every day she threatened to kill me, and every day I eked my life a little farther with an adroit metaphor, a catchy adjective.

"All right, I'm stronger now," she'd say, striding briskly into the chamber where I waited for her, reading, and she'd walk up to me, hand lifted, teeth clenched, while my tongue scrambled for a sentence to deflect her blow. "Did I tell you about the time I stole from the dead?" I might say. Or, "Once, as I was fondling the Pharaoh's favorite wife . . ." and her resolve would founder like a wave subsiding on the shore. She'd stand a few minutes, hand raised, while I gabbled, but her arm would slowly descend, she'd sag to the ground and put her head on her knees and berate herself.

"You're a wizard!" she shrieked.

"Hush, what if the others hear?"

"Let them hear, let them come. They'll be stronger than I am."

She'd beg me to leave the library for good. "Look, no one will ever know. I won't tell. You don't have to leave the city; just don't come to the library anymore."

"All right."

"Agreed?"

"Agreed."

And I'd tell my story and she'd drink her glass of wine, and when I broke the story off and stood to go, was almost through the doorway, she'd whisper, "Balthazar."

"Yes."

"You'll come tomorrow, won't you?"

I'd nod. And she'd sigh and tell me which room to meet her in.

. . .

There was always a space between us, even if we sat side by side on a sofa. Our ankles never clicked together, our hands never lighted on the other's shoulder or knee, as if we were strange magnets, simultaneously attracted and repelled. She had no hair to fall accidentally against my arm. I could still feel the bright stripe on my neck where her hand had rested the first day. Sometimes I saw her place the tip of her bitten finger against her lips, so I knew she still felt my teeth in her flesh. I knew that if I raised my hand toward her she'd sway back, as though a breeze moved through me. I knew precisely how close I could move my skin toward hers before she'd shy away.

We read to each other, reviving that lost art. Certain books are loveliest shared this way. We lay side by side on carpets, the magnetic gap between us, and took turns reading. Reader and readee. The best books to read aloud have shortish chapters, cadenced sentences, songs and verses, lots of illustrations. We gloated over pictures. The tattered *Dawn Treader* at anchor on Dragon Island, the waterpipe-puffing caterpillar, the cat walking by his wild lone. We pored over maps of imaginary lands, more real to us than any country on the actual globe. We pointed out Oriathon and Minas Tirith, Arrakis and Selidor. Just as rereading is utterly different from first readings, so reading aloud is such a separate experience from solitary reading, a new word should perhaps be coined. To read a cherished book aloud to someone who also knows the book by heart is an experience closer than any conversation, closer than making love; the same reefs and swells crossed at the same time, the chuckles rising in tandem. You feel you're speaking into her blood.

She read more deeply than I: "You see, Balthazar, how dangerous desire is—the tiniest craving can rearrange the world inordinately. Take Lucy. There's nothing she likes more than the touch of fur. So she enters the wardrobe. A hundred pages later, the king of beasts is on his way to sacrifice himself for her brother, and for all believing Narnians, but that sacrifice is not the climax of the book. The climax occurs on the walk to the Stone Table, when Aslan allows Lucy to do what she has longed to do: place her hands in his mane. Place her hands in the fur of God. The whole book has led to this point."

Sometimes her voice would break as she read, sometimes mine, and then we'd pass the book to the other, riding the emotion, like passing a morsel of plum between mouths, taking in the other's saliva along with the taste of the fruit, trying to extrapolate the other's taste. I imagined touching her. I imagined her continuing to read while I inched the cotton of her robe up her thighs. But we never touched. As our hands passed the book back and forth, our fingertips never met. Only our voices curled toward each other. I imagined her body as a book. I imagined holding her as I would a book, opening her, turning her, being drawn in, perhaps tearing a page, folding a page, jotting a note on her inner thigh, her armpit. The small poetry of her eyelashes, the incunabula of her bones.

We were sitting in a room of books about rainstorms, some so vivid their pages were permanently drenched. I could hear, faintly from the shelves, the muttering of thunder, and the candlelight was augmented by pins of lightning escaped from blue bindings. I had been telling her about the thieves in the

Kanisa.

"Tell me about Zeinab," she said. "You said you'd . . . that you'd . . ."

"I fucked her."

"Is she your lover?"

"No."

"Why not?"

"A true thief should never make a permanent liaison, especially not with another thief. It goes against the nature of our art. Anyway, I don't know who she is. I don't know what lies beneath her veil."

"She's scarred."

"It hardly matters. I'm sure she'd never lift her veil, and I have no desire to rip it away."

"Yet you have to lift every cover of every book you come across. Are you afraid, Balthazar?"

"Call it fear if you like. This is what I know: she cursed in her orgasm. The bells tinkled. Then she burned my book."

"Tell me about your books."

So I told her about the books in the Pension Scheherazade, the single shelf of my private library, and could see the need in her face, the look of a child after her first lick of peach sherbet.

"Bring them to me," she said.

"No."

Her lips quivered. Then I saw a craftiness enter her eyes. "We'll copy them, it will take a month. You can have them back."

"You'll give me the copies and keep the originals. No thanks."

"I have to read them." She stamped, really angry now.

"You can."

"How?"

"Come with me."

She was silent for a minute. Then: "You rascal. After all I've done for you, to try to trick me into leaving the library."

"What have you done for me?"

"Let you live. Let you read the books I love."

I spread my hands. "You're right. I owe you my life. And in return I'd like to show you my collection. But I'm damned if I'll bring it into your prison."

She stared at me. "Ogre!" she shouted. "Leave!"

So I left.

Walking along the corniche, I imagined her face against the sea, the sky. I imagined her hand on the corroded coral of the sea wall. I had only seen her by candlelight. What color would her skin be in the light of sunrise? Noon? Full moon?

I gave her a week. A week in which I returned to my old life, drinking macchiatos on the terrace of the Trianon, reading poetry on the corniche at dusk, dining at the Elite, visiting my booksellers, playing chess at the Kanisa Prometheus. I even went out thieving one night. Nura had given me a tip, and I broke into a palazzo on Sharia Rafaffa. Entering the little library, I bunched scarves beneath the door, drew the curtains, then lit a candle. Not two paces away, a veiled figure sat crosslegged on a sofa, a book in her lap. My candle shook, sending her shadow leaping across the stacks.

"Can you read in the dark?" I whispered, trying to control my voice.

"I was waiting for your light."

"Let me see your wrist."

"No."

"You were a librarian once."

"Who have you been talking to?"

I was silent.

"Do you know the danger you're putting yourself in?"

"Reading is a dangerous art," I said sullenly.

"You have no idea how dangerous. What's her name?"

"Shireen."

"And you're in love."

"Well . . ." I fingered the strap of my swag.

"Of course. How could you resist. Is she pretty?"

"Oh, yes."

"Describe her."

"She's not like the other librarians, not like any other girl I've met. Her blood is blue, her pupils are pages. I can't read the letters of fire in her eyes. She's never left the library, it's all she knows. When she reads, she falls into a book, like falling into the sea. I love to watch her read."

"Oh. That girl."

"You know her?"

"The library is a primal soup of pages and poems. It was only a matter of time before it gave birth to a child. I'll meet her some day."

"You can't go back down, can you?"

She stood, whisper of cotton, wash of silver: "I've got a book to burn."

"Wait," I said, but she was gone.

I raised my candle to the shelves. But, though the collection was extravagant and contained several fabulously rare volumes, I completely failed to achieve my customary thrill. The Library of Alexandria was so enormous, its treasures so outlandish, the

KEITH MILLER

dangers so precipitous, that ransacking these meager
overworld collections seemed a child's game I could not
imagine having played. Nevertheless, once I'd grabbed a few
volumes and stepped from an upper window, there was some
nostalgia in traipsing across the rooftops with my swag,
looking out over the shimmering sea lit by moon, lighthouse,
stars. The stars which are, I imagine, the shorn locks of the
virgin librarians, escaped from their underground sepulchers
to form arcane constellations.

Riding a late-night tram, I closed my eyes a moment, then felt
fingertips like feathers on my thigh and, turning, saw Amir's
sad smile, the brown lenses of his spectacles. "Any luck?" I
asked, and he held up a sealed envelope, a diary, a pressed rose.

"Few pockets lack secrets," he whispered.

The tram stopped, disgorging its contents, admitting a new
flock, and Amir excused himself with a murmur and shuffled
through the aisle, laying a hand gently on a shoulder here and
there to ease his passage, whispering apologies. Returning, he
fanned his treasure like a pack of cards, all hearts, in his lovely
hands. As we approached Mazarita, he leaned to me and
murmured, "Come. Dinner in my rooms."

Amir wears a somber uniform of three-piece suits and a
lavender cravat. His thick-rimmed spectacles curdle opaque
brown at the least light. When he takes off the spectacles to
polish them on his cravat, his eyes are startlingly beautiful:
violet, heavy-lidded, lashes thick as moth antennae. He haunts
the trams, sidling up behind young men and divesting them of
the contents of their pockets, but he's not after money, and
will often leave the fat wing of filthy notes on the tram seat, or

116

return it surreptitiously to its owner. What he seeks are secrets. All of us keep on our persons secrets—postcard, tram ticket, bookmark, letter—and Amir ferrets these out, hoards them. He is himself a cipher. Meeting you on the street, he'll inquire where you are headed, then regretfully inform you that his destination lies in the opposite direction. Nothing in his countenance or attire sets him apart, yet he seems to stand at a slight angle to the crowds, and the sidewalks he paces seem to carry him forward at a slightly slower tempo.

We walked to Sharia Lepsius, where he had an inherited apartment above a bathhouse, flanked by church and hospital. The rooms, at first glance, resembled Tutankhamen's tomb, as glimpsed by Howard Carter through the hole drilled in the doorway (and through which the djinn passed that would carry him off). They were redolent of candle wax and semen, crammed with steamer trunks and Zanzibari chests, chiffoniers and orange crates, stacked on each other, overflowing, the cases bulging, the drawers stuffed with all manner of objects dredged from the pockets of Alexandria.

He sat me in a scrollwork sofa stained with ochre islands like a map of a mythic archipelago and adjusted the shutters to angle the failing light onto the coffee table. While he worked in the kitchen, I examined the contents of the tabletop: bottle caps, driftglass, handkerchiefs, seashells, shopping lists, envelopes, photographs—the spoils of his latest excursion.

He returned with anis and salted almonds.

"Any luck?" I asked, nodding at the loot.

"Oh yes, look here." His elegant fingers delved, gathering photographs. "These are his family—mother, sisters, you can see the resemblance." He laid them before me one by one. "And then there's this." His trump was black and white, webbed by creases, the face dark and handsome, framed by fez

and galabiyya. Even through the crazing, I thought I
recognized the face. Amir turned the photograph over, and I
saw it was cohered only because a tram ticket had been glued
to the back.

"Ah, I think—"

"Yes, you know him. The conductor on the Bacchus route.
These are the contents of a searcher's pockets. There are so
many secret obsessions in this city. Businessmen in love with
shoeshine boys, princes with jarveys, priests with flower sellers.
Sometimes I imagine the relationships of this city as fine
threads knotting palace window to garret, steeple to minaret,
culvert to asylum, netting its citizens. After a heavy dew, from
the peak of the lighthouse, you might see the bright web,
obscuring the tiles and stones. With its burden of struggling
prisoners."

In a tiny indigo dining room he lit black candles, then filled
our glasses with Château des Rêves. On antique porcelain, he
served me smoked salmon with brown bread and butter,
followed by a prawn curry on fragrant basmati. We talked
about our work. He described the arduous training a
pickpocket requires, the years of practicing in the dark, and
assured me that he could undress me as I sat across from him,
without my awareness.

"I've searched your pockets, book thief, but only came up
with a paperback." I clapped my hand to my trousers and he
held up the tattered pages, fanned them, then handed the
book across. "Where do you keep your secrets?"

"Who says I have secrets?"

"You have secrets." I could see a flutter of violet behind the
sepia lenses.

"I have a secret, you're right, Amir, and this paperback will
tell you as much about it as anything. My secret is also a secret

to me."

"Careful there."

"I'm always careful," I said, but his lenses had turned smoky once more. "Why the obsession with secrets?" I asked.

"Secrets serve the same function spirits do."

"And what is that?"

"They bind interior and exterior. They can cause untold havoc if released from their graves and pockets, but also inordinate beauty. I read through my stash sometimes. They're so lovely and sad, the unsent love letters, the unused suicide notes. An unsigned postcard, a stamp-sized photograph with just a date on the back. Sometimes they're small, a bead or a pebble, a tiny bone. You're about to throw them away, and then see how they've been worn and tarnished by fingering. Look." Reaching behind him, he pulled from a drawer a chambered box. Nested in kapok were seeds and stones, morsels of ivory, fragments of lace, gathered from the pockets of Alexandria.

After the curry, he brought out an immense quivering trifle drenched in cognac. The conversation turned to love. "Sometimes," he said, "I'm so obsessed I can't think. I find it's dangerous to try to pickpocket in this condition. My fingers shake. I have panic attacks. The only cure is pursuit. I'll ride the trams till I see him again, I'll find out where he lives. Then the seduction. Perhaps I'm rejected. All right. That I can live with. But obsession is not a state one can survive indefinitely."

"What about Zeinab?"

"Those sloe eyes are killing me. I've started hearing his whisper everywhere: in the waves, in the tram wheels, on the radio. He whispers his secrets, but his voice is so quiet, so distorted, I can't understand what he's saying."

We retired to the living room. Amir played Abdel Halim

Hafez 45s on an old Victrola. The room was filled with candles. Candles on windowsills, mantelpieces, in bottle necks, the bottles stuck to surfaces by pleated gowns of wax. As the evening deepened, he lit more candles, bending to me and excusing himself in the midst of the conversation, rising and roaming the room, lighting wicks here and there with stolen matches, lifting a few more cobwebs from the gloom. I've heard that if he wearies of a visitor he'll snuff the candles one by one till he sits silently before a single candle, staring at the flame as if willing it to burn down. But the night of my visit the house was illuminated like Diwali by the time I left.

After we'd finished the wine I negotiated my way to the water closet, down a labyrinth of corridors with eroding wallpaper. The corroded mirror reflected only ghosts and memories. I took a wrong turn on the way back and wandered into a bedroom. The room was entirely filled by a four-poster bed, lavender curtains parted to reveal a youth asleep on disturbed sheets. One ankle was bound to a bedpost. Semen had dried to a lace doily on his brown stomach.

VI
Lions and Roses

WHEN I RETURNED to the library the next day it was clear
Shireen had been weeping for hours. "I have to see them," she
said. "Take me to your books."

She was shaking as we stepped across the threshold, her
words strangled: "It's just . . . it's just another door."

"Come."

She took my hand and we walked up the steps to the
sarcophagus. I could feel her heartbeat in her fingertips. She
knew the way of course, knew the visions she'd encounter, but
was unprepared for the stench, the sparkle of candlelight on
the gold of the dead, the crunch of her sandals on the bones of
inept book thieves. On the ferryboat, she cringed as the bats
whirled like black vellum blown free of bindings. At the base
of the lighthouse stairwell she crouched, head in her arms.

"Let me go back," she said.

"You can go back."

I watched her in the light of the candle flame, her head
bowed, sobs quaking her narrow shoulders. "You're the devil!"
she wailed.

"Thief," I corrected.

She started sobbing again but I held up my hand. "Listen."

She hushed and we heard, faintly as a stroked earlobe, the dash of waves on the corniche, and at the same moment a chance trickle of briny breeze threaded the stairwell to our nostrils. "The sea," I said.

She sighed, polished the tears away with her sleeve, and we started up the steps.

As we entered the base of the lighthouse, I took her hand again and helped her up the last step. We stood in the doorway looking out. She stared at the sea.

"Here." I pulled a blue niqab from my satchel. She slipped into it, adjusted the eyeholes. I handed her the gloves.

She put her glasses on over the veil, glared at me. "You prepared for this. Kidnapper."

I shrugged.

Like a pair of conservative newlyweds we walked down to the corniche wall. A gust of spray spattered our glasses and we took them off to wipe the lenses, glancing myopically at each other.

"It's—" her voice faltered.

"Well?"

She put her glasses back on, spread her gloved hands. "Much more . . . chaotic than I'd imagined. I'd imagined the waves going tap tap tap on the shore but the pattern is looser. The waves are all different sizes. I hadn't thought of that."

"Come. It will soon be dawn."

The corniche seems straight as you walk, but every time you look up the skyline has shifted drastically, as if each step shoves the world out of alignment. I peered at Alexandria through her dewy lenses that night, saw the fresh rinds of moonlight on the domes and minarets. We walked slowly. She refused my arm, though she stumbled often on the misshapen stone. I noticed for the first time, seeing her walk in the open, that her shoulders were slightly bowed, her head curled slightly forward on her neck like that of a dove. She did not know what to do with her hands, fingers still caressing phantom pages. And I recognized my own posture in hers: the reader's slouch. A sleuth might have guessed us siblings from our pigeon-toed gait, our wire-framed spectacles, the sense of something missing.

We came to the green bite out of the center of the corniche, crossed the road and walked round the back of the Cecil to the Scheherazade, up five flights, past the snoring proprietor, to my rooms.

And now the time has come to reveal that my rooms are not precisely those you entered, how many pages back. There is, for example, another demitasse, brown-and-gold, beside the black-and-gold one on the shelf. In the wardrobe are several extra hangers with new cotton dresses and blouses. And beneath my bookshelf, in the hidden room, is a cot, with new linen folded over a new quilt, and a new pillow plumped. Beside the cot is a small escritoire with a burgundy leather writing surface, and upon it a green half-leather notebook, a slender silver fountain pen, a bottle of blue ink. There's a pot of strawberry jam beside the candle on the end table.

She scented the bookshelf as soon as she stepped across the threshold. Passing blind into the wardrobe, she shoved through the cotton with a clacking of coat hangers. Her belief made of the back a curtain of shadows. Dashing into the room, heedless of the wine and jam, she rushed to the shelf. But she swooned as soon as she began reading the titles, swaying into my arms. I carried her to the chair, lifted her veil, and fanned her with a chapbook till her eyelids stirred.

"I was dreaming," she said.

I shook my head, pointed to the shelf.

She started up again, a drunken gleam in her eyes, but I gripped her arm.

"Slowly," I said. "You've had plenty of excitement for one night. Eat something first, drink a glass of wine."

She closed her eyes, nodded.

I opened a hamper of bread and salads and laid out a little picnic on the carpet—saucers of white cheese with tomatoes and dill, olives, tahina, watercress, marinated aubergine.

She ate daintily, frugally, tearing off neat fragments of bread and dipping into each plate in turn, placing the olive pits in a row at the rim of a saucer. She sipped the wine. Constantly her eyes strayed to the books. "How?" she said.

"A lifetime of labor, that," I told her. "Each book on that shelf is a year of my life."

"I can't believe it. I can't believe it, Balthazar." She swayed, and I reached toward her, afraid she might faint again. But she brushed me away. Setting aside her glass, she knelt before the bookshelf. "These are the missing books. The books I've known were out there. Every time a box arrived from overseas, I ran to check, to see if these books were among them. So there are two libraries in Alexandria. May I read now?" she asked plaintively.

"First the dawn," I told her. "Bring your wine."

She could not go onto the balcony. "Too much space," she said, and made me set a chair inside the doors. She'd seen the sunrise only as dove-colored lozenges among the palm leaves or angled stems in the great reading room.

As the sun welled from the sea, she exclaimed: "Why is it so big? Is it the end of the world?"

"The beginning."

"Look how wide the sea is. Look, look, and boats, and how the light dances!" She'd never seen a palm tree or a fountain. Standing and gripping the jamb so she could peer over the balustrade, she laughed at the urchins chasing each other around the statue in the square. Then she sat again, looked into the room. "It's too much," she said. She had to set the wineglass down with both hands. "Too much all at once, the books and the sea. I don't think I can manage it."

"It's time for thieves and librarians to turn in, anyway," I said gently. "Would you care to bathe?"

"I'll wait till morning. Or afternoon, I suppose. Goodnight, Balthazar. I don't know whether to thank you or slap you."

She passed into the wardrobe.

I ran a bath and soaked a long time. When I got out, candlelight still glowed within the wardrobe. I lay in bed, holding a book but not reading. It was pleasant to lie there, listening to the sea and the sounds of morning, and imagine her lying in bed in the next room, sheltered by candlelight, reading my books.

I woke once during the day and saw her candle was still lit, slept again, and when I woke in late afternoon her room was finally dark. I tiptoed out and ordered coffee from Abdallah, drank and read on the balcony while night rose. The moon tangled with the flags on the Trianon. I read all night, and still she slept. Finally, as dawn broke once more, I heard a footfall and turned. She stood framed in the balcony doors. One cheek was creased; a morsel of sleep lay like a seed pearl in the corner of one eye.

"Hungry?" I asked.

She nodded. "I'd like to bathe first, if I may."

I showed her the new towel and washcloth laid out, the toothbrush in its case, the fresh bar of Pear's.

The Trianon was open by the time she was ready and we stepped out past the astonished Abdallah, down the stairs and across the tram tracks to where the waiters were shaking heavy cream linen over the outdoor tables.

"I've never eaten breakfast here," I told her.

"Why not?"

"I'm always asleep."

"Of course."

A waiter set menus in front of us and stood by politely.

"What will you have?" I asked.

She looked at the menu. "Oh, everything. I don't know. You choose, please."

I ordered croissants and white-cheese omelets and macchiatos and glasses of strawberry juice.

A tram ground by and she watched it pass. "I'd hear that sound, in the distance, while I was on sentry duty. I had no idea what it was. Some animal, I thought." In the square, palm leaves shivered, spraying needles of light, and the light was salt on the sea.

The waiter came with the coffee. She took a sip, lowered the cup, then brought it back to her lips. "This coffee," she said. "What makes it . . . ?"

"Sunlight," I said. "Sunlight and the view of the bay enhance the taste."

"I'd imagined sitting here, tearing the corners off a croissant, drinking a macchiato, like you'd described. But how foolish I've been, thinking my dreams could match reality. I'd forgotten about colors. And smells. And the sound of the tram and the harness bells, that hadn't even occurred to me. Or my breathing." She touched a gloved finger to her veil, leaving an ultramarine blot on the blue. "I don't know why I'm crying. I'm not suited to this. Perhaps I should go back underground."

"Finish your croissant first."

"All right."

She read three books in the next nine hours. I slept, and when I woke looked in to see if she wanted lunch or coffee, but she held up a hand absently, without glancing from the page. I did a watercolor, hiding eyes and *o*'s in the archways and windows of the city. I turned at a footstep, saw a woman veiled in blue, and wasn't sure who it was.

"I'm not a ghost," she laughed.

"Sorry, I . . . you startled me."

"It's lovely." She touched the painting.

"Dinner?"

She nodded.

We walked along the corniche with the evening crowds. I could sense her flinch as the young men jostled past, holding hands or punching each other, shouting insults, all perfumes and pomades, testicles like ripe boils in their tight trousers, chins and foreheads spangled with amber and garnet pustules.

"You're hidden," I whispered. "They won't touch you in your disguise," and she nodded tightly.

We passed the swath of public beach, the water seething with bathers, men and boys in undergarments, women fully dressed, hegabs swiped by the waves across their faces, the cold sea bringing up their nipples even through the layers. Then the corner of fishing boats, reflected colors gashed by ripples. Boys were jumping off prows of caiques and yachts, light slipping on their brown bodies, sliding supple as oil across their shoulders and abdomens. They belly-flopped and somersaulted into the bay, smashing open the gold dabs of their own reflections.

Crossing the isthmus into Bahariyya, we walked beside the shipyards to Restaurant Samakmak. The stares of the fish in their nest of ice made her shiver and she turned away. "You order for me, please."

We sat outside under an awning, with a view of the sea between the skeletal boats on stilts. The boat builders were grilling their own suppers on the sand, over fires of castoff lumber. A waiter smoothed newsprint on our table, then laid out salads: baba, tahina, khadhra, hummus, badingan, and a basketful of toasted pita.

"Careful," I said. "There's going to be a lot of food. Pace yourself."

"I don't know why I'm starving."

"Reading makes me hungry too."

"Oh, Balthazar. I'm not really here, you know. I'm still in those books. How many lives I've lived today. Your wardrobe is outside time, outside this universe."

So we talked about books. Have you talked about beautiful books with a beautiful girl, while sampling fried aubergine marinated in garlic and lemon and waiting for your calamari to grill? The air was perfect that evening, slightly scented with myrrh and charcoal, just this side of cardigan weather. We watched the seagulls resting their elbows on the wind. A young father walked with his daughter down the sidewalk. The girl was picking up shells and bottle caps and running to show him and he held them carefully in his hand. They laughed about something and he lifted her and tossed her in the air, then nuzzled his beard into her cheek and she giggled and squirmed.

The waiter shoved the saucers of salads to one side and the seafood began to arrive. Grilled prawns and calamari, sea bream stuffed with cilantro and garlic, mussels in parsley and clarified butter. We drenched it all in lemon juice and set to, she with knife and fork to preserve her gloves, I with my hands, teasing the white flesh from the fish bones, nibbling the purple fronds of calamari. After a while she stopped eating.

"What's wrong?"

She shook her head. "I had no idea. All this. I had no idea."

"You eat well, in your underground lair."

"I thought we did. But this calamari. I've never tasted anything so fresh. It's like eating the sea."

A waif wandered by with a fistful of tattered stolen roses and I bought the lot, arranged them in my water glass and set it among the plates. "Red roses," I said. "I don't know what they smell like anymore. They smell like roses. You tell me."

She took one and held it under her veil for a minute. "Brown sugar, peaches, a drop of blood." She began pulling the petals off, round and round, till she was left with a tiny burgundy vase. When later she picked up her napkin she left a dot of blue on it so I thought at first the dye had run on her gloves, then realized she'd pricked herself on a thorn.

Beneath the city, time was dead, but aboveground, Alexandria was a city of clocks, cased in brick or granite, high on tiled walls, set like twin-pupiled cat eyes into archways, the numerals virgin or evolved Arabic, or Roman, or merely their sideways shadows, the hands chopsticks or spears or wrought-iron filigree. Each clock told a different time, as if the city was caught halfway through a wormhole, and I sensed this, the warping of time, as I walked through the streets, my heartbeat dancing or shuffling. Some clocks had stopped altogether, or perhaps moved so slowly you'd stand a lifetime waiting for an hour to pass, and the hands of some whirred like windmills, grinding who knows what temporal grain. Ask two waiters in the Trianon the time and it would become apparent they were not inhabiting the same week, let alone the same hour. In Victoria Station, you had to rely on chance and rumor to board your train. Only the muezzins, tethered to the sun, kept accurate time in this city, and my heart had developed five chambers that filled in turn with sand as the earth revolved. The dawn chorale I loved, a new composition every morning, marriage of Schönberg, Orthodox chanting, and women wailing for their demon lovers. All dissonances, and then the occasional resolution, the more precious for being happenstance.

But her presence skewed time like a nearby star, expanding and shrinking the days. Two weeks. Fourteen days. And half the time she was reading. Does it sound like time enough to you? But time is water, time's a mustard seed, time's a molecule of plutonium.

I took her into a city of hands. Palm prints of blood on doorframes, on donkeys, blue palm prints of children on walls, staving off djinns and book thieves, little silver hands on silver chains on the breasts of Bedouin women. We watched the hands of the fatiir-seller slap his dough and fling the fat pale hillocks into wobbling paper circles, then strew the olives and cilantro and old cheese on them, crack an egg, fold the dough, and slide it into the oven. We watched the falafel-seller dab wet green circles into crushed coriander and sesame seeds and flick them to buzz in brown oil. We watched men twist paper cones for nuts. Bricklayers, ironmongers, their hands so educated they could forget about them, look around and chat while their fingers flailed like deft fish.

I took her into a city of lights. The lofty bonfire of the lighthouse, of course, but also the festival lights strung across alleys, and the street lamps, those not burnt out, and the sparks of the tram and the incessant glittering of matches across the city as cigarettes were lit, the glow of embers, swelling and subsiding with each inhalation.

I took her into a city of smokes. Apple tobacco and clove cigarettes in sawdusted ahwas. The fragrant wood smoke of the sweet-potato roaster. The sandalwood saunas of the Nubian households. The incense-sellers, swinging their chained braziers into shops for a guinea. And of course the smoke—heady, alarming—of burning paper, because there was always a book burning somewhere in Alexandria.

I took her to the street of booksellers, and she walked through, nodding. She'd read all the books, and though to most tourists the bookstores of Alexandria seemed miraculous in the rarity and variety of their stock, none equaled a single chamber in the underground library. And none, of course, could match the shelf within my wardrobe.

She wanted to see the zoo, so we took the tram to Nouzha, bought two tickets for a guinea, and wandered among balloon men and sticky children, past the diseased elephant and insane monkeys, to the terrible echoing hall of lions, which stank like an abattoir. The scrawny lions with their outsized paws slept, or trod soundless ellipses, shoulder blades pistons, while keepers urged children to thrust skewers of rancid meat at them. Some paid a piaster to let a snarling cub worry their collars. One beast groaned enormously and gnashed at the bars.

Shireen stood mesmerized. "What do they dream?" she wondered. "If they were born in these cages, do they only dream about iron bars and screaming children, or can they imagine running? Can they take their bowl of water and make a lake, or that window and make a sky?"

We sat by the enclosure of the white oryx and her delicate child, watching the rickety ferris wheel. Rusty speakers mangled a lovesong.

كم بنينا من خيال حولنا   هل رأى الحب سكارى مثلنا
ومشينا في طريق مقمر تثب الفرحة فيه قبلنا
وضحكنا ضحك طفلين معاً وعدونا فسبقنا ظلنا

I bought her cotton candy, which she consumed with relish, strands melting on her cheeks, tangling in her eyebrows, and a blue balloon, which she clutched solemnly.

"Our myths of unicorns, they say, come from sightings of oryx that snapped off a horn in a fight," I told her.

"This oryx is the myth for me. I've met more unicorns."

She was as interested in the picnicking families as the animals, and kept exclaiming over their antics. "Oh, look at that boy! Is he going to do a cartwheel? Oh, that baby just fell over! What are they eating? What are those leaves?"

I laughed and tried to keep up with her questions. The families had brought squares of quilted funerary-tent cloth and laid them out on the scant grass and opened pots and tins. She relished the textures, the circles of salads—beetroot, baba ghanoug, watercress, radish—and the knotted blossoms and polka dots and tiger stripes on the hegabs and blouses, and the unfurling fists of cigarette smoke.

"It's all so pretty," she said. "You know what I like? I like to see how they sit beside each other and touch each other. In the library we touch, of course, but we're not a family. We say we are, but we're alone, each of us with our books. Look at how the mother holds her arm to the child. What a lovely gesture. If I could keep something, put it in my pocket, it wouldn't be a rose or a lion's claw. It would be that gesture." She sighed, and I looked at her. "Some things up here are so much stranger than the images I'd taken from books," she said. "The sea, coffee at the Trianon, sunlight on palm leaves. And some things hadn't occurred to me. Like the wind on your balcony, or how the horizon shifts as you walk along the corniche, or, well, the boys, the men, how they jostle and stare. And all the noise—trams and seagulls and radios. But other things seem strangely diminished or altered. Not less beautiful—it's all so beautiful—but the roses aren't the huge potent blooms of stories and poems, which cause so much heartache. They're just flowers. A little tattered, with thorns. And the lions— where are the golden manes and the earth-shaking roars?"

"Are you disappointed?"

"Not at all. And that's strange, isn't it. Somehow these lions, because I've seen their scrawny ribs and their ragged coats, because I've seen them walk around their tiny cages, are more beautiful than their avatars. What will Aslan be for me now, with mites in his ears and his mangy tail? The rose Beauty's father steals, with its bruised petals and aphids—how will this change the story?"

133

. . .

We took the tram back to Midan Saad Zaghloul. Sidi Gaber, Hammamat Cleopatra, Riyadha, Ibrahimiyya, Moaskar. . . . As the tram swayed on, I saw a figure step down into the doorway. I wouldn't have noticed him if he hadn't turned his sepia lenses to me for a moment. The doors slapped open and he was gone, folded into the crowd on the platform. Terrified, I clutched my pockets, but my paperback and lockpick were safe.

She was not a fast reader. Like all true readers, she savored words, allowed the books to walk at their own pace. Some books she read in a single gulp; others needed plenty of air, evenings strolling on the corniche, macchiato breaks. It was as she meandered through one of these denser books that she said to me one evening: "You promised to teach me to steal."

"Why would a pretty girl like you want to learn to steal?"

"Balthazar, you promised!"

"All right, but we'll need to get you some shoes."

We went to a certain cobbler's on Sharia al-Zeitun and he had her place each foot in turn on a polygon of hide while he traced their contours with a pencil. We picked them up two days later and she tried them on, executed a dainty pirouette en pointe.

"They're like wearing feet," she said. "Like putting on someone else's feet. I could run up a wall like a gecko."

"Let's see you do that."

. . .

Two a.m. Late tram to Moharram Bey. We walked up among the art deco villas, gardenlets of dwarf palms and bonsaied bougainvillea behind lacy ironwork. Moths spun frail cocoons around lamp-posts, bats gave voice to the stars. In the sparse light, caryatids and gargoyles watched our passage with shadow-eyed sentience. I am a connoisseur of likely houses, scouring for a taint of decline, for neglected flowerbeds, flaking paint on sashes, speckled panes, and a hint of the romantic: a bouquet of dusty roses hung heads-down, petrified puddles of wax on windowsills. If a house is too freshly painted, the shrubs too neatly pruned, I know the denizens have no time to read. Likewise, I shy away from fashionable wallpaper or spartan interiors: the inhabitants of these houses spend their evenings baking casseroles and reckoning their accounts. I passed a couple of possibilities that I might have entered on a less momentous night; then, at the end of a cul-de-sac I'd never noticed before, I found the house I craved—cherry pits in the hedgerows, crumbling steps, a sofa on the balcony, its armrests darkened by soiled soles, empty wine bottles beside it. I could see a blunted profile behind a curtain, but the head did not turn.

I helped her over the fence and we circled the house, listening at shutters. Jimmying one open with my bodkin, I peered into the darkness, then straddled the sill and helped her up. We sat for a minute, my knees against her thighs, gazing into the darkness. I could hear the jostling of her heartbeat in her breaths. We entered a lumber room—old packing crates, a rickety rocking chair, vacant picture frames—but the stench of dust and rat piss could not conceal the odor that sharpened my hard-on: gilt leather, old pages.

A librarian's step is not so removed from that of a thief. She was not silent, but to a sleeper's ear she might have been a breeze in the curtains, a rustle of jasmine leaves. We passed through the salon, a plaster bust of the old scribe of the city on a marble plinth. No need to pause or look round, her breaths were a leash. The book scent led up the stairs and past the rooms of sleepers, loud with Arabic snoring (خ خ خ) and outbursts of unconscious invective. We glanced in at the twitching dreamers, the children drooling on calico camels, the somnambulating grandfather pacing the balcony, the sightless tossers convulsed by solipsistic epilepsies. A baby sat up suddenly, stared at us, said "Da," and subsided into her cot. Onto a landing, up another flight, and still the scent of pages trickled down.

Three flights up we found the little door that led out across the roof. I looked around, baffled. Was the perfume falling from heaven? But then I spied the hexagonal tower, its shaky staircase. I took her gloved hand and we tiptoed among bat bones and discarded carnations. Wooden steps are tricky. I nudged corners and edges with the ball of my foot till I found the sweet spot that would take my weight without whining. Once inside, I drew the curtains, closed the door, lit a candle, and we found ourselves in a perfect little library, someone's private obsession. Rosewood shelving, worn sofa in the center of the floor, rack of wine bottles, cedar humidor.

With my bodkin, I pried the cork out of a bottle. We prowled the room in opposite directions. I could hear her fingers on bindings. She lifted down a volume, vanished for a page, slotted it back. And I likewise fondled the books. Thievery always turns me on, but this night my fingers rattled on the spines; I saw the titles through a veil of blood. When I pulled down a book, the words were full of innuendo, like inscriptions within a pyramid, decipherable only on this night, in this palpitant light. My mind was ripe with openings, but when the shelves brought us round to each other I could not speak. She clutched a book to her breast, stared at me. I handed her the wine bottle and she tipped a ruby gurgle down her throat, passed it back. I touched the corner of the book she held.

"Balthazar," she said. Her voice so exotic my name seemed a word in a foreign language.

"What have you found?"

"I don't know." She looked down at the volume.

"Let's read it." I moved to the sofa and after a moment she followed, sat beside me, inch-wide gulf between our thighs where dragons whirled, comets smoked. She opened the book, equally on her lap and mine, and we bent over the pages. Poetry, perhaps. Her fingers brushed the paper.

"I can't read the words," I said.

She lifted her veil. "Read my lips." We took off our spectacles. I bent to her. Our fingers met in the trough of pages and we kissed. Flavors of ink and wine. She fended my hand from her breast, so I abandoned myself to her mouth, the inept and avid fumbling of her lips. I had forgotten about kissing, most intimate of the erotic arts. Her eyes were closed. I curled my palm over her shorn scalp, the fine nap. She drew away, gasping, head back against the sofa. I tasted the mole on her neck, spice of Zanzibar, then ran my tongue in the bitter seashell of her ear.

I woke within the perfume of her breath, as the afternoon breeze shifting the curtains still stirred the pages of my dreams, sweet book of lies. She slept, book for a pillow, its pages mauled, marked with the spittle seeping from her mouth. Opening the curtains and shutters, I stood in the book-lined birdcage and looked out across gables and minarets to the bay flashing like a gorget on the headland of Anfushi, the sky

137

teeming with clouds—buoyant, it seemed, only because of my good cheer. She joined me, rubbing the sleep from her eyes. A crow rocking on a palm frond looked us over, laughing obscenely.

"Well, we're trapped," she said.

"Perhaps that crow could carry us away on her back."

"Or we could just spread our wings."

"Anyway," I turned into the room, "there are worse places to be caged."

"I'm so hungry."

As if in answer the rooftop door below us opened and a young girl stepped out bearing a plate of sandwiches. She was dressed in white and wore a circlet of jasmine on her brow. There was no place to hide, so we watched as she creaked up the wooden steps, focus on her feet, then looked up. Her lips formed a soundless o, then softened. "Are you angels?"

"Quite the opposite," I smiled.

"What kind of sandwiches are those?" Shireen asked.

"Kofta. Would you like to share?"

"Yes please."

She set the plate on the floor and we sat around it cross-legged. The sandwiches were delicious, the plump kofta slathered with tahina, garnished with tomato and onion. The wine bottle was still a third full, and Shireen and I passed it back and forth. I offered it to the girl. "Do you drink wine?"

"I've tasted it before." She took a dainty sip, made a face. "Sour. Is that my grandfather's wine?"

I nodded.

"How did you get up here?"

"We came in the night, while you were sleeping."

"Are you friends of my father?"

"No."

"Why did you come?"

"We're thieves. Well, I am. She hasn't stolen anything."

"Yet," said Shireen.

"What were you going to steal?"

I waved a hand at the shelves.

"Do you like to read?" she asked solemnly.

"Oh yes," Shireen and I said in unison, leaning forward. "Do you?"

"This is my favorite place in the world. I come up here after school. Mama makes me sandwiches and I'm allowed to read till my father comes home. When I grow up I'm going to become a librarian. Or a tram driver. I haven't decided yet."

"This is your grandfather's library?" I asked.

She nodded. "He comes up here in the evenings sometimes to drink wine and read. But he doesn't remember very well these days. I think he just holds the books, because that's what he used to do."

"What books do you like?" I asked, and we talked about books for a while. I watched the slow blossoming of her face as she realized she'd encountered beings like herself, whose lives were more than half fiction.

The sun had candled a minaret. "When does your father come home?" I asked. She looked to the west. "Any time now."

"We have to get out of here. Can you help us?"

"I thought you were going to steal."

"We'll leave them here for you." I smiled.

But Shireen picked up the book she'd used as a pillow. "I'll take this," she said.

"Can I come with you?"

"I wish you could, darling. But not now. I have a feeling we'll meet again, though."

She looked down, then into our faces. "All right. Wait here.

When you hear a noise, go down the stairs and out the back. There's a place you can climb over the garden fence."

"You're the angel," Shireen said.

The girl took the plate and empty wine bottle and trotted down the steps. A minute later we heard a crash and a shriek, voices and footsteps, and we dashed down the stairs. I looked back as we passed out the back door and saw the bust of the scribe in fragments on the floor of the salon, and the girl with her ear in a woman's grip. But she was smiling.

The next evening, Shireen stood on my balcony, looking down across the midan. A wedding party clattered by, beating time on the sides of carriages, the horses decorated with wreaths of jasmine and streamers of triangular primaries. Shedding flowers and colors, they chanted past under the date palms, down the tram tracks. I placed my hand on her nape and she shied, turning to me, lips bending, then bitten, her eyes brimming. I reached out a finger to touch her eyelid where a crumb of tear stood, and she raised her hand as if against a blow.

"I thought . . ." I said.

"No."

"What did last night mean?"

"Too much wine."

"You didn't like the kisses?"

"I didn't say that."

"What are you saying?"

"Let me read, Balthazar." She left the balcony, and I heard the hangers clacking as she entered the wardrobe.

I fell asleep reading, and continued reading in my dream,

though the book seemed to have been grafted into my fingers. My face sank closer and closer to the pages. Then from the ditch emerged a hand. The fingers touched my face. I woke, and fingers moved on my cheek. I could feel the weight of her body on the mattress. She brushed her lips against mine, sideways, twice, thrice, till they stuck, and I lay still, rocked by my heartbeat, succumbing to her flavor.

We went to the rose gardens in Nouzha one afternoon. It was full of hoopoes and torn paper. The flamboyant trees were on fire, quilts of flame thrown across the leaves, almost too bright to look at. I'd brought a pocketful of little apples and we ate those as we strolled along the flagged paths, tossing the cores into the mulch. She bent to the roses, sampling colors.

"Yellow are nicest," she said. "Caramel and sunlight."

"You've been reading too many books."

She gathered a handful of petals and held them to my nose and I puffed a fragrant apricot flurry about our heads. I loved to hear her giggle, fresh as a child's. Couples sat on benches beneath the flamboyants, faded love notes shuffling about their feet. We spied on their slow-motion struggles, a boy's arm sidling across the bench to descend gentle as a moth on the girl's shoulder, her careful flinching, his casual shifting so his knee nudged her thigh, her drawn breath, the sudden emergence of her nipples against her bodice, his elbow trying to stanch his hard-on, and meanwhile their faces tilted up and out and they chattered aimlessly, while the boughs clashed behind them and petals fell in drifts of flame about their feet.

"What happens to the couples?" she asked.

"You're witnessing the high point of their petty lives. Soon they'll start bickering about the trousseau, about whether the water glasses should have little gold lines around the rims or the faucets porcelain handles. Then they'll get married and instantly the boys will discover that the erections which were ubiquitous as pariah dogs are suddenly rare as unicorns, the simper they'd found so endearing reminds them of their Aunt Fagr, those thighs which had seemed so butter-soft under the pressure of their knees are pitted and rancid as old cottage cheese, and they'll discover a latent talent for judicious beatings, ostensibly to keep her in check, but really because it's the only thing that turns them on anymore."

"You sound bitter."

"Honest."

"Are there no marriages that work?"

"Only thieves can have true marriages. Thieves, maybe whores and desert explorers. I'd like you to meet some friends."

We took the tram to Loran, walked two blocks toward the sea, then up six flights to Koujour and Hala's apartment. One of the twins, Zara, let us in, curtsied, and went to fetch her mother. Hala came from the kitchen, adjusting her hegab. "Balthazar, you've been lost." She touched my shoulder, then laid her fingers in my palm. She turned to Shireen. "Welcome. This is your house." Then back to me. "Koujour's working. Shall I fetch him? You'll stay for supper, of course."

"Let him work. We don't want to bother you."

"Balthazar! The children are always asking about you. I tell them you're too busy. Anyway, you sit." She waved an arm to the chairs by the bay windows. "I'll make tea. Zara! Aziza!"

The girls came running, hands full of pictures they'd made and special jewelry and new dolls. Zara sat on my lap and counted my fingers while Aziza showed us the dance she was learning. She put a tin coronet in her hair and held a scarf in her little fists and swung her head this way and that. Zara bounced onto Shireen's lap. "Are you going to marry Balthazar?" she asked.

"I'm just a friend."

"Are you a thief?"

"No."

"Balthazar's a thief, Abba said so."

"Yes, I know."

She didn't know how to touch a child, her hands on Zara's shoulders awkward as the boy's in the rose garden. But Zara was a gentle tutor, squirming into her embrace so she was obliged to cradle the girl's body. She smoothed a corner of Zara's skirt. "How old are you?" she asked.

"I'm five, but I'm older than Aziza."

"We're the same," said Aziza.

"Yes, but I'm older. Why are your eyes like that?"

"I'm not sure."

"Have you ever seen a goat's eyes?"

"In pictures."

"Have you seen a frog's eyes?"

"No."

"Your eyes have a bit of gold like a frog's eyes."

"I see."

Hala came in with the tea, hanks of mint soaking in the glasses.

"Are you ugly or beautiful?" Aziza asked Shireen.

"Aziza!" Hala scolded.

"Well, I can't see her face."

"It's not something you ask."

"I think she's beautiful," said Zara, "because her eyes are like a frog's eyes."

"That's not very nice."

"I think it is. I like to look at frogs' eyes. We find them by the lake in the park," she told Shireen.

Koujour came down the steps. "Who's this?" he asked. He was drenched in colors and patterns as if he'd been dipped in a vat of kaleidoscopes. One eye hooped in marigold, peacock stripes on either cheek, a turquoise tika between his brows. He'd been sketching in oil pastel on his forearms—geometric palm trees and crocodiles, bark and hide textured by his ornamental scars. Ignoring me, he stood in front of Shireen. She looked up at him, then at me.

"Ah, my friend," Koujour hauled me up and embraced me. "Your beautiful."

"You see," Zara whispered to her sister.

"What do they say?" he asked Shireen.

"Sorry?"

"The words, there." He jabbed at her eyes.

"I can't read them."

"Balthazar will read. Tea? Yes. Good. Hala will make food." He embraced me again. "My friend." He turned to Shireen, his hand on my shoulder. "My friend," he told her and she nodded.

"Could we see your studio, Koujour? Shireen would love to see your work."

"Today yes. Yesterday no, today yes. Come." We climbed the steps to his breezy loft, chockful of sunlight, slathered with sunlight, as if it accumulated on the surfaces like dust. Holy fragrance of linseed oil and cigarette ash. Zara and Aziza danced. Paintings paneled the walls.

"Oh," Shireen said. "But this is . . . and this . . . isn't this by . . . ?"

"She begins to know." Koujour grinned and nodded. He

circled the room tapping paintings. "Salah al-Mur, Abushariaa, Tahir Bushra, Rashid Diab."

"You're a—"

"Yes, yes."

"But they're perfect."

"Yes."

"Do you make your own paintings?"

He spread his arms.

"Yes of course, but—"

"In the beginning I learn from them. Now they learn from me. In Abushariaa's house he has on the wall my painting, with his name. He tells his girlfriends he can't sell it. Of course. Too beautiful to sell. He bought it from a gallery. My painting."

"Books are—" she pressed her fingers to her veil.

"I know you," he laughed. "Don't hide. Balthazar loves you, you love books."

"All right. Yes. The more you read the more you realize how books are trampled into each other, muddy footprints of other books all over the pages."

"Thieves!"

Hala called us for supper. She had laid the meal on a mat beneath the windows and we took off our shoes and sat. No cuisine rivals that of Sudan. There were chickpea falafel, kisra with weka, and cinnamon-flavored kamoniyya. There were stews of pumpkin and okra, aubergines stuffed with rice and spiced meat, kofta in tomato gravy. There was a dish of salata beidha and another of salata dakwa. There were little saucers of red pepper and salt and cumin. There were glasses of helomur and abrey.

"Eat, eat!" Koujour and Hala urged if we showed signs of slacking.

When Shireen paused for a moment to glance out the window Hala looked dismayed. "Is the food not tasty?" she inquired, and Koujour bellowed "What's your disease? Why aren't you eating?"

I grinned at her flustered scrabbling. I knew the routine, and paused long before I was full to receive the first volley of good-natured vitriol. I parceled out the admonishments till finally, belly a calabash, I lay back and shook my head.

Shireen had already conceded. "I wish I could go on and on," she said. "Food like this makes you contemplate suicide by overeating."

The girls helped their mother clear the mat. We moved to the chairs, moaning and soporific till the ginger coffee arrived. The girls fell asleep on the sofa in a tangle of dusky limbs and locked hair.

That evening I heard for the first time the tale of the courtship of Koujour and Hala. I had gathered fragments from Koujour's abraded outbursts, but this night Hala told the story, so it came whole. She sat straight-backed, legs folded under her.

"My father, may he rest in peace, was descended from the Mahdi and was thus a member of the ruling caste. We lived in a mud-brick mansion in Omdurman, to which rooms had been added over the centuries, so it was a termite hill of gossiping women and politics. There were always elderly men in jalabiyyas and loose turbans knocking at the door with their ebony walking sticks, coming to see my father. And when they glimpsed me they'd arrange meetings with their sons, spoiled dandies with their own pleasure boats on the Nile. I had bribed my mother to let me act in a play, something by Aeschylus, pieced from scraps of papyrus used to stuff mummies. I was a princess, of course, and wore the gold of my inheritance, and my mother's wedding tobe. Koujour was the set painter. I didn't see him—he was of a lower caste."

"My father was a slave!" Koujour shouted. The girls twitched in their sleep.

Hala went on. "He was someone with whom my mother would not have shaken hands for fear of contamination. But I was backstage and needed to rehearse my lines and he was sitting on an upturned paint bucket. So our first conversation was a dialogue of fraught love written millennia before. Later, I saw that my face had been cunningly concealed in the set, in the pattern of windows and the flight of pigeons, and still later I saw my face in a downtown gallery. I bought the painting and invited him to my house for sweetmeats and guava juice. How naive I was. My mother shrieked that there was an afriit at the door and ran screaming into the house. My youngest sister fainted. My father threatened him with a sword.

"Next morning I woke to see a painting on the road outside our house, drawn with spilled water in the dust, so it vanished even as I looked at it. A painting of my face. He invited me to his parents' house, south of the city, in the refugee quarter. They were poor. His mother sold her wedding veil to buy pigeons to roast for me. But the house was fabulous. Koujour had built it himself, using colored mud, and had worked Nuban designs into the walls. I saw how beautiful he was. We could only meet rarely, clandestinely. We met among the ancient mausoleums or in the date groves along the Nile. We kissed once. Then, by chance, my mother's maternal aunt's paternal cousin spied us together one evening, holding hands by the water's edge, and I was confined to my room. Shortly after that, Koujour began drinking and fell afoul of the authorities. He fled to Asmara, beyond the eastern hills.

"For five years, we wrote. I have one thousand, eight

hundred and eleven letters from him. All contain drawings. Some are burned by cigarettes. Many are stained with tears. His or mine, I no longer know. I still read through them once a year. Each of those years was sadder than the last. He told me he'd become a drunkard, he'd started smoking hashish, he'd taken to using whores, he'd become rich. Come back, I wrote him, even with your red eyes, even with your pain, even fresh from the embrace of another, come back. But he could not. I knew I had to make a choice."

Koujour seized the story. "Asmara. In the evening I walked down the boulevard. Drunk, always. I looked for whores that looked like her. I saw her at the other end. Red dress. Too far away to see her eyes, but I knew. I walked above the street like a bird. We talked for three days."

"Without sleeping," Hala laughed. "We drank coffee in Café Sheba and chewed qat and talked."

We walked back to Midan Saad Zaghloul along the corniche.

"Are you asking me to make that choice, Balthazar?"

"I took you to see Koujour and Hala because they're my friends."

"I won't make that choice. I belong to the library, you must understand that. These days in the overworld are part of my work as a librarian, as a reader. I'm here to read your books. You won't understand this, Balthazar. I should never have kissed you. You think I'm like your other girls. I'm not like your other girls. I'm not like your one-night lovers. I'm not like Zeinab. I'm a creature of dark passages and silence. I was born among books, and from books. This overworld is a strange and beautiful place, but it's not real. Only the reflections of this world are real, you know this, and the reflections of the reflections. That's where I belong, in my halls of mirrors. You have a gap on your shelves you need to fill, that's why you want me. Isn't it?" She turned to me, suddenly vivid, as if she were being spoken to rather than speaking. "You want another book on your shelves, to gaze at, take down from time to time and coddle. To read. And then put back on your shelves. Let me tell you something, Balthazar. No, be quiet, let me say this. You think you're freeing me. You're not freeing me. You're locking me into your wardrobe. I'd rather be Zeinab, burning books, than locked in your wardrobe. Let me go back down."

"You can go back down."

"I just came up here to read some books. Can't you understand that?"

"That's the part I understand."

"If you won't accept that, I'll just leave."

"Didn't you like the twins?"

"Oh, they're lovely, aren't they?" She looked out at the sea and sighed. "I never knew other girls, other children. Only those in books. I had such long conversations with them. I'd be sent to bed early and I'd lie awake and have these conversations with the children in the books. Out loud, so the rumor spread I was conversant with spirits. But they weren't spirits. You know that. I could meet them again. But also they weren't flesh. How I longed to meet a real child. I willed secret doors to open. I willed children in illustrations to brush aside the tissue paper and step out of their engraved cages, but it never happened. Then I grew to teenage and girls arrived at the gates, girls close to my own age, but still, my childhood was bereft. In some ways. In others, rich beyond compare." A pack of boys jostled past but she didn't notice them. "I don't mean to sound ungrateful," she turned to me suddenly. "I loved your friends. Thank you for taking me to them."

"I have other friends, but it might be dangerous to go to them."

"If only I was stronger."

"What do you mean?"

"If I was stronger I'd just stay in your rooms reading. I'd order you to bring me food, I wouldn't talk with you. But I'm a coward. I had no idea how seductive moonlight could be. Roses, lions, the sea, all this," she lifted a hand.

"You don't have to go back."

She moved to the corniche wall. The water was a morass of shadows, all sparkle drowned. After a while she said, "I need to read. Quick, take me to the books."

Zeinab had told me that rare books are more satisfying to burn. Likewise, a reading environment shapes the books we read. Though we claim to vanish between the pages, though we cannot drag our eyes from the print, yet reading a book on a night train, cross-country, and reading the same book under a parasol in a rainstorm are utterly separate experiences. I took her to my favorite reading spots. A certain café in al-Atariin, where the waterpipes drew nicely and the cardamom coffee was potent. The breakfast room of the Cecil. The derelict dancehall over Chatby beach. The balcony of the Yacht Club. Montaza beach. We read our books side by side. Sometimes, by chance, we turned the pages in unison, as though our reading was a ritual, choreographed, and sometimes our rhythm was syncopated, pages waving like slow semaphores.

. . .

We still read together, before we slept. Once, as we pored over an illustration, I jostled the book and we each received a paper cut from the same page. Gently, I tugged the finger from her mouth and pressed it to mine. Our joined blood turned purple. I dabbed a purple bindi between her eyes.

Then we kissed. But in the throes of her lips a whiff of the city—carrion, brine, ash—snuck over the balcony. Eyes closed, I imagined a veil beneath my face.

I was constantly terrified Zeinab would appear, but I never saw her. Or rather, I saw her everywhere, in every archway, sieved through mashrabiyya, silhouetted behind curtains. Among the mermaids in the sea, beneath every niqab, every time Shireen donned her blue garment. I smelled her when I stepped onto the balcony. Daily I imagined her slipping into my rooms. I imagined her laughter, like a crow fried on a tram-wire, like spectacles crunched underfoot, like lightning in the radio, like the clashing bells on the fringe of a veil.

I took Shireen dancing one night, at the Tempest. Her niqab exotic as any punk paint in that space. Ignoring surly stares from whores I'd had, I led her through the fug to a leather sofa. We held hands and drank arak, watching the revelers jig and stomp. Colored lances of light sliced across her eyes. When she'd drained her glass I pulled her up, tugging against her resistance, and led her to the floor. She shouted in my ear but I could hear nothing but Asala. The glitter ball sprayed a tinsel spindrift over the churning bodies. Dancers making clothed love, tongues braided, hips a single pendulum. The jerkers, the tremblers, those whose buttocks possessed independent buttock-brains. The comic dancers. The drunk staggerers clutching bottles. She danced like a leaf, twisting away from my side and blown like a blue leaf through the crowd, wafting miraculously among elbows and knees, arms at her sides, then raised like boughs. Buffeted, riveted, I stood still to watch her. After a while I fetched my arak and squeezed into a seat near the dance floor. She danced for hours, the leaflike quivering and gusting, finding gaps in the throng, bare feet scattering coins of light, toenails polished by colored light, eyes lifted into the smoke, or closed as if she slumbered there on the dance floor, sleepdancer.

Deaf, we did not speak as we walked back to my rooms at dawn. She was still dancing as we slipped between the sheets. The room tipped like a boat about our locked lips. She pulled my hands onto her breasts, crushed them into her ribcage, but slapped me away when I tried to undo a button.

She woke with a moan, pressed the heels of her palms into her temples. Her lips crackled open. "Water," she said. I filled a glass at the tap, held it while she drank. Then she staggered over to the sink and let the water spill into her cupped hands, dunked her face in it, gulped it down. She hawked up a clot of gray phlegm, then coughed till she threw up. Vomit all over the mirror. Stench of bile and warm arak. She looked at me aghast. "You're the devil!" she said, strings of vomit swinging from her lips. Gripping the porcelain and howling, she puked again. I shouted to Abdallah for tea.

"Here," I said. I wet a washcloth and dabbed her face clean. She had vomit in her eyebrows and her ears. I led her to the bed. Abdallah arrived with the tea and I made her sip it slowly while I wiped the mirror and floor, sluiced the sink. When I finished she was weeping into her cup.

"Enough," she said. "I want to go back to the library. Why did you take me to that place?"

"I wanted to see you dance."

"And throw up."

"I'm sorry about that."

"Well. How did I dance?"

"Like this." I ripped the flyleaf from a paperback, cast it out into the afternoon, where it curled and caught the sun, floating, falling.

"All I remember are lights. Lights in my ears, lights on my tongue. If I close my eyes I can see them."

She ran a fever that afternoon, eyes glittering, face the color of damp sand. I sat by her, read to her. She would not let me hold her hand. But that night, when I thought her asleep, while I read beside her, she murmured: "I didn't make a fool of myself, did I?"

"You were the most beautiful dancer," I told her. "They're still talking about you. Men are wanking to your memory as we speak."

"Balthazar!" She swatted my arm feebly, then drew the sheets to her chin.

"What about Zeinab?" she asked.

"I don't know where she is. I haven't seen her for weeks."

"But what about her?"

"What do you mean?"

"You're in love with her."

"Oh. That." I sat back and laced my fingers across my chest.

"Don't think I'm trying to hold onto you."

"What are you trying to do?"

153

"I'm just curious."

"I see. What do you want me to tell you?"

"What would you do if she walked into the room right now?"

"She wouldn't walk into the room."

"How do you know?"

"She's a thief."

"But if she did?"

"She'd probably throw you over the balcony, then stick a knife in my wrist." I placed a fingernail on the scar, the burred I.

"What do you talk about?"

"We argue."

"About what?"

"About what we should talk about."

"Does she ever just talk?"

"Sometimes."

"What does she say?"

"She tells me about the books she's burned."

She passed her hands across her face, as though wiping away tears, but there were no tears. "Do you like that?" she asked. She sounded timid.

"Of course."

"How does she make you feel?"

"Does she make me feel like you do? Is that what you mean?"

"Does she?"

"No."

"Then what?"

"I don't know her. I know you."

"You think you know me."

I nodded.

"Would you like me better if I never spoke?"

"No."

"Would you like me better if I never took off this veil?"

"No."

"But if she came back, if she came back right now, who would you choose?"

"Are you saying you're in love with me?"

"I'm asking you a question."

"It's possible to be in love with more than one person at the same time."

"I don't want to believe that."

"But you're in love with more than one book."

"All right, but still, there's always a favorite."

"Anyway, I don't have to make that choice."

"I think you do."

"No. I can't afford Zeinab any more. And you're going back underground. Or so you threaten."

"Am I just another of your whores? What do you want from me? I'm not going to be another book on your shelves, to gloat over. I'm not going to sit on your shelves."

I was silent.

"Make your choice."

"Here, in this hour, I choose you, Shireen. I'm obsessed with you. But you'll go underground and I'm a thief."

She was quiet a moment, then smiled sadly. "Go away. Can't you see I'm trying to read?"

Nura called to us as we walked along the corniche near Chatby one night. She was crouching with some friends around a fire lit in a square charred tin. We descended the steps to the sand.

"Balthazar, Zeinab, where have you been?" She stood up as we approached.

"Morning, Nura. This is another friend. Shireen. I haven't seen Zeinab."

"Oh. I see, yes. Sorry." She took Shireen's hand. "Come get warm. Meet my friends."

Her friends were two skinny men with lank hair, eyes at once ravaged and ravishing, the eyes of saints and insomniacs, surfaces burnished by visions. They nodded to us. Nura upturned tins for seats, offered cigarettes. I took one and held it to the flames.

"Balthazar, I was just about to come looking for you. I thought you were gone, but people saw you. At the Tempest, along the corniche. Why don't you come to the Kanisa?"

"I'm busy."

"So I see. Do you steal books as well?" she asked Shireen.

"I'm a novice."

"But you like to read?"

"Oh yes."

"That's wonderful. Sometimes I worry we aren't much fun for Balthazar to talk to, we thieves. He's so smart."

"What do you do?" Shireen inquired politely.

Nura displayed her ravaged arms without compunction.

"But you're a thief as well?"

"Just to feed my addiction. I'm not as professional as Balthazar, I'm afraid. I break in, take what I need." She smiled at Shireen.

One of the men stood and unbelted his trousers and let them drop. Shireen looked at him in alarm, but he sat again and rummaged in a paper bag. His inner thighs were colorful with bruises. She watched fascinated as he prepared the poison, drew it into the syringe, pecked for a vein. When he

156

had crushed the plunger he pulled out the needle, passed it on. His companion shot up in the neck, which caused Shireen to suck in her breath. Nura held the syringe to us. "Will you share?" We shook our heads. "I know how awful it seems from the outside," she said apologetically as she readied her dose, "but it helps me. It's so delicious, the rush. Otherwise I get sad."

"How did you start?" Shireen asked.

"My father was a priest in the Orthodox church. You didn't know that, did you, Balthazar? Yes, I'm a daughter of the church. Look." She touched the blue cross tattooed on her wrist, nearly submerged under needle pricks. "I went every day. I prayed to all the saints. When I was little I saw miracles. Miracles are all around us, of course, happening on every street corner, in every tramcar and every handshake. In every kiss. Often at night—miracles love the darkness—but sometimes in daylight as well. Not everyone can see them, though. A miracle might happen in front of you, your karkadeh suddenly turning to wine or a fever cured by a touch, but your friends will talk about chemical processes and phases of the moon. But whose hand joins the molecules, whose hand nudges the moon through the sky? God is present everywhere." She lifted the syringe, tinkled a fingernail against its surface. "Even here. God lives inside this glass, a djinn I set free every evening.

"I was an unruly child. I saw visions. The virgin, once, above the cross on the bell tower, shining. She had tears on her cheeks. She was so beautiful. I was in love with her. I fell in love with her, and with the icons of the messiah, his face was so sad. Young girls love sadness. My father at first welcomed my love of the church, but he soon got frightened. The visions I saw weren't right. They didn't fit inside his gold frames or under the covers of his books. At breakfast I'd tell what I'd

157

seen in the night, the coupling archangels, their feathers rustling together. The demiurge, master of this world, striding along the corniche in his top hat and boots, his goatee brilliantined, handsome as a ringmaster. The thirty-ninth angel, banished from heaven for the sin of loving too much, tossed out of heaven and into the world. My father would snort to erase my revelations, and then forbid me to talk. My family knew when I had received a vision, though. 'There's a shining about you,' my mother would whisper, and she'd let me stay home, in bed, while she put my father off with the mysteries of women. Seeing visions is wonderful, but also exhausting.

"One night I stole my father's keychain and went to the church and lay naked on the altar, my eyes on the messiah. This was in the hours before dawn—I've always loved the night. He winked at me. He was lonely. I wanted to comfort him. Then I fell asleep. I woke when the priests came into the church to get it ready for the Sunday service. I tried to tell them about my vision, but they really had no choice but to excommunicate me. They couldn't explain why the icon was suddenly smiling, though.

"I wandered through the city. I was fifteen. Friends turned their backs. I lay down in the gardens of rich relatives and they set their dogs on me. So I walked along the corniche and it passed me into the hands of the real saints: the addicts, the thieves, the only people who would take me in. They showed me the way to heaven, the easy way. Daily heaven, daily hell. But it's better than the constant horror of the nun's life. Or the terror of the fanatic. At least I'm certain I'm going to paradise, if only for an hour or two."

Other denizens of the night joined the circle around the fire. A white-bearded man who seemed about to collapse but

THE BOOK ON FIRE

perked up once the drug entered his veins. He pulled out a bamboo nai on which he played a vagrant melody, tapping his foot on the hot tin, his fingers trapping and releasing the harbor lights. A boy and girl arrived, dressed in peasant rags— he in a stained galabiyya and embroidered tagiyya, she in a frock of pink and lilac, a green scarf on her head. They held out their arms to Nura like children begging cookies, and received their treats. The girl still child enough I could read the transformation in her face, the blossoming of bliss as the drug took effect. They sat for a while holding hands, then moved to the edge of the ring of firelight to rut in the sand. A frantic woman, half her hair scorched off, came up and gripped Nura's arm and whispered in her ear, and Nura emptied her purse into the woman's hand.

The moon passed behind the triangular struts of the cranes. Shireen had fallen into conversation with the old man. I walked down to the water's edge and crouched there watching the moonlit refuse wash onto the shore and get swept back, new patterns settling each time. Ships rested in furry gold cocoons on the horizon. I looked back at the group around the fire. It seemed a gentle community, Nura its benign mistress. The old man had started to play again. Nura joined me at the water's edge.

"She's lovely. Who is she?"

"Just a friend."

"You seem content."

"Maybe. For a little while."

"Is she leaving?"

"I think so."

"Over the sea?"

"Underground. You won't tell, will you, Nura?"

She touched my arm.

"She's up here to read my books."

"I see."

"I'm scared, Nura. Is it possible to return to the old life?"

"You're welcome to join us here."

"Thank you. Perhaps I will. It would be nice to forget now and then."

"When will she go?"

"Soon. She's reading the last book. Slowly. I'm trying to distract her, take her out, but the book's so good."

And as if she'd heard, Shireen came up behind us. "Balthazar, I think I have to go back now."

Abuna Makarios banged into my room the next afternoon while we lay kissing on the bed. I had just coaxed open her gown, the first sighting of breast. "Pastoral visit!" he trumpeted. Shireen shrieked. He bore a wine bottle in each fist, a net bag of communion bread dangled from his wrist. "No no, don't let me stop you," he gestured expansively. "I'll watch," and he sat down at my desk chair, which moaned alarmingly. But kisses and giggles don't mix, so I rolled away from Shireen and we sat up. She turned away, closing the gown, tying the knot.

"Nice tits," he nodded at her. He sucked the cork out of a bottle and tipped half the contents down his throat. "Small, the nipples well-defined. Would you like to see my testicles?" he inquired.

"No thank you."

"Just as well, they're none too pretty. And none too clean. Balthazar." He stood and subsumed me in his black garments. Priestly reek of stale lees and incense. "I came to see how you were, but looks like you're happy," and he nodded at my straining zipper. "Wine?" He sucked the cork out of the second bottle before we could answer and tossed it to us. "Special stuff," he nodded as Shireen peered at the label that depicted a drunken savior. "Contains the saliva of the Pope himself." She drank cautiously, then laughed.

"Who's the girl?" Makarios asked me.

"Ask her."

He jutted his black beard at Shireen, raised his eyebrows.

"My name is Shireen. I'm here to read Balthazar's books."

"Good, good. Are you a churchgoer?"

"I don't know. I've never had the opportunity."

"You're welcome to stop by some evening. Good drink, good company. All the host you can eat. Do you play badminton?"

"I never have."

"Balthazar here is champion. Snappy wrist, quick feet. Karim's getting cocky in your absence, Balthazar. I'd be good, but my gut weighs me down. And I can't see out of my eyebrows. And these robes aren't designed for sport. Well, I thought we might take communion together. What do you say?" He cocked a caterpillar eyebrow at Shireen, who nodded. "Fantastic!" He pulled out a gold loaf, broke it across the stamped skull, releasing a gout of steam. "Fresh from the oven," he said. "Baked it myself." He passed the bread around—"This is my body"—pulled out a wedge of cheese and a jar of olives. "Go to it. Fondling always brings up the appetite. Mind if I smoke?" He hauled his pipe from somewhere within his garments, tapped the stale ashes onto my rag rug, filled it, and set a match to the bowl. He ate and drank as he smoked, spewing crumbs with each exhalation. "You have a nice perch here, Balthazar. But where are the books?"

"Hidden."

"Best policy. Read any theology lately? Of course, it's all theology. We try to fool ourselves, we say they're just stories, just entertainment, but it's all theology. And you're a reader too, sister?" Shireen nodded with her mouth full. "Excellent. I can't keep up with Balthazar, of course, too many widows to comfort, but I like a little book chat now and then. He's read everything. Well, you know that, being a reader and all. But I do try to keep abreast of the latest heresies. Even tried to write a gospel myself once. Didn't go so well. I'm a preacher, not a scribe. But I thought it would have a nice ring: The Gospel According to Makarios. Everyone should write a gospel, in my opinion. Have you written one?"

"I'm afraid not."

"Give it a go. You'll find it very liberating. Are you a thief?"

"Balthazar's trying to teach me."

"Couldn't have a better tutor. Myself excepted, of course. Come along to the Kanisa some night and I'll give you a few tips. Might even show you my little collection of gnostic blasphemy. Are you sure you don't want to see my testicles?"

She laughed. "Quite sure, thank you."

"Well, I must be off. Appointment with a grieving widow, you know," he winked. "She likes nothing better than to juggle my filthy nuts." And he was off, leaving behind two bottles of sweet wine, his sacred stench, and a triangle of black cloth like a pirate's pennant on the jamb where he'd squeezed through the door.

. . .

She read all morning to finish the last of my books, then slept all evening. She woke at midnight. "I'd like to go to church," she said.

"I don't know if that's a good idea."

"The priest invited me."

"Well..."

"Am I a prisoner?"

"All right."

We dressed and walked to the Kanisa. Abuna Makarios opened the door to a congregation of Karim, Amir, and Nura. Karim clutched his heart as Shireen pulled her veil aside.

"Zeinab?" he stammered. "But you're bald!"

"This is Shireen," I said. "A friend."

"Is she a thief?" Amir asked suspiciously.

"Indubitably. Look at her shoes."

"What do you steal?" Karim asked.

"Leave her alone," Nura said. "She's my friend," and she put an arm around Shireen's waist and led her to the table.

"No, I want an answer. What does she steal?"

"Can't you see she's shy?" Nura scolded.

"I'll answer." Shireen's voice was quiet. "I've come to this city from far away, farther than the north pole or the moon. You want to know what I steal, what I'll take away from here? The sun on the bay at dawn, a croissant at the Trianon, curtains in a breeze, moths in jasmine, blue palm prints on whitewashed walls, crows, flamboyants, minarets. And Nura's smile, and Balthazar's kiss."

Karim looked dubious, but luckily Makarios, who'd been rummaging in the sacristy, now blew through the curtains like a black gale, bearing a tray with drinks and communion bread slathered with olivada. "Ah, my pretty sister, welcome, welcome. Delighted you could come. Choose a drink, my dear:

ouzo, arak, karkadeh. Blood of Christ, of course."

Karim subsided with his ouzo but still glared at Shireen. He brightened when I challenged him to a badminton match. We played with our drinks in our hands, ice clashing as we zigzagged the court. On the brink of fifteen I thought better of it and lobbed the shuttlecock into the shadows. It nosedived into Amir's glass. I let Karim snatch the game and he smirked as he walked off the court. "Balthazar's lost his touch. Distracted by the bald interloper, I believe. Better luck next time, book thief." Sitting down opposite Shireen, he called for a celebratory round of ouzo. He downed three in succession and was soon beetroot and bellicose. "So why Balthazar?" he said. "What does Balthazar the bookworm have to offer?"

"He likes to read."

"Reading's for children and grandmothers. Pages filled with fake ghosts. When you've seen a real ghost you can't be bothered with the paper variety."

"You've seen ghosts?"

"Every night."

"Could you take me to see one?"

"All you'd see is dust, you'd feel the wind on your neck. I know readers. You fuck around with belief so much you don't know what's real anymore. You wouldn't know a ghost if it bit your ass. This city is filled with ghosts and dreamers, passing each other in the street. I watch them walk through each other. Only those of us who spend time with the dead, with bones and winding sheets, can see the spirits."

"But books are filled with ghosts."

"Books are wood chips and oak galls. Don't fool yourself, darling."

"I love to fool myself."

"That's the problem. Right there," said Karim. He shook

up cigarettes, held one out to her. She shook her head. "You've boxed yourself in with books and have to squint at the world through little chinks between the pages. Of course you've never met a ghost. Here's what I suggest." He lit his cigarette, inhaled, then held the burning match out to her. His words came out on a raft of smoke, tousling the flame. "One little match, darling. Solve all your problems. Clear the cataracts from your eyes. Take my medicine."

Shireen looked at me in alarm. "Teach me to play." She gestured to the badminton court. So I showed her how to hold the racket, made her practice swinging it, then served to her. She shrieked and closed her eyes as the shuttlecock descended. We tried again and again. I finally got her to keep her eyes open, but then she'd forget to swing. At last, when the shuttlecock had bounced off her forehead, she collapsed giggling, racket clattering to a halt beside her.

Abuna Makarios seized Shireen's arm and dragged her away. "Come see my books," he said.

"Careful with that rascal," Nura called as they went up the stairs. "If he gropes you, pull his eyebrows." Makarios winked at me and mimed buggery behind Shireen's ascending derriere.

They were gone a long time and, concerned, I climbed the stairs to Makarios's belfry hideaway, but they were sitting side by side on his bed, bent over a heretical text and deep in discussion about the existence of angels. Shireen seemed shocked that some denied their reality. "But surely," she was saying, "I mean, they come into so many books. And it seems natural that some people would have developed wings."

"I agree. Haven't seen them myself, mind, but I'm sure they're out there. Perhaps further north. Or east. Ah, Balthazar, what do you think? Do angels exist?"

"Why not?"

"Excellent answer. Well, shall we join the others?"

We descended the stairs. Shireen was beside me, and I felt her stiffen. Looking up, I saw only the pockets of candlelight, eyes of icons. But then a blue shadow detached itself from the doorframe. Zeinab had arrived.

She and Shireen stared at each other. I couldn't breathe, let alone speak. "Aren't you going to introduce us?" Zeinab laughed. Her voice, after Shireen's murmur, clashed like rusty cymbals.

"I don't think we need introductions," Shireen said. Her voice shook. I thought it was fear, then saw the brightness in her look.

Makarios looked from one to the other, bewildered. "You know each other?" he said.

"Not yet," Zeinab told him. She seized Shireen's hand and, before I could muster a word, whirled her out the door, into the night.

I was the last to leave the Kanisa that evening. I waited for Zeinab to return with my prize, but the hours passed. I played badminton and chess, drank arak. I held a book on my lap, but couldn't see the words. Makarios was yawning. "I'm off to bed, librarian. Blow out the candles before you leave."

All that night I walked through the city, peering into every doorway, veering into every alley, horrified by the imagined conversations in my head. Horrified and mesmerized. I tried to hush the voices, shove them under by blabbering poetry, but they surfaced, insidious. Returning to my rooms, I fell asleep athwart my mattress, fully clothed, and immediately entered a vision.

Two girls are dancing across the rooftops of Alexandria, books in their hands, matches in their hands, leaving comet tails, peacock plumage of sparks in their wake, two girls in blue, blue-veiled against the sky. Their thin-soled shoes are so light on the tiles and crenellation they seem to scamper on a wafer of oxygen, never touching down. They pirouette on minarets, shimmy down domes, slipping gravity's leash so they can tiptoe eave to eave, their steppingstones sparks and gnats and fraying smoke rings. The books in their hands are flowers, kites, fireworks, balloons. One lights a book and passes it to the other, who holds it heavenward like a burning offering, and it is accepted, gathered into the sky, lifted on the cord of the smoke it generates. And they are dancing and opening books, the leaves ripped unread and lifted on their own hot breath across the sea, above the towers and domes of the city, torn apart by their own wings, and each morsel, bearing its cargo of word or syllable beneath an evanescent parasol, rising to join the stars.

Lying on my bed, I whispered to them, my dancing figments. This was a new species of sadness. The sadness of starlight traveling a million years to crumple in the bay, of Oum Koulsoum's contralto detailing the remnants of a lover's campsite, the sadness of writing a letter you'll never send. I imagined them dervishing on minarets over the bay, blue skirts parasols, sea breeze whalebone, fingers plucking stars like figs, slipping them beneath their veils.

A veiled figure shook me awake. I sat up, my head a heart. "What did you do with her?" I gasped, then saw the book-shaped pupils. "Oh. Sorry. Welcome back." She lifted her veil and I could see in her face the afterglow of something.

"Where were you?"

"Out for a rooftop stroll."

"What did she tell you?"

"Secrets."

"I have to know. Did she . . . did she light a match?"

"You know I won't say."

"What did you talk about?"

"All secrets, Balthazar."

"Did you talk about me?"

"Hush."

We went onto the balcony. Skyful of ash. Now she could lean over the balustrade, thirsty for the light and space. She took a bath, read a little, went to sleep. I lay beside her all that day while she slept, watching her breathe, watching the small struggles of her face, the ebb and flow of her dreams. Sometimes she said a word, in a language unknown to me. Sometimes her eyelids would part and she seemed to look at me but she saw her secret pages. Twelve hours she slept, then woke at dusk.

"This is the last night, isn't it?" I said.

She nodded.

"Is there anything I could . . . ?"

"You've been wonderful. These have been the most lovely days. Oh, the books. I'll never forget reading your books in your room. That shelf is on fire, I see it in flames and unconsumed. And those wonderful meals. And the city, so many things, the lights, the faces. Lions and roses. The night we went stealing, the girl who found us—the angel in her nightgown, bearing kofta sandwiches. And your kiss, of course. This has been my two-week marriage. To my demon, my thief." She turned her small fist in my hand. "But now I have

THE BOOK ON FIRE

to go down again. This has been a necessary holiday, more beautiful than I'd imagined, but I'm a creature of dark corners, dusty passages. The books are my family, I have to return to them."

"I'm . . . I'm angry."

"Yes."

"I'll see you again. Down there."

"No."

"What?" I gripped the edge of the sheet.

"You're forbidden to enter the library again."

"By whom?"

"By me."

"Why?"

"You want another book in your wardrobe, Balthazar. In a blue dust jacket. I don't want to be pawed and cosseted. I don't want to be cataloged. All my life I've been stashed away, folded up, handled with care. I don't want to be a book on your shelf."

"Zeinab put you up to this."

"No."

I was silent a while. Then: "How will you stop me?"

"The librarians won't be sleepwalking this time. I'm going to have to tell them I was kidnapped. They'll be more vigilant. And you forget that I'm trained to defend the books." As she had during our first conversation, she brought her hand down in a semicircle, laid its edge against my neck. "Are you crying?" she said. "Don't cry. Here, sweetheart, sweet dreams, silverfish, don't cry." She touched my face, let her fingers rest on my cheek a moment, then put her hand in her lap.

For a long time we sat side by side, without touching. At last she said, "Well, Balthazar."

"Would you like coffee? Something to eat?"

"No. I'll wait till I'm underground. Thank you, though."

"You seem happy."

"Do I?"

I tugged her fingers, bit one gently.

"Don't fret," she said.

"No."

"I'll get dressed."

She went into the wardrobe and came out after a while, wearing her niqab.

We walked along the corniche, past flower girls and perfume sellers and distraught lovers. When we reached the lighthouse she put her palms on the corniche wall and leaned across, looking at the sea. She closed her eyes and inhaled, then took off her glasses and buffed them on her veil. She turned to me.

I uncovered the trapdoor in the lighthouse floor, lit a candle, and we descended into the dark. The stations of the way to the library—the dark river, the tombs of the scribes, the bones of the book thieves—which had been holy because they led to her, were now nightmarish as they had been at my first entrance. At the threshold of the room with the sarcophagus I turned, placed a hand on her arm.

"Come back with me."

"Balthazar."

"All right. All right. Kiss me, then."

Her lips were so soft, tasted of cinnamon. Then she entered the sarcophagus. I closed the cover.

VII
Winter Rain

IF YOU'RE GOING to stare and sleep, Alexandria in winter is a fine place to do it. Here you can wander along the corniche, laying your forehead on the cool lampposts while waves shatter on the stones. Here you can sit for hours over cups of coffee, smoking waterpipes. Here you can nurse a bottle of Omar Khayyam through a bereft evening at the Elite, watching passing djinns through misted windows.

I slept and slept, sometimes escaping daylight altogether, so the world seemed to have entered an age of darkness. I could not read. The book on my lap grew heavier with each turned page, as if I held a slab of wood, glass, iron. I laid it aside and simply stared at the ceiling. Some serial plumbing catastrophe had left concentric brown rings above my head, like the orbits of erratic moons. I followed those orbits for hours, listening to the trams groaning like whales as they ferried souls through the city.

I slept so well. Early winter in Alexandria is excellent sleeping weather, the air just chilly enough you don't want to leave your cocoon. I'm not ordinarily a talented sleeper: too many books to read. A jangling bell or quarrel in the square and I'm instantly awake, salivating for cardamom coffee, a page of metal Bembo. But now the effort of dragging off the blankets and pulling on my robe and walking to the door and unlocking it and turning the handle and opening it and calling to Abdallah seemed inordinate labor, so I'd stare at the ceiling a while, then close my eyes. Sleep was always there, a blink away. While I slept, Abdallah brought sandwiches and fruit. I woke and ate a few bites, slept again, and the plates had been cleared. I told him to turn visitors away. I heard Nura gently chiding one evening, Koujour hassling him on another. I wouldn't have minded a visit from either, but couldn't pull free of my pillow.

Then one afternoon the proprietor came in demanding the rent. I asked him to hand me the trousers I'd slung over the back of my chair and my jacket from the wardrobe but dredged up a single guinea. Grudgingly, he granted me a week's grace.

Astonishing what a week in bed can do to one's appearance. I peered into the face of a mendicant or desert father: crushed, bearded, hair soft greasy spikes. I shaved, showered, drank four cups of coffee, and set out groggily over the rooftops.

That night, for the first time since the expedition with Shireen, which had yielded only her kiss—priceless, but not currency enough to buy a cup of coffee—I moved through the city with my satchel. Being horizontal for so long seemed to have affected my balance, because I slipped twice on the gables, once escaping a plunge to the street below only because my belt buckle caught in a rain gutter. Trying to jimmy the window of a house in Mahmoudiyya I first broke my lock pick, then tore a fingernail, then yanked the window open so violently I smashed the glass. A dog barked in a neighboring yard and lights came on in an upper floor. Still I stood leaning on the windowsill, staring stupidly into the dark house, till I heard shouts and footsteps, and I turned and lumbered off.

Running cleared my head a bit and the second break-in went more smoothly, though I realized once I'd entered the house that it was uninhabited, barren of books. On the third burglary the scent of paper finally entered my nostrils like smelling salts. I found my way to a room of shelves, but my skills were eroding or my timing was off, because the stash I encountered was savorless. The delicious books were gone, stolen or burned, and I ran my finger in the slots where they had stood, trying to imagine the titles, trying to imagine the hand that had snatched them away. Do you know what it is to lose your art? Your skills foundering, as though your fingertips crumbled like a leper's at the touch of paper or skin.

I read through the books on my shelf, as she had, and they were changed because she had read them. And though they sustained me in my sorrow, though I felt that without my shelf of books I would long ago have let go, they were not enough. Though I possessed the most beautiful books in the world, they were not enough.

. . .

Season of winter rains. Kassem veering into al-Faida al-Sughayara. The sky steeped in ink, crows hurled across rooftops. Shivering, I walked along the corniche, cigarette fuming within my fist. The water spilled down the striped awnings of the seafront cafés, pocking dents into the flagstones, and I imagined the drops denting my skull as well. The chairs lay tipped against the tables, forgotten ashtrays overflowing onto the tin. Everyone else had taken shelter behind shuttered windows. They sat indoors, heads wrapped in blankets, sipping tea and whining about the weather, but walking in the rain seemed the only sane activity to me.

Alexandrian women, learning of the departure of a loved one, enter a series of practiced, ritualized gestures and cries, beating their faces with stiff palms, a tuneful animal in their throats. Thus they tame their grief and keep the djinns at bay. I was heir to no such ritual. Abandoned, I succumbed to my sorrow, drowning, and thought I might never surface.

In Midan Saad Zaghloul I sat on the edge of the fountain and listened to the chattering palm fronds and some half-remembered song on the radio.

وانتبهنا بعد ما زال الرحيق   وأفقنا ليتنا لا نفيق
وتولى الليل والليل صديق   يقظة طاحت بأحلام الكرى
وإذا النور نذيرٌ طالع وإذا الفجر مطلٌّ كالحريق
وإذا الدنيا كما نعرفها وإذا الأحباب كلٌّ في طريق

The rain entered my collar and trickled down my spine. I tried to remember conversations with Shireen, but couldn't summon a single word. They survived, on this afternoon, as texture and weight, as one might remember holding a starfish or an artichoke. The words fell away and I was left with a roughness beneath my breastbone, an ache in my shoulder blades, as if I'd been carrying something heavy, as if huge wings had recently been hacked away.

What was she reading now? I imagined her sitting in her owl-colored armchair. If I closed my eyes I could almost dream myself into the book she read, the rain on my nape her fingers on the spine. An empty tram slished past, turning up silver sillion of rainwater. After a while, I went back to my rooms and took a bath.

I cannot let you go, Shireen, and cannot fathom what you are becoming. Sitting in these cafés, by the sea, in this harsh season, staring at rain, at panes and pages washed by raindrops and unshed tears, I cannot tell you, cannot speak you, but I hold what you were for me like a pebble, hot obol on my eyelids, under my tongue. How many words passed between us? And now, in the throes of my soliloquy, I recall only one, the sound of my name, spoken in your voice, which is the subdued, impassioned voice of a reader, of someone who occasionally whispers words, testing words on the tongue, of someone who samples conversations and gestures, shrugging them on and off like clothing.

Could you let me go? Have you already let go, cast off, books in hands and pockets to weight you, to ensure your descent? The blue thicknesses of water and air closing over your face. You will not turn. Are you reading, Shireen, in your cozy jail? What might have kept you by my side, in the overworld? Another book, perhaps. Another kiss. How could I have clutched you to myself? Forever, I want to say. All right: forever. What would it take? I imagine flaying you, peeling away your skin, using my paperknife to pare the meat from your bones, and desiring even the bones. I would keep them in an acacia box with a little gold clasp, each bone individually wrapped in silk. Every evening I'd take them out and polish them with silk and olive oil. I'd place your finger bones in my mouth to cleanse them of dust. I'd lay your arm bones along mine, press the hoops of your pelvis to my groin. I'd leave your eye sockets turned into the box.

There seemed no hope. Yet I persisted. Why? Habit, perhaps. The ordinary is often the only savior from drowning. I could feel my grip sliding. What bliss to sink beneath the lights, into the weightless deep, where obsolete gods slumbered among angelfish. Not yet, though, not yet. Cling a while to the edges of this city. What keeps us going? The bitter-chocolate aftertaste of a macchiato? A phrase of Oum Koulsoum on the radio? A breath of apple tobacco? A pickled lemon? The sum of these?

I returned to the Kanisa Prometheus. Makarios opened the door, opened his arms to embrace me, then gripped my shoulders and held me at arm's length. "What happened to you? You look dreadful."

I mumbled something.

"Where's your friend?"

"Gone."

"Dead?"

"No. Well . . ."

"Girls come and go, Balthazar. Get over it."

"I'll be all right. Where are Karim and Amir? And Nura?"

"Karim and Amir have been spending more time together," Makarios smiled. "My sermons must have had some effect. Or the communion wine." Then his eyes lost their crinkle. "Nura's in hospital again."

"Will she be all right?"

"She's in God's hands."

"I'll visit her."

"Can I get you anything?"

"Give me some of that wine."

Koujour and Zeinab were bent over a chessboard. I sat on the arm of Koujour's chair and watched the game. He looked up and grimaced. "She's killing me."

Makarios came back with a wineglass in each hand.

"Badminton?" I asked.

"I'll swat it around with you."

We didn't play a game, just batted the shuttlecock across the net.

"What have you been reading?" Makarios asked, puffing slightly, though I planted the shuttlecock on his sweet spot every time.

"All the old books. But they've lost their savor."

"What's that?" The shuttlecock bounced off the cross on his chest. He picked it up laboriously and preened the feathers while he peered at me across the net.

"I've been looking for a good book. Something new, something fresh. Among your gnostic gospels, is there one for thieves?"

"They're all for thieves. Even the act of writing a gospel is an act of thievery. All they can do, the writers of the gospels, is hold their papyrus, their notebooks, to the sky, and hope they catch fire. Some do, some don't."

The shuttlecock was swinging again. Pop of cork on gut,

the ring of feathers wobbling into the shadows, plummeting in a smooth arc, past the stares of the saints, into the candlelight.

"Have you ever thought of writing a gospel yourself?" he asked.

"I'm a thief, Makarios. Quite the other thing."

"The opposite of something is not necessarily its enemy."

"What do you mean?"

"One way to God is through the demiurge."

"Have you seen him? The demiurge?"

"Several times. He haunts the cafés of al-Atariin, sharing waterpipes with his lover."

"What does he look like?"

"Oh, he's a handsome bastard all right."

"And his lover?"

"She wore a veil, color of shadows."

Later, after Koujour had left and Makarios went to bed, I sat across from Zeinab.

"Where did you take her?" I asked. "What did you teach her?"

"That's a secret. But tell me—why her, book thief? What is it about her?"

"She was born from a book, umbilical cord a bookmark sewn into the book's heart. Somewhere in the library is the book that is her mother. To feel her mother's embrace she folds herself into pages. Her blood is blue as ink. When she blinks pages turn, but I can't read the letters of fire. She was born with spectacles on her nose. She has a mole on her neck, embedded like a clove, to keep silverfish at bay. She reads like I breathe. I love to watch her read. Like watching a beautiful woman fall from a tower, endlessly, the same tug at the gut. Like watching a beautiful woman drown herself. Her skin is the color of fallen leaves, of rivers in flood. A particular brown

I've found so elusive and so desirable. Kissing her is like reading. I'm obsessed with the image of her holding a book."

"How does she hold a book?"

"Here." I tucked Zeinab's feet under her thighs, artfully ruffled her skirts, laid her cheek on her hand, head tilted down and to the side, and placed a book on her lap. I showed her how to stroke the book. "Not like that. Like this. Like a cat. As if you were stroking a kitten. Yes, that's better. Now read." I sat back. She turned a page but her eyes were on my face. I smelled her perfume. Odor of ripe kelp, sautéed garlic, frangipani, myrrh. Then she began tearing a page.

I sat back and watched her, involved in the act that is the opposite of reading. Dismantling a book is hard work, and as she labored she shifted positions, leaning over the book, taking a better grip.

Prying off the covers, she peeled back the cloth from the boards, and I saw the brown flesh of the book. Even this she savaged, shredding the cartonnage, itself the layered strata of dozens of destroyed volumes. The boards removed, it was easy work to pluck off the flyleaves and endpapers, tearing them into marbled plumage. Now I could see the complicated cords and needlework and stacked folds of the spine, the rainbow headbands. She yanked out the red tongue of the bookmark, then set to work tearing the signatures apart. They separated with a series of dull reports as the cords pulled through the paper. She ripped each signature meticulously into shards, each loaded with markings: severed words, or specks and scrapings of ink from illustrations. In a few minutes the dismantled book lay about her feet and in the blue trough of her lap: petals of paper and stamens of cord, noded with dried glue, a few stiff blue rags. She brushed her hands together, satisfied: "This is the future of all books."

179

I was suddenly vertiginous with desire. "What would you cost?"

"You couldn't afford me, book thief. Not anymore."

"Name your price."

"All the books."

"What?"

"You heard me. All the books on your shelf."

"So you can burn them."

"Of course."

"Never."

"Your books will burn, Balthazar. This city will devour them."

Coming back with a modest haul from a house near Stanley Bay, I noticed Koujour's light was still on and climbed up to his studio. He had just finished a painting, executed in sand, shoe polish, and blue ballpoint in the manner of Tahir Bushra. Long-horned cattle, symbols from Saharan rock faces, geckos on a dark ground.

"Good," he said when I stepped in. "Drink merissa." He poured me a gourdful and we sat looking over the sea.

"Merissa will make you strong," he said. "You are thin."

"I need help. Advice."

"Yes."

I told him I had lost the only woman I could read with.

"The eyes."

"Yes. Shireen."

"Where?"

"Well . . . dead. Buried, at any rate."

"You sleep?"

"Too much."

"You fuck?"

"I . . ."

"Ah, yes. Yes. Merissa is good. Drink merissa." He topped up my gourd. "In my country if someone is sick we go to the priest. I am a priest. Did you know? Yes, in my country.

"When I was young, eighteen, nineteen, I dreamed. Strong dreams. A leopard put his feet on my shoulders. A snake bit my tongue. I could feel the kuni coming, like the rain. One night, lightning. My house on fire. Only my house. I saw no fire. My mother pulled me out. I shouted, they told me. My eyes were white. This was the beginning.

"I prepared for the tir, to open the head. My clansmen came. I was kuni da koyidi: the spirit came to me. My family made a house of grass. Fifteen days inside. My clansmen did not touch their wives. They touch, their children die. Then the big feast, many animals killed, merissa, dancing. The drums. The kuni came. Now I am koujour. Look." He touched his jewelry. "Four iron bracelets, here. This bead, white." He touched his throat. "These rings in my ears. Scars. Touch." And he grabbed my wrist and drew my hand over his textured cheeks. "We must decorate, Balthazar. Do you hear?"

I nodded.

He was leaning into my touch, pressing my palm against his face. "You must decorate. Do not leave your life smooth. Make a scar, make a color. Do you see my brushes?" He pointed to a gourd stuffed with feathers, chewed twigs, knives, matchsticks. "You paint with what you find in your hands. Even this . . ." He seized my hand. "Even this." He gripped a finger. "Even this. Paint with this."

I staggered away from him, laughing at myself for having applied to a drunken Nuban for advice.

. . .

Carrying a bright bouquet of stolen paperbacks beneath guttering bulbs, I moved past walls graffitoed in blood, past bloodstained gurneys. In a wastebasket, among apple cores and yellowed gauze, a fly preened its wings on an eyeball. I had to ask directions twice before I found Nura's room. Her lips were covered in flies and she was so pale I thought she was dead, then saw the sheet tremble at her breast.

She had gorgeous bones, and as they rose to the surface she became lovely. I could imagine her as pure skeleton, unadulterated by flesh, lying in the sand, or beneath the sea, opalescent as mother-of-pearl, her phosphorescent crosses glowing green in the gloom.

She opened her eyes when I waved away the flies. The platters on the bedside table had been subsumed under pastel mold. Her lips parted, but her throat was too dry to speak. I filled a glass at a tap in the hallway, then propped her up and she sipped, the water spilling onto her throat and the sheets. Her eyes glittered in violet bruises. She stank of urine and crushed bedbugs.

"Balthazar," she said.

"How are you, Nura?"

"I'll be all right. This is one of my homes. I'm friends with the nurses."

"I brought you these. I don't know if you'll like them." I held up the paperbacks.

"Thank you so much. I'm sure they'll be lovely. Just set them over there. Clear a space. Balthazar, look at me. You're haggard. What happened?"

"It's been a rough winter. My addiction finally caught up with me."

"You need to be careful or you'll end up in here."

I looked around. "It's not so bad."

"It's a good place to rest," she agreed. "Where's your friend? Shireen."

"She left."

"I'm so sorry."

I shrugged. "Do you need anything?"

"No, I'm fine. Well, if you see any of my friends you could tell them to bring me some stuff. You know."

"Are you sure, Nura?"

She nodded. "I feel much better."

"Would you like me to read to you?"

"Yes please."

I chose a paperback and sat at the foot of the bed and started reading. She closed her eyes, smiling. After a while I realized she'd fallen asleep. Flies gathered on her lips. I finished the story silently, then placed the book on her bedside table and tiptoed out.

That evening as I sat at my corner table in the Elite, nursing my Omar Khayyam and staring out the window, Karim and Amir walked in. They saw me and came over. "What's this?" I looked from one face to the other. "A reconciliation?"

They looked at each other and smiled a little awkwardly. "It's like this . . ." said Karim.

The waiter came over with menus. "Have you eaten, Balthazar?" Amir asked.

"No."

Karim ordered a steak, Amir moussaka. I waved the waiter away, then called him back. "Another bottle," I said, flicking my glass with a fingernail. I divided the remaining wine between their glasses.

"Are you all right?" Amir asked.

I shook my head.

"It's your bald friend, isn't it?" said Karim.

I nodded.

"Anything we can do?"

"Sit with me." I laid the glass against my forehead, pressing the rim into my scalp, hoping it would shatter.

"I searched her pockets, you know," said Amir.

"What? When?"

"The Gianacles line. She was holding a blue balloon."

"What did you find?"

"At first I thought they were empty. But then—the strangest thing—I felt a prickling in my fingertips, like a series of sparks. As if braille was written in sparks on her skin."

"What did you read?"

"Nothing. But I felt there were words. I could have read them if I was blind."

"How's your work?" I asked.

"Good, good," Amir said. "Karim took me on his rounds."

"I thought you two were at war."

"We were. But then one day he caught me." Amir undid the top two buttons of his shirt and displayed the scab, stroke of rust on his olive skin.

"I thought I'd killed him. We were on the roof of the theater."

"*La Traviata*. The lovers' song. You know the one. I had to glance in, to the stage."

"My knife met his body. He grabbed his chest and fell. I thought I'd killed him. And in that moment, I didn't know what I'd do if I had."

"Karim carried me back to his apartment. He made me tea and soup. Lovely soup. I had no idea he could cook."

"And now you're ransacking graves," I said. "Have you seen any ghosts?"

"I'm learning to look. I think I saw something, like a bit of cobweb in a corner, but I couldn't be sure. I'm teaching Karim to pick pockets."

"Is he any good?"

Amir smiled. "He's dreadful." He picked up Karim's hairy, calloused hand and pulled at the fingers, ran his palm over the burred fingernails. "He couldn't pick a quadriplegic's shoelaces with these bananas."

Karim didn't pull away from his touch, and their hands lay side by side on the table, little fingers overlapping. The food arrived. "Eat something." Karim held out a forkful of charred meat. "You're thin."

"I'm not hungry. I'll eat later."

"This moussaka is delicious," said Amir.

"Can I try?" Karim bent to him and they put their forks in each other's mouths.

There is no sorrow like the sorrow of abandonment. If she'd been on another continent, if she'd disappeared leaving no address, if she'd died, perhaps I could have reconciled myself to it. But she walked beneath my feet: the mole on her neck was a clove-shaped pea and I the tossing princess. Sometimes, pacing the alleys, I imagined we were magnets on either side of the earth's crust, the turnings I chose dictated by her rovings through the library labyrinth. I dreamed I was watching her reading. For hours I paced the perimeter of the library fence, peered into the face of every shaven-headed witch. "Where's Shireen?" I called to the librarians. "Tell her Balthazar greets her." But their glances brushed my face and moved on. They were accustomed to madmen.

Through every thought ran the golden-brown thread of her memory. Every book I read, every meal I ate, every sunrise I watched, I wanted to shout to her. Constantly I conversed with her, another zany muttering along the corniche. Sudden outbursts as I sat alone. Abrupt gestures at the Kanisa. Nura, recently released from the hospital, told me I displayed all the symptoms of withdrawal and wondered if I needed someone to sit by me and bathe my forehead with cool cloths.

In front of the mirror, as I shaved, I'd pause to argue a point with Shireen, stabbing the air with my razor, then catch sight of myself in the glass. I'd admonish my image, waggling a finger at my nose. "Watch it, Balthazar. This is how it starts. Soon you'll be barking like a dog, dragging your sack of paperbacks through the streets." But as I sat on the balcony she'd invade my skull again and I'd give in, jerking my wineglass about, mumbling to my djinn, while the urchins in the midan giggled and pointed.

At last, as I was leaving the Kanisa one night, drunk, wacky as a monkey, Koujour and Makarios each seized an elbow and dragged me back inside, into the sacristy, stripped me naked, laid me on the altar, and bound my wrists and ankles to the horns with chains ripped from censers. The messiah gazed from the ceiling, T to my X. I saw for the first time that the thorns on his brow in fact grew from his scalp, their tips pen-nibs dripping blue blood on my forehead, an emission like ink or sap or semen, natural and salubrious. Priest and painter performed over me that night an exotic exorcism, conjoining the lore of Coptic Orthodoxy and Nuban spirituality.

Koujour wore a mask he'd carved himself, not so distant from his own daubed visage, with stained eye sockets and stippled cheeks, though the mask bore horns and a beard of strung mirror fragments. He shook a calabash rattle in one hand, a colobus-tail flywhisk in the other. Makarios, clad in his own ridiculous costume, brandished a cross and a censer. They sang and danced for me that night, cavorting like the ambassadors of Oberon himself, their chants and dancing at first clashing, so they banged elbows, and censer and flywhisk knocked in a spray of sparks, but as the night wore on they learned to dance with each other, round and round the altar, fat priest and masked Nuban, in a haze of incense and mirror-sparkles, and their songs learned a harmony. Koujour brushed my body with powdered color—karkadeh bellybutton, sky-blue cock, saffron rings around my nipples, and Makarios double-crossed my forehead with holy ash. At last, as the dawn prayer calls flooded the city, Makarios placed his hands aside my skull and Koujour flailed my belly with his whisk and they shouted the invocation at the same moment, summoning my demon. I fainted.

When I came to, Koujour had doffed his mask and Makarios was blotting his brow with a corner of his cassock and they were examining in the dawn light a blade-like object. I sat up.

"Do you feel better?" Makarios inquired.

Closing my eyes, I did an internal assessment. "I feel a bit washed out."

"Yes, washed," said Koujour. "Look. From your stomach." He held up the object for my inspection and I saw it was a palm leaf. As he shifted it against the stained glass I saw the bright prickling and read the message.

I lay back. "I see," I said. "Thank you."

VIII
Catching Fire

FOR YEARS THE RELIGIOUS factions of Alexandria had been honing their rhetoric—those who trusted in a single book (but which one?), those who claimed the purpose of human existence was to amass as large a library as possible, those who insisted illiteracy was the only way to salvation, those who believed we were all characters in a book read by the demiurge. Each sect had developed an architecture codifying its beliefs, and so the churches, mosques, synagogues, and temples had sprung up in the hinterlands of the city, with symbolic stained glass and friezes, and even the proportions of minaret to dome, of lintel to post meaningful.

. . .

Some zodiacal catastrophe had occurred in this fateful year to cause a confluence of the festivals of Eid al-Adha and Orthodox Easter, a marriage that had never happened before and, according to the magi shuffling their horoscopes, would never happen again. Bedouin led flocks of sheep, fattened on delta alfalfa, across the bridges and through the back streets, till every lamppost supported its tethered beast and steaming dung speckled sidewalks, and the city was buffeted by their alto bawling. Knife grinders worked through the nights, wedges of sparks sprinkling every alley as they pressed blades to whirring stones. Overhead, stars of woven palm leaves hung from windows, and children on doorsteps plaited palm leaves into abstract basketry, spangled with scarlet flamboyant flowers and sprigs of bougainvillea. Choirs practiced Easter carols, and the poetry of God spiraled from every minaret, the beautiful rhymes coiling in the air and dissipating. Every house was made ready, swept and scrubbed, and the steps and streets were swept and doused in preparation for the feast. Even the maimed cats of Alexandria, with no fish heads to pick at, washed themselves, and the filthy sparrows preened their wings.

I was sitting on my balcony at twilight, eve of the double feast, a book on my lap, but not reading, just rubbing a page between finger and thumb, smoking a waterpipe, and pondering the kisses I had lost, the books I'd never see again. An elaborate moon, incised like old ivory, passed behind the rotting silk of clouds, drawing across gables and minarets huge silver brushstrokes that evaporated like water on hot pavement. The sea was a mess of silver and shadows.

Suddenly I realized that the window across the curve of the bay, that I'd been resting my eye upon, was changing. The light pried at its box, tearing the frame of the night. And suddenly I was awake, after the weeks of sleepwalking. I leaned over the balcony, peering at the flag of light, fiery semaphore. Then I was up and running, caroming though the stairwell like a cotton-clad billiard ball, then across to the corniche, scampering over the crooked cobblestones. The first siren brayed, and I arrived on the scene minutes before the fire truck. A crowd had already gathered, composed of neighbors in nightcaps and galabiyyas, infants clutching dolls, a couple of journalists popping bulbs and bending toward faces, pencils agitating. And the owner of the burning books, on his knees in the dust, whacking his cheeks with his palms, calling the names of the lost characters like the names of burning children. None comforted him. There are no words adequate to comfort those who have lost their libraries.

The burning room was in the upper story of a Turkish house, balcony cantilevered over the street on carven struts. The window was entirely fire. Broken pages erupted to the stars, lit, ripped, and tossed among the stars by pale hot fingers. Almost impossible to pull my eyes from that beauty, but I turned my back on the fire and peered through a scrim of afterimage at the surrounding rooftops. And, a moment before it spun and vanished, I saw the slim bell-shape, smokeprint, blotting stars.

The fire truck clanged into the alley and disgorged its fat crew, cigarettes plugging their maws as if they had learned to live without oxygen. But as they began laboriously uncoiling the hose, I shouted, startling them: "Wait!" I ran to the nearest facade and swarmed up, dipping fingers and toes into mashrabiyya perforations and eye sockets of alabaster saints.

From the rooftop I caught a glimpse of her fleeing form, and dashed after her, tripping along crenellation, swinging one-handed around minarets, sliding down gilded domes, leaping gaps. Across the streets of the city lay strings of lanterns and colored light bulbs, and, like hasty high-wire artists, we scampered over these. The lanterns were patterned: silk-and-paper cobblestones etched like evanescent fossils with dragons, butterflies, crescent moons, alphabets, our footsteps jostling the flames within, so they flared briefly behind us, the shards of flaming paper soaring.

I chased her, my shadowy book burner, through the quarters of Alexandria that night, across the art deco friezes of al-Atariin, over the gabled hillocks of Kom al-Dikka, the spires of Ibrahimiyya, the rococo doorframes of Kafr Abdu, into the steep meadows of Italian tile in Zizinia and Loran. Sometimes I'd catch sight of her, far ahead, like my own shadow thrown against the stars, but mostly I was chasing a scurry of blue, a whiff of ash. She circled back, and I lost her in Moharram Bey.

But almost immediately I heard the sirens, and once again rushed through the streets. The new fire blazed in a villa in Glymenopoulous, home to a famous collection of erotica I'd plundered more than once. I watched the flames catch on vellum, lick like the blue and orange tongues of incubi across intaglio labia, hand-tinted lilac glans. Dismembered bodies flaking up. Breasts and thighs gnawed by fangs of flame. By the time I arrived, breathless, the top floor was entirely alight. I scanned the surrounding towers and rooftops, but they were barren of the silhouette I desired. Then a gasp from the crowd, and a figure leapt from a dormer, blue-headed comet, fists trailing fire, hem of her garment on fire. Buoyed by the heat, she scampered en pointe across fence posts, shimmied up a wall like an indigo gecko shedding a bright tail, and vanished.

In a moment I was after her. Once again I chased her across the rooftops, along the tram wires, through the courtyards of Alexandria.

Across the beautiful light-webbed city we raced. I knew I'd never catch her, though this was my domain, though she was hampered by her shroud. She was too swift, too light, could too easily vanish into alcove or grotto. Yet I had to chase her, as though hoping to catalyze her transformation, as though by the act of pursuit I might lift her veils, press her face into pages, into story.

She set a dozen fires that night, leading me across the city. And before dawn, I almost caught her. I came upon her in Moharram Bey, looking over a church and mosque that stood side by side, steeple and minaret leaning together, making a mandala of cross and crescent. She was holding a book in each hand, and must have just lit them. Smoke trickled from the pages. I stood mesmerized, unable to move or call out, while the pages caught and blazed. Then she tossed the books like grenades through stained glass and pointed arch.

I thought I heard her laughter, though it might have been distant church bells or a premature mosque call. Then she winked out, my blue angel, and during the roll-call of tram stops back to Mahattat Ramleh my mind's eye chased her afterimage, complementary orange against ultramarine flames, the successive prints of her fleeing form on minarets and bell towers, perched momentarily on caryatids, hurdling fountains and palm fronds. The tram's topple was the fugue against which the images played. The rectangles of sea slid, each incrementally brighter than the last, between the hotels to my right.

I passed the scene of the first crime, where the fire was dead and the onlookers and journalists had dispersed to their beds.

Only the owner remained, soot-stained, trying to piece fragments of sodden ash into a word, just one word, a single word, as the burnt odor sanctified his lamentation.

I sat on the corniche wall, the thrill of the chase still within me so I was loath to return to my rooms. I shook up a cigarette and lit a match and at the same moment a single cry to God severed the silence, immediately followed by a gunshot. The sun burst the skin of the night, the shadows fled across the bay, and the air was suddenly filled with fireworks and gunshots, mosque calls and Easter carols. In the excitement I had forgotten the date: the celebrations had begun.

I finished my cigarette as the mosque calls tailed off, then went walking in the dawn. The city erupted. From every doorway children in pajamas danced, strewing firecrackers, lighting rockets, filling the air with small thunder. Here and there a firecracker exploded in a child's hand, or ignited a child's trousers or hair, and then there would be a spasm of yowling, quickly drowned by laughter. Men, adjusting tagiyyas or jacket collars, hurried to mosque or church for prayers and dawn mass, and the collective chanting made a great hum across the city, while indoors, women began to cook, buttering phyllo, rolling vine leaves, for today would begin the great feasting.

After prayers, the slaughter. Fathers emerged with their knives, called their sons around, invoked the name of God, and slit the throats of sheep. How strange, and strangely compelling, to watch a creature die. One moment standing. A gesture, and the next moment it shivers on its side, coughing thick blood from its new orifice. The children, hungry for this sight, dashed from slaughter to slaughter, watching the moment silently, then commenting volubly on the death. Blood ran under their feet and they left small bloody prints on the cobblestones. The fathers sank their hands into the slit throats and placed bright palm prints on walls and doorframes, urging their sons to do likewise. Long drips ran from the prints, so they resembled wet flowers on slender stems. Then they struggled to hack up the animals, leaping back as the guts spilled, yanking at the skin, cursing at the tenacity of the spine.

It began to rain. I walked through the blood-soaked streets. Everywhere lay hacked heads and opened bodies. Blood ran with the rainwater across the macadam, in long veins the color of karkadeh, and in the brief paragraphs of sunshine the puddles sparkled like troves of garnets. Blood surged into the gutters and then out rainspouts along the corniche and into the rain-roughened sea. Men in crimson smocks staggered under soaked fleeces and cats squabbled over severed ears and a boy carried roses and a ram's head in the basket of his bicycle.

Young men had already formed processions. Handprints of blood on faces and banners. They emerged from churches and mosques and bookstores, singing carols in the ancient liturgical tongues. All carried books in their hands, Bibles or Qurans or favorite novels, books and palm fronds, books and knives, books stained with blood. And as they marched they chanted favorite verses, favorite passages, the words gathering power by being uttered in unison. I eavesdropped on the rumors: this faction or that had burned the books in the night, the veiled ambassador had come from this mosque, that church. The other side, they whispered, had been abroad at two a.m., on a mission of fire.

I never read the daily newspaper, but the paper-boy's cry caught my attention, and I turned back. I grabbed the paper from his fist, flapped it open and pored over the photographs, read the paragraph of wide-eyed prose: "Caped enigma with a

poetic vendetta . . . struck a dozen locations without warning
. . . our photographer, who happened on the pyromaniac in
the act of . . . despite every effort of the . . . incalculable loss to
. . ."

The ephemeral—fire, mirage, rainbow, djinn—
photographs superbly. Against a pattern of flaming
bookshelves a shrouded figure danced, seeming to pirouette
within the very inferno like a bibliophobic Abednego. Spent
matchsticks in her hands. Close-up of a burning book. Shots
of ash and pages spinning from windows on curtains of smoke.
I knew the gestures of those hands, and I knew the color of the
niqab she wore. I could have tinted the photographs with my
watercolors, indigo and pale orange.

But even as I read, I heard her voice, the voice I craved:
"Balthazar—" Turning, I saw Zeinab seated with other
mendicants before a communal tray of fried mutton.
"Balthazar," she said. "Come, break your fast." And suddenly I
realized how hungry I was. Casting the paper aside I joined
her. We ate in silence, guests of some rich benefactor, beneath
an awning outside a mosque. The meat was fatty and delicious.
We dipped it into saucers of salt and cumin and red pepper,
then wiped our greasy fingers on fragments of bread, and ate
the bread.

When we were done we walked together through the
bright rain. In the midst of the slaughter, a girl stood beside a
basket of rain-washed strawberries and I bought a paper bagful
and paid her what she asked and we ate strawberries and
walked among the dead and dying beasts.

. . .

She led me to the cemetery in Azarita. Daily I'd walked past its walls, or ridden past them in carriage or tram, and never thought to enter. The dead possess no books, and anyway I'd seen them, the cadavers, the underground citizens of this small metropolis. But now she took my hand and led me through the ruined archway into the acres of winged people and sleeping lions. After all the seasons in Alexandria to come at last into this lovely, forgotten oasis. The miniature houses of the dead, with pediments and porticoes and tiny flowerbeds where burly bumblebees rootled. The spaces between the stones were rich with wildflowers and grass gone to seed, that gorgeous fleeting pale gold. Within the tombs were small benches and plates of clean bones and dry seeds, petals and butterfly wings. In coming days it would be shadowed with black-robed women gibbering extended animal howls of pain while they flailed at their cheeks and bosoms and ripped their palms on fresh plaster. But now this was a zone of stillness. We negotiated our way around canted crosses and lovers whose lips would never meet and never draw away and one-winged angels and vases containing a finger of green flower-broth. Sepulchers rose like elfin apartment blocks, a dozen niches, each with its contents of two hundred and six bones arranged in various patterns. Among the bones cats slept. Near the gate, the flowerbeds were tidy, the photographs pristine behind glass, but as we pressed deeper she led me through shrubs whose names surfaced as we crushed their leaves underfoot— thyme, lavender, bay laurel—among stones from which the lettering had been entirely scoured by centuries of weather or libations, and statues eroded to knobs and spindles.

At the back of the cemetery, neglected jasmine formed a messy bower. And beneath it, like a tiny temple, a little tomb stood, jasmine up its pillars, no door. On the swept space before it, a bench flanked the libation brazier, which was filled with ash. I peered into the tomb. Clean bones. Medallions of candle wax decorated with triangles of moth wing, a worn cushion, a waterpipe, coffee paraphernalia, and, in a corner, a pile of postcards, tram tickets, pressed flowers, old lace. "Bookmarks," she said. "I collect them for Amir."

"So you are a ghost," I said. "As Karim claimed. As I'd guessed."

"Of course. But which of us is more alive?"

I sat on the bench while she brought out the waterpipe and banged the stem free. In the brazier, using a paperback for tinder, she lit a fire, arranged charcoal, and set a pan of coffee beans among the coals. She tamped the apple tobacco into the pipe, then with brass tongs added an ember and handed me the nozzle. As the beans began to shine and smoke, she shimmied the pan, wafting the fragrance to my nostrils with the side of her palm. Once they had achieved a glossy darkness, she tipped them into a mortar and ground them savagely. She poured the ground coffee into the round-bellied earthenware coffeepot, added water, and set it on the coals, murmuring the coffee rhymes. When the liquid had frothed up the prescribed three times, she plucked the pot off the coals and poured me a thimble cupful. It was thick, fragrant, potent. Not till we had drunk three cups did she sit straight-backed on her cushion in the manner of the old storytellers, arrange her blue skirts decorously about her, and turn to face me. And while I gathered her tale, as if her words spawned violence, the festive gunshots and chanting swelled, became myriad, punctuated by the knocking of bombs, so that she finished her telling beneath a sky of scudding gunsmoke.

ZEINAB'S TALE

I was raised a princess in a great palace along the eastern seafront. A palace of a thousand rooms, a hundred staircases. I grew up surrounded by canaries of gold wire that sang in human voices and mirrors that reflected, on moonlit nights, my soul, and clocks that not only told the time but decoded my dreams. Rooms of magi bearing gifts of frankincense and liquorice and rooms of choirs of blinded castratos. Trained monkeys wearing tasseled fezzes swung from chandeliers. Belly dancers slept all day in silk-lined chambers while Nubian lutenists murmured lullabies. A house of uncountable treasures but only a single book. A single book that lay in a room of its own, in a locked case, to which my father possessed the only key.

My father, though of royal lineage, had not allowed vice or gluttony to destroy him as had his predecessors. He ate sparingly, a little rice with lamb, he drank only water. He smoked thin brown cigarettes he rolled himself. He was dreadfully scarred, resembling a man roughly pieced together from fragments of other men. A great slash had cost him one eye and half an ear, he was missing two fingers on his left hand, and he walked with a limp. Yet he carried his scars with dignity, for they were the signs of his accession. He had survived a dozen assassination attempts. On one occasion a crow had overturned a poisoned glass of coffee. On another, he had insisted that his enemy take the first puff of a poisoned waterpipe. And on a certain autumn evening he had placed his royal cloak around my mother's shoulders as they stood on a balcony and an assassin had planted the dagger between the wrong shoulder blades.

I had a single brother who, though younger, was of course in line to succeed my father. But as a child he followed me like a dog, echoing every word I said, demanding to wear what I wore. During the day, my father held court beside a fountain in the center of the palace, alternately stroking his hennaed beard or the white mane of the blue-eyed lion that slept beside him. Sometimes he allowed us to attend those sessions, to bang his scepter on the floor and play ninepins with rubies the size of pigeon's eggs, for, though a steward of violence, he indulged his children.

My father was frugal in his personal habits, but exceedingly generous toward those he hosted. His guests reclined on hand-embroidered silk, helping themselves to choice sweetmeats, opulent tobaccos, rare coffees. Once a visiting ambassador, at the height of summer, expressed a longing for cherries. My father dispatched a message by pigeon post across the sea to a caliph in Lebanon. The next morning half a hundred pigeons arrived at the palace, each with a pair of cherries tied to its feet. But on another occasion, after a visitor had displeased him, he sent us from the courtyard. Glancing back, I saw the fountain spout pink. The impassive eunuch mopped blood from the tiles while my father wiped his dagger meditatively on his shawl.

Once a week he took us to the sword room, where we watched as he fenced with the master, for he kept himself in fine fettle. If he was in a pleasant mood, he'd hand me a curved dagger, cumbersome as a scimitar in my little fists, and teach me to lunge and parry. I remember the day I first drew his blood, a pinprick on his forearm, and he tossed me in the air and declared that I was more worthy of his name than my brother, who in truth was of a timid nature.

Every evening, after the day's business was completed, and following the prayers, my brother and I joined my father in the sacred chamber. There he would dredge the key from his robes and unlock the case and take out the book. Seating us on either knee, he held the book before us and read the tales it contained. The book was huge, its cover inlaid with emeralds and aquamarines. The pages were the color of old ivory, textured like linen. Their borders were decorated with petals and vines, stars and birds, painted with brushes of a single hair, in vermilion and peacock and liquid gold. Each page a month in the making, the labor of a battalion of the finest miniaturists, who had been ceremonially blinded upon completion of the task. And in the center of every page lay the pool of snarls and speckles that I did not yet know were precious to me, that I did not yet know were forbidden.

My father, as he read, followed the lines with his finger. He read slowly, in the singing voice he reserved for those tales. He allowed me to turn the heavy pages. Those were holy hours. I remember his stiff beard against my cheek, his scent of tobacco and ambergris, for he always kept a little silver box of the precious substance among his garments.

But the day my first blood appeared, when as usual I followed my father and brother into the chamber of the book after the evening prayers, he turned at the threshold and crouched and took my shoulders in his maimed hands. Then he explained that I was now entering my maidenhood, and that reading was not an art appropriate for princesses. I wept and clawed and would not leave, twining my fists in his robes, and at last he slapped my cheeks and called for a servant to take me away.

So, while my brother learned to fence and ride, to hunt with the bow and the spear, to debate and to read, I was tutored in the arts of a princess. I learned to apply kohl and pluck my eyebrows and embroider cushion covers. I learned to lower my eyes and speak in soft tones and walk with soundless tread. But also I learned to dance.

Only the dancing lessons kept me from insanity. A monk of Shaolin or a Zulu warrior leads a life of strawberry sherbet and goose-down coverlets compared with the rigors a novice dancing girl must undergo. I was forced to stand on my toes for entire days. I spent days walking on my hands. I trotted the ten thousand steps from the dungeons to the highest minaret, and back down. I learned to move each muscle of my body independently. The madame was an exacting tutor. She would teach me a pose, nudging an elbow a hair's-breadth this way, that way, adjusting the angle of a finger, then have me repeat it over and over, beating the soles of my feet with a silk knout until I could reproduce it precisely. Those were long and terrible days, naked in the room of mirrors, my body writing an impossible, erotic alphabet in the silvered glass. But the pain and the immersion in my body were welcome, because they distracted my memory from the book, the pages I craved.

And then one day it was over. The madame sucked at her cigarette, squinted at me, and said "So, you are free to go. You have been a good pupil." I had learned the dance of the veils, the dance of the knife, the dance of the flame, but now I was confined to my chambers, attended by slaves, to practice my art and while away the hours with music and daydreams till my suitors should arrive.

I was a sad princess in a house of wonders. All day I sat in the topmost tower, gazing over the sea, where the sails and dolphins were an affront to my incarceration. My maidservants tried to tempt me with acrobats and baubles and midgets, but I turned them away. I refused to eat. All I saw, sleeping or waking, were the beautiful pages, harboring the rectangles of magic. Forbidden.

Reading is the strangest art. Your eye takes a shape, turns it into music, then story, then spirit, so a curl of ink laid long ago by a sliver of reed can become, a thousand years later, your own breath. I had, unwittingly, swallowed those stories, whole, and they crouched within me. In my dreams my father's finger still pursued words. I heard his voice, singing, which became my voice. The shapes of ink spoke. I learned to read while sleeping.

One night, two a.m., I stole down the stairs and entered the chamber of the book. In my hand I held a length of bent wire. It took me many hours, but at last I managed to pick the lock and take out the book. This is what my father taught me. In caging me, this is what he taught me: the arts of dancing, and of thievery. That first night I read only the contents of a single line, perhaps half a dozen words, the art was so new, as painful as learning to dance. But I returned the next night, and the next. I read a page, then a chapter. For many nights following, I read the sacred book by candlelight while the palace slept. I read it once, then over and over. Though I contained the entire text within me, I could not stay away from the voluptuous leaves, abrasive on my fingertips, the borders like flower gardens, the marriage of the letter shapes with the words in my mind, my eyes dancing with the ink. I loved the scent of the book, the weight of the book on my lap, which was also the weight of a newborn child.

And then one night, as I sat in that room, the book on my thighs, the candle in my hand, I felt a cool drop on my neck, rippling down my spine like heavy rain. I looked up. My father stood behind me, an unlit lamp in his hand. He must have woken and needed to refill it. A second drop quivered on the spout, poised to fall. For a moment we stared at each other. Impossible to read his expression through his scars. Then he emptied the lamp over my head. The fall of oil met my candle flame and my hair caught instantly. I looked down through a frame of fire at the burning book, at the burning pages. That was my first death.

I began to run, down the staircases, through the hallways, out into the streets of Alexandria, a girl on fire. I ran along the tram tracks, my face burning away, my voice charring away, to the library, where I begged entrance. Which was granted.

Cages have tremendous power, Balthazar, because they keep the energy—the words and dreams and stories—pent, under pressure. If you want to ensure that a thought will catch fire, put it in a box, lock it up. When I first entered the Library of Alexandria, I imagined I'd come home. I'd lost my face, but that was a small price for the riches I'd acquired. To read unfettered, after the years of believing that a single book existed in the universe—I was a blue butterfly freed from my cocoon, in fields of flowers. But years later, after all the books, I realized I was still caged, and that I was caged because the books were caged. So I began to release them. I gathered a dozen books, the choicest volumes the library contained, and handed them through the bars, into the eager hands, before the flesh was ripped from my bones and my bones were cast outside the library fence.

The citizens carried me to this tomb. I was given the burial of a princess. But I could not sleep. My work was not yet done. So I donned another blue cocoon, wrapping it around my spirit. Twice I have died, once at the hand of my father, once at the hands of my sisters. And someday I will die again, the death I crave, the final death, which will allow me to sleep. For centuries I've been stalking my death.

. . .

203

Zeinab looked down into her coffee cup. She looked up. "So you see, Balthazar. You see, I know what a burning book becomes, in the heart."

"You released the books. The books on my shelf."

"Yes. I released them, knowing they would return. The books you gathered around the world, from the continents where they had alighted. The books you returned to Alexandria. You did not understand your task, but you knew the books, knew they were meant to be together, to come home. I've been waiting for you, Balthazar, waiting and waiting, burning books to keep myself awake."

"How did you know I had them?"

"I didn't."

"But you asked—"

"I asked that question of every visitor to this city. You were the one who answered."

"So now what?"

"'I have cast fire upon the world, and see, I am guarding it till it blazes.' The day's not over. I have hope for you, book thief."

This is what it comes down to: a few bright moments, hot in the hand, rising to the stars. And what then?

I remembered the book she had burned, the book from my holy shelf, which I had only read because it had been freed by her hands, how many centuries before. But though I knew the words by heart, could place my fingertips, like a lutenist, against the chords of its phantom spine, the memory of the book was entirely usurped by its demise, the afterimage of the burning book falling into the sea. And certain sparks had fled upward, obliterated in the darkling sky. In my mind's eye I followed their traces, trying to read the bright scars whose dotted arcs on my inner eyelid were composed as much of my stuttering consciousness as of light (as the words you read are only rudimentarily ink). Surely the paths they took were not random, but informed by the words they had been. Words now ash.

What happens when a book is burned? The only copy in existence, unmemorized, so the words are gone, dispersed into the sea and the dust. The words have vanished, and the beautiful pages have vanished, but something remains. Where does story lie? Once the words have been erased, the story resides along our bones, remains tethered within us like a beast, which we can listen to, translating the animal cries, giving the story breath, wrapping it once again in a cloak of words to make it visible. And this act, the act of embracing the djinn, raising the dead, is sacred. But in the spaces between the words, the space after the burning of the book and before the telling, where does the story live, and what is its nature? Seed, swelling; or flesh, worm-ridden? Icon or architecture? Wordless, in us, in our deepest parts, the stories crouch, unborn. They make us. We live by them, we are host to them. We are maker and made, ship and spark, insane, blind, wounded, sounded, singing.

Zeinab and I emerged from the cemetery into a changing city. And now began the strangest journey I have made in any land, a journey as evening fell, my companion a ghost. As thieves, we are always taking the alternate routes, across rooftops, through side alleys and shady quarters, but now, with Alexandria at war, even these zones were treacherous, and we had to move with extra stealth. I led her to an empty villa and we crept up a faulty staircase, the steps crumbling away even as we mounted them. At the top we exited through a window and pulled ourselves onto the roof, and looked out across the cityscape. Smoke lifted here and there like tall blue palms. On the rooftops to the west, snipers crouched, lone figures in somber garments, backs to parapets, nests of bullets like brass eggs beside them. As we watched, they angled their weapons through crenellation and gashed walls, sighting carefully into the streets before touching forth their venom. We could not see the fruit of their labor, but saw them draw swiftly back to cover, take a pull from a bottle, reload.

Beneath us the battles raged, groups of boys in holiday finery rallying and retreating past carcasses of sheep and men, books and knives in their hands, calling out the ninety-nine names of God, their ninety-nine favorite titles. They huddled behind corners, behind art nouveau gratings and toppled wardrobes and barricades of books, into which bullets thudded, spewing paper dust. We heard the tish of books thrown through windows. Glass like salt in the streets. Citizens of all ages ran through the streets with armloads of books, wearing the mask of panic and glee common to looters everywhere.

Whispering to each other, we mapped our route, sketching zigzags through the air, tapping the villas and mosques we'd step across to get to the Kanisa Prometheus. Then we set out, in an artificial twilight of gunsmoke and plaster dust, teetering along tram wires and tree limbs, moving through houses, entering a window on the third floor and exiting through a skylight, then leaping across an alleyway. Zeinab was a blue cat beside me, so silent I had to will myself to notice her.

As we tiptoed over a tram wire, battalions surged from either end of the street below, brandishing banners and butcher knives, books and scimitars. The slogans and verses they yelled, distinct at the outset, became a general clamor, the superb joy of young men hankering for blood. The clang as they came together was louder than I'd anticipated. Sparks and dust and scraps of paper seethed over us. But then the battle settled to grunts of effort, the surprise of the wounded, bodies joining in embraces, some falling and trampled, some stumbling into alleyways, clutching bellies or eyes. We moved on.

The city we passed through was changed and changing, new vistas of the sea where buildings had hemmed the gaze, sudden thoroughfares where buildings had fallen. Interior became exterior, so we looked into a salon, complete with framed portraits and porcelain figurines, teacups and sliced cake, perched at the edge of a precipice where a façade had fallen away, the carpet draped across the edge, one chair in gilt smithereens below.

We came to the church and mosque in Moharram Bey, through whose windows Zeinab had tossed the burning books. From a rooftop vantage across the street, we watched as the congregations boiled out the doors. Priest and imam fought toward each other like rival princes, and finally met, swinging rosaries like bicycle chains, cassocks ripped, beards glossy with blood, each wielding a book. A nun, stabbed in the belly, lay in a gutter clutching her cross and yelling as if in labor. A man smashed an icon of St. Horus across his neighbor's bald pate, splintered dragon tooth and horse hoof spraying. Bodies lay bleeding on prayer mats, heads angled southeast. A woman gnawed the tattooed cross from another's wrist and grinned through a mouthful of bloody tendons. In a font babies lay immersed in the fluids of their opened bodies. Housewives dropped books from balconies onto heads, their victims swaying a moment before splashing headlong into puddles. Books lay in the puddles, swollen to twice their normal size. Torn leaves were stuck to bodies with water and blood. We moved on.

On the outskirts of Anfushi we climbed once more the minarets of the Jamiat Abu al-Abbas al-Mursi. This time I did not slip. Curled in the copper moons, we smoked, looking across a cityscape no longer static. Darkness had entirely fallen, but no stars looked down on Alexandria this night. The city at war was as pretty as a thunderstorm, with pockets of flickering brightness and seams of roiling ink. The chants of the militants echoed, primal and enticing. Tracers bent like thin rainbows out to sea. We smoked three cigarettes each, flicking the matches back and forth, while windows and balconies blossomed, and we watched falling girls on fire, and falling lovers clutching each other, their descent slower than gravity warranted, as if buoyed by their burning garments. In a nearby apartment, a mother comforted her daughter with a lullaby. To that gentle soundtrack, we watched a skirmish in Midan Saad Zaghloul, silent from this distance, elegant as ballet, the parties chasing each other down to the seafront and back to the Trianon, banners rippling, blades winking.

Zeinab snapped her cigarette toward the sea, then pocketed the matches and swung down. I followed.

Near the Kanisa Prometheus, we descended through a vacant stairwell and crept through the alleys. But rounding a corner we halted, suddenly vertiginous. As though endowed with x-ray vision, we stood looking through the walls of the church into the sacristy. The curtain had been blown away, revealing the altar. On shards of wall here and there a few icons hung askew. Someone had shot St. Isaiah between the eyes. The dome had collapsed onto the badminton court in a heap of rubble, but the armchairs, palled with plaster dust, still lay about, beneath a ceiling of gun smoke and rain cloud. The bats had flown.

And as we watched, from behind the altar emerged a fat ghost decorated with illuminated fragments, limping, blood soaking through the white dust on his vestments. In each hand he bore a glass filled with dark liquid.

"Welcome, welcome," Abuna Makarios bellowed, hearty as ever. "Don't mind the clutter, we'll soon have this swept up." And he handed us our drinks.

"Are . . . are you all right?" I faltered.

"As it happened, I was arranging my bookshelves when the bomb came in. The books are blown to bits, but I escaped with a few paper cuts, nothing to fret about. Have seats, don't let me keep you standing." He slapped at an armchair and vanished within a cloud of dust.

So we sat in the ruins of our church, sipping wine and karkadeh, while bullets and hurled books riffled over our heads. We could hear the clicking of magazines being changed in the next alley, and the screaming and prayers of the wounded. The battles surged along the isthmus and subsided into Mansheyya. A man walked slowly out of an alley carrying a book drenched in blood, passed through the church without seeing us, and disappeared into another alley.

As night rose, other thieves emerged. First Nura, fireworks and tracer bullets racing on the surfaces of her huge eyes. She kissed our cheeks, her lips dry as fingertips, crosses knocking against our chests, then took a seat. Koujour next. Makarios handed out drinks and cigarettes. He brought forth a platter of day-old communion bread, ash-dusted, arranged around saucers of tahina and spiced cheese, and we ate without speaking while the gunfire rattled and grenades popped. The fighting seemed to have moved into Kom al-Dikka, though there was sporadic gunfire nearby as pockets of resistance were cleaned out.

I asked Koujour about Hala and the twins. He told me he had sent them into his studio with a supply of food and books, anad locked and painted out the door so it would be invisible to looters. He had left all the money, with a basket of fruit and paperbacks, on a side table beside the door. Nura had escaped the mobs by joining them, chanting with this procession and that through the streets, till she was close enough to the Kanisa to slip away.

As she was talking, Karim, normally so ebullient, staggered into the circle. Thinking he'd been wounded, I sprang up, caught his shoulders, and lowered him into a chair.

"What is it?" Nura asked, voice barely audible.

He looked around at us, the muscles of his neck bulging and writhing as if he strained against a harness. Bringing his hands to his face as though to grip the words, he tore them suddenly away and in a terrible broken bark shouted, "Amir, Amir!" the name deteriorating into retching.

"No! Oh no!" Nura knelt beside him, embracing an arm. We crushed round him, laying our hands and cheeks on his seizing body, for the minutes while his spasms diminished, though his cries of grief continued, as they continued throughout the city. Makarios helped him hold a glass of arak, as one holds a cup for a child, and he sipped awkwardly, alcohol mingling with tears and ash on his chin. At last he scoured his face with his shirttail and told us what had happened.

"We were in the catacombs when the fighting began, so we

heard nothing till we came out. Then we saw the gangs entering houses, burning. I wanted to go back underground and wait till it was over. Amir . . . Why, Amir, why? Why?" Again we waited till his shouting diminished. Karim looked around blankly. When he spoke again his voice emerged too loud. "He had to go to his secrets, of course. I begged him not to. As we got near his apartment we could see it was on fire. I tried to hold him, but he can be slippery. He ran up the stairs. The doorway was on fire. He didn't look back. I shouted to him, but the fire roared. The stairwell filled with smoke, and I had to go back down. From the street I saw him at the balcony, emptying boxes into the air. He was on fire, but didn't seem to notice. He rushed inside, came out with handfuls of letters and photographs, tossed them down. I called to him. I shouted that I'd catch him, that I could put out the fire, but he didn't hear me. Or wouldn't hear me. The secrets rained down. Finally the fire swallowed him. Look, though." He pulled from the watch pocket of his tuxedo jacket something brown, oval. A leaf, I thought, then saw the passage of a tracer across its surface. "This fell," Karim said, his voice too soft now. "This fell. It's all I have left. More precious than any emerald. I will build a shrine. It will lie on a cushion of lavender velvet, under glass, on a marble pedestal. I will polish it with silk. I will endow a feast day in his name. Only the chosen will be permitted to look through it."

Within the lens Karim cradled, I could see, tiny and topsy-turvy, the strange pietà we formed, beneath the uncertain light, within the skeletal walls. Its corpse already ashes, reduced to this remnant. In the dark glass, a figure detached itself from the group. I looked up. Abuna Makarios had moved to the sanctuary. I heard his whispering as he readied his vestments and prepared the tools of the Eucharist, though the chalice was dented, the platen gouged, the prospherine scorched. He placed the chalice within the ark, the spoon on top, and spread the prospherine over all. Then he set the paten on the altar and folded a cloth upon it.

The Orthodox liturgy, as Makarios has explained it to me, is not adjunct to the world, but is in fact its foundation, the still point in a whirling, burning universe. It is the continual renewal of the world, in an elaborate architecture of smoke and song, texture and text, culminating in transformation: the mystery of mysteries: bread to flesh, wine to blood. And from this foundation spring the arabesques: gnosticism and blasphemy, sins and flames. Someday perhaps the liturgy will become entirely surface—tone and clash and smoke, the sense of the words veiled—and still it will be performed, and still the magic will occur, renewing and sustaining the world.

The ceremony began with the whispered invocations, inaudible. Makarios washed his hands thrice with stylized gestures, then paced around the altar, muttering, casting crosses over every surface. He circled with the bread, then with the bottle of wine and a candle in upraised fists. At last he turned to us, spread his palms, and bellowed the opening words: "Let us give thanks!"

Normally the liturgy in the Kanisa Prometheus was background, a soundtrack to our lies and chess games. But on this night Makarios corralled us into participation, handing an icon to Nura, the censer to Zeinab, cymbals to Koujour, a box of incense to me. Only Karim remained in his seat, his mouth a cut, his eyes dead. We marched around the hillock of frescoed rubble, our ruckus joining the battle noises and lamentations throughout the quarter.

Makarios invited me to read the Gospel passage, from a book more than half destroyed. The hand-drawn, illuminated letters slowed my eye and voice as I stood at the lectern, making my speech unwittingly ponderous. I took in, along with the words, the decorations, the tiny sketches of winged beasts and crosses, the wavy margins of burnt paper, and the stuttering of my eye entered my speech.

During the litany for the dead, Makarios added to the censer a spoonful from the box I carried, speaking Amir's name as he did so, and we wept as the fragrance enveloped us.

He welcomed us to the altar while he prepared the magic. From this moment, the instant of the transubstantiation, he would not look back. He must stand facing the altar, through bombs and gunfire, through earthquake and conflagration, till the ceremony was complete. He swung the censer to the directions, then removed the prospherine and waved it over our heads, the rattles shivering. Lifting the loaf, he broke it into unequal parts. He traced the edge of the cup with his finger and made the sign of the cross within it, then broke the bread into fragments.

As we filed past, he placed the bread on our tongues, spooned wine into our mouths. And whether because of the afterimages of the scarred city, or the emotion of Amir's death, or because at last I was fully participating, I wept again.

When we had partaken, we returned to our seats while Makarios swallowed the rest of the blood and scraped up the last of the lamb. Finally, laughing, he turned from the altar, holding a basin, and splashed holy water across us, and we raised our hands and laughed with him. Then, palms outstretched as they had been at the beginning, he said the benediction, ending with the words: "Go in peace." And I realized, in the stillness, that this exhortation was the simple truth: the violence had abated during the liturgy, the guns had ceased, and the day dawned with doves and hoopoes.

The thieves left in the new calm, Nura and Koujour supporting Karim, who was snarling and raging. Makarios went to sleep on the altar, the shredded curtain his counterpane. And at last Zeinab and I sat in the ruined church facing each other once more.

"You started this, Zeinab. Where will it end?"

"Who knows? The path of fire is unpredictable. That's why we love it. You light a match, sit back, and watch the fireworks."

"But Amir is dead."

"So am I. Most of the citizens of Alexandria are. Anyway, it was his choice."

"It broke Karim's heart."

"Karim has his djinn, at last. Even if he has to create him, summon him by rubbing the lens of his spectacles. And there is this: Amir has finally released his secrets. They are settling over the city. Who knows what flowers will sprout?"

We left the church together, through the aftermath of violence, sidestepping corpses, splashing through pools of blood, and she stayed with me as I scrambled to the rooftops, lowered myself onto my balcony. We stood side by side, looking out over Alexandria. The sky was occluded, underlit by fires here and there in the city.

"It's the end of the world," I said. "What do you talk about at the end of the world?"

"You don't. You go to your bed, you go to sleep."

"And when you wake up?"

"Everything will be changed."

"You sound so certain."

"The city has burned before," she said. "The foundations of these houses are words and ashes, like a book whose writing has been traced over, like a tattoo renewed. The phoenix has its rebirth here. Few know this: the tamarisk it nests in stands in no Arabian desert, but on the outskirts of Alexandria, in a hinterland of rubbish, among bones and fallen tram wires and broken glass. And few know, as well, how the phoenix desires the fire, craves the fire like a lover, seeks it like an embrace, and clasps it to her breast. Her plumage is blue, her wings are tattered, she is flying across Alexandria with the seagulls and doves and hoopoes, searching the tree that will char her bones."

"What about your dream? The mountain town, the tram across the sea."

"The tram exists, yes, number 99. It exists as the phoenix exists, its circuit as lengthy and elliptical as that of a comet. It rattles and spits among the stars, celestial streetcar, joining the dots of constellations, ferrying angels on their errands, till it returns at last to Alexandria, touching down among fish heads and spent needles and stray cats. Hoping to pick up a passenger or two. But I'll never abandon Alexandria. I am tethered to this city, she holds my bones.

"Καινούριους τόπους δεν θα βρεις, δεν θάβρεις άλλες θάλασσες.
Η πόλις θα σε ακολουθεί. Στους δρόμους θα γυρνάς τους ίδιους."

I watched the smoke a while, then turned, but she was gone. The blue niqab lay across the balustrade. How many veils did she possess? I realized that I was exhausted: I had been awake for a day and a night. I stumbled to my bed, kicked off my shoes, and slept.

IX

Tram 99

I WOKE AT TWILIGHT, into a strange calm. The scent of gunsmoke still in the air. "Everything will be changed." Zeinab's voice still soughed in my ears.

I felt like reading. I called for coffee, then entered the wardrobe. Lighting a candle, I crossed to the wall where my shelf stood. I raised my hand, then sank to my knees, my heart emptying itself into my head, because my shelf was bare. The wall behind it was slightly paler than the surrounding paint: the jagged ghost of my library. And at last, kneeling before my barren bookshelf with my face in my hands, I began to guess the awful conspiracy.

Suddenly furious, I slammed out of the wardrobe. Seizing the niqab Zeinab had left behind, I leaped over the balcony. In the shadow of a doorway, I pulled on the garment, like pulling on her smoky skin, then followed the curve of the corniche westward to the lighthouse, seeing nothing but my bare shelf. I entered through the octagonal aperture, lit a candle and began my descent. The jackal in the prow of the ferryboat looked into my eyes, accepted my obol. I opened the sarcophagus, descended the steps.

A librarian rose as I entered. "Zeinab . . . ?" she faltered. I raised my hand and she backed away. I forced myself to walk slowly for a couple of chambers, then began to scamper, thief's soles silent on the carpets and leveled stone, choosing turnings at random till I was deep within the library. When I paused for breath, I found myself in a room of books about bibliodelirium, cautionary tales concerning readers who became so obsessed with particular volumes they abandoned their homes, their families, their countries, in many cases their selves, to wander the world like plaintive ghosts, crying the title of their beloved. Suggested cures included pomegranate juice, mud baths, and bloodletting, but most authorities admitted such remedies were seldom efficacious. I waited, listening for some minutes till I was certain no footsteps echoed after me like ellipses, and then began my search for the youngest librarian.

She was not in the room of the owl-colored armchair where I'd first spied upon her, nor was she in her bedchamber, nor in the great central reading room. I passed through the rooms of books she'd loved, touched each volume as if it might give me some clue, and indeed, reading those titles again was like taking hold of a piece of her, like gripping a finger or an earlobe. The want rose like grief in my gorge.

At last, as if by chance, I found myself once again in the chambers through which she'd fled the day we'd first spoken. And now my thief's nostrils picked up the trace of cinnamon spiked with a single clove. I found her in the room of the books of the doomed. She knelt on the floor in her blue niqab, head bowed. Around her were scattered my books, the books from my shelf, returned at last to their domain. Some were open, some face-down, as if they'd been flung aside. She looked as if she might be praying over the candle in her hands. When she raised her face, I could see she'd been crying. "Who are you?" she asked.

I lifted the veil.

"No," she said. "No. I told you not to come."

"You stole my books."

"I didn't know what else to do. It took me all night. I got the last books out just as dawn broke, so I heard the beginning of the feast. I'm exhausted."

"Zeinab put you up to this."

"No. Well . . ."

I knelt in front of her, the books between us. "What did she whisper to you, that night?"

"Just a date: the eve of the double feast, she said. She told me you'd be out of your rooms. I didn't understand what she was saying. Then I came back down and couldn't find anything to read. I wandered along the shelves, looking for books. Miles and miles I walked, deep under the sea, looking for a book. But all I could think about were the books on your shelf, the books I'd read aboveground."

"So you stole them."

"I didn't know what else to do."

"The city is burning above our heads, do you know that? She set the city alight to lure me away from my books."

She said nothing, just laid a hand gingerly on one of the spread pages.

"They're back where they came from," I said.

"What?"

"Haven't you guessed? These are the books she passed out of the bars, how many lifetimes ago. She's been waiting all this time, to get them back underground. But she needed our hands."

"Why does she want them underground?"

"I think she'd say the day's not over; the story's not finished yet."

"Balthazar—"

"Listen," I said. "No, listen, I have to get this out. This is what I wanted to say. I love to watch you read, I love the way your fingers touch the pages, I love the way your eyes move behind your glasses. I love your voice when you read aloud. At last I've learned who I am. I'm a thief. I'm here to steal. Come with me . . ."

"It's too late. Have you forgotten?"

"That you can kill me? No. And how many nights have I lain awake desiring that death. Listen Shireen, I can't read. The books have lost their savor. You've unmade me, unbound me."

"It's too late," she said, and suddenly placed her hands over her eyes. "Oh, what have I done?"

"It's not too late."

But she held up a hand. In the sudden stillness I heard the rushing, like an incoming tsunami, of a thousand bare feet, of wind in robes.

"Would you rather be torn apart by a thousand librarians? Or will you receive my hand? Come, Balthazar. I'm not afraid anymore. Such a long journey you've taken toward this touch." She lifted her arm. We knelt facing each other in that terrible room, while the sound of footsteps swelled like rain.

. . .

THE TRAM TOUCHED down on iron rails at dawn, far to the north and east, and immediately veered inland, upward. Peering out the windows, we could see the mountains above us, turbaned in rainstorms. We wound up through the zones of euphorbia and eucalyptus, jacaranda and bougainvillea. Lovebirds beat among the boughs like escaped illuminations. Then we were among pines. The air grew cooler and we could see our breath. We pressed together on the wooden bench and I took off my jacket and put it around our shoulders. As the grade steepened the tram slowed, tottering through tunnels, racket battering off the walls. We passed a little station, flowerboxes crammed with geraniums hanging from the eaves, the mustachioed stationmaster with his feet up, smoking. Rich whiff of hashish. The tram was moving so slowly he was able to hand earthenware cups of milky coffee through the window. We shouted our thanks and sipped the sweet coffee as the tram teetered over gorges, on delicate stone arches, the curly ice-green rivers hurtling below.

One hundred and thirty-six tunnels to the mountain town. The sky had cleared by the time we pulled into the station. It was deserted. We got out and thanked the driver and she touched a finger to her jasmine circlet and tinkled the bell and the tram pulled out, empty, heading farther up, into the frozen landscapes, among polar bears and icebergs, and then, I imagined, on rails of northern lights, deeper, higher, past the moon and the planets, into the zones of galaxies and outer space, gathering speed, mauling time in its celestial circuit.

We took a room at the hotel behind the station. Polished concrete floors, dusty paintings in the hallways, at which I peered as we walked up the four flights. Goddesses with a dozen breasts, a dozen hands clutching roses, flames, hearts, books. We had to pause for breath on every landing. My fingers shook so I could hardly match the brass key to the hole, but inside, the fire was already lit on the hearth. We leaned our elbows on the sill, noses pressed to the cold glass, looking down past angled tin roofs through gulfs of blue. Hills, cities, seas, all lost under leagues of oxygen.

The bed took up half the room, the eiderdown turned back on the linen. On a scroll-top table was a box of watercolors, and bone folders, burnishers, brushes, a book of gold leaf. She turned to me. Slowly, I undressed her, and laid her, brown as a stain, on the white sheets. I imagined placing a color on her skin. I loaded a sable brush with alizarin crimson, moved to the bed, and lassoed her navel with a tangerine *a*. She squirmed under the brush stroke. I dragged the desk over to the bed and calligraphed a rainbow alphabet across her body, pale *o* circling a nipple, burgundy *b* across the ribs, summer-sky *k* at her heart, lemon *m* and azure *n* on her eyelids. I slashed a liquorice *z* on her left sole, and she cried out. Then I took the booklet of gold leaf and set about gilding my lover, laying down the sizing, tamping the thin gold with a wooden spoon, teasing away the excess. I led her to the mirror. Drenched in mountain light, she was an illuminated goddess, hands full of nascent poetry.

We made love in a welter of color and a nimbus of breath, letters offsetting onto the linen, onto my lips, gold in the blood on her thighs. The windows misted over.

In the enormous bathroom we bathed together, limbs dovetailed in a tub the size of a dory. I sponged her skin to cinnamon. Gold leaf in the lavender foam. We dried ourselves on the enormous towels, leaving puddles on the polished concrete, then scampered naked back down the hall to the room. The veil cast by our lovemaking had diminished to a silver fringe about the small panes.

We put our clothes on, and the thick sweaters provided by the hotel, and went out onto the promenade. It was full of monkeys and balloons and boys playing cricket and children flying kites. To the north the peaks stood, ripped white against the voluptuous, astonishing blue. From genial vendors I bought her a red balloon and a chain of marigolds, a cup of tomato soup and six sandalwood bangles, and we watched the kite-flyers battle. The kites dipped to each other and the strings bent around each other, and then one would suddenly lose its energy and waver gently into the valley while the victor flickered higher.

We strolled down to the lookout point. I bought coffee and pastries and we sat on a bench looking at the mountains, colossal and silent, intricate with glaciers and crevasses, speckled with screes. Snow leopards and frozen climbers folded into their slopes. It was very cold. We cradled the coffee cups in our palms, sipping slowly, then tossed the cups onto the heap of shards below the railing.

I bought more pastries and we walked back up among pony riders, dancing children with their kites and balloons, and strolling lovers, flowers in their hair. Clouds had smothered the mountains, lightning bristling within them. By the time we reached the peak of the ridge the first clouds had swung across the town. There was a moment of triple rainbows before the rain hit. Hurriedly we bought umbrellas, while the wind smacked our clothes about us. The ridge was deserted except for the kite-flyers, who could not let go of the strings. Several, in pursuit of other kites, toppled over the edge and were carried off into the storm or plunged down among the trees. Lightning roared down kite-strings, reducing children to little heaps of smoking ash, which their companions scattered as they ran. Then, as quickly as it had come, the storm blew over and the temperature dropped. The rain turned to snow. Sudden hush. The ash of kites and children was soon subsumed under a white coverlet.

We went into the restaurant on the first floor of the hotel and took a table by the window. Snowflakes fell against the blue pane with small silent blows. She made petals from the melting wax of the candle. We ordered a complicated dish of white cheese in a sauce of almonds and coconut and cream. White wine. After the meal we ordered hot chocolate. It came in huge blue mugs, capped with cream, foxed with nutmeg. The snow had stopped falling. We carried our drinks onto the terrace and looked down over the town. The streets were constellations of stars. Fireworks boomed and crackled, dyeing the snow suddenly ruby and saffron, illuminating the rooftops. As I bent to kiss her we heard shouting to our right, then the noise of shattering glass. Flames licked from the windows of the theater, where they were performing, on the longest night of the year, *A Midsummer Night's Dream*. More windows burst as we watched and we saw a frantic shadow pantomime against the flames. Then the actors came tumbling out through a back exit. Cobweb, Peaseblossom, Moth, and Mustardseed on fire, rolling about in the snow to quench their flaming wings. Puck, bright as a girandole, cartwheeling down to the lookout point, shouting: "If we shadows have offended . . ."

As the roof caught, the air grew warm enough that we could take off our sweaters. The restaurant was deserted—the waiters and diners had all gone out carrying glasses of water to dash them with beautiful, futile gestures against the walls. We knocked the snow off the wicker and sat cradling our drinks and laughed. She was so lovely against the flames and the snow. Her hair had begun to grow in, dark halo. I leaned over, tasted the cream and spices on her lips. The fire was bright as morning, bright enough to read by.

She reached across and put a slim hand into my pocket and drew out a book. Opening it, she began to read aloud, slowly, looking up at the end of each paragraph.

What book is that? you clamor. What book is she reading? And how did we escape?

Listen . . .

This is how you burn a book: you light a match, you hold it to a page. It's not an uncommon activity: biblioclasms illumine history texts.

Choose a book you love, light a match. How pretty it looks in its jacket of flame. Some books don't burn well, you have to fan the pages, stir them with a stick. Others seem hungry for the flames. They'll keep you warm on chilly winter nights. An average novel is good for ten minutes of toasty fingers.

Imagine a world of books. Imagine a planet entirely usurped by a single library, every tree mashed into paper pulp, every animal slaughtered for leather bindings. And imagine the inhabitants of that planet, librarians every one, pacing the hallways with their feather dusters, snacking on dried rat and salted silverfish. They have no time to read, the library is too enormous. And then imagine, on that planet, a single match. A splinter of pine, a dab of phosphorus, held between finger and thumb.

When you burn a page you're releasing sunlight. Centuries of sunlight cupped into leaves, trickling through twigs and boughs, stored like mica in the wood, stacked in the wood like bright words waiting to be spoken. Years of quiet toil on some forgotten hillside, beneath a shifting burden of jackdaws and butterflies, toes among gemstones and earthworms, hair wet by rain, dried in the wind. Much later: chainsaws, pulp vats, rollers. The benison of the type. The laying on of hands. And then, one day, a match. And all the days have led to this moment, are caught up in this moment of brightness.

Imagine the planet of books, parched, winds gusting through the hallways, stirring the dry pages. And then imagine a single match, struck. You're an astronaut, peering from your astral shuttlecock, and you watch the envelope of fire, like a new species of hot flower, a pretty plague of marigold, flamboyant, bougainvillea, blowing itself out, blowing you into the stars.

The deep space probe lands millennia hence on a landscape of ash, afterburners spewing a soft tempest. The bemused explorers fill their hands with ash, trying to trace from the gray fragments with their iridescent filigree the genesis of this catastrophe.

This is what happened: we knelt facing each other in the room of the books of the doomed, the storm of enraged librarians approaching. And then I made a simple gesture. I tipped my candle forward, touched the flame to a page. At first nothing happened, but then I saw a flaw in the air at the base of the book, and a blue thorn snuck over the text. All at once it was wholly alight. A single burning book, like a lone blooming rose in a garden of buds. I stood back. The next book crackled into flame. For a minute we watched, mesmerized, as the pile caught. Fire is beautiful.

She stepped forward with a cry and took my hand. Laughing, we raced through the library, hand in hand, while the fire dervished through the chambers behind us. Out the back door, through the burial chambers. Across the dark river, neglecting to pay in our haste. No more obols for the silent jackal.

We exited through the lighthouse into the aftermath of celebration and battle. Still holding hands, walking now, we stepped through broken glass and pools of blood along the seafront. Before we reached the center of the corniche, we heard the first sirens and soon saw the spines of flames and the storm of underlit smoke. People were calling to each other from the balconies and pointing to the library grounds. Citizens rushed by, carrying jam jars, wine glasses, demitasses of water. We followed them through the streets to the iron fence, beyond which the flames spouted from the library roof like the wings of seraphim. The crowds gathered at the fence, holding their vessels. And within the fence, the librarians stood, watching the fire. Some of their robes were scorched, some held cloths to burns on arms and foreheads.

But then, as we watched, a figure appeared on the roof, veiled in blue, dancing among the flames. For a moment she danced, alone. Then, with a sound like a great exhalation, the roof collapsed, the flames curling inward, and she was gone. The watching crowd echoed the sigh. Shireen clutched my arm. I stroked her fingers. "This is the death she craved, the death she has been seeking all these years. Her third and final death."

"But all the books," Shireen cried. "My family . . ."

"Yes. Let us weep for them."

We turned back and walked, weeping, to the sea. She still gripped my arm, but I could not have made it without her by my side. Midan Saad Zaghloul was deserted. Far away I heard a tram approaching, the barest rustle, like water trapped in the cochlea, swelling to a reef, a drum-roll.

"Here," I said, as the tram mashed and shrieked into view, drenched in sparks.

"Number 99," said Shireen through her tears.

The tram driver was a girl in white, a circlet of jasmine in her hair, both feet up on the console, a book in her hands. She winked at us and, though we weren't at a station, the tram stopped. We got on, the only passengers. In front of the Trianon the tram curved left, crossed the corniche, then rode the rails of moonlight, soundless now, across the sea, east and north. Looking back, we saw the lighthouse topple silently into the bay, the beacon glowing a moment beneath the water, then doused. Instead of sparks, falling stars hissed about us into the waves. I turned toward her. I touched the mole on her neck. She blinked, her pupils brimming. And I saw that her eyes no longer harbored pages. The pupils were as round and dark as mine. But in her hands was a book, a new book, a book I'd never seen before. She passed it to me.

And what book is that? Ah, that is the book we've been striving for, you and I, the book for which we've raveled labyrinths, crossed seas, the book we've chased across rooftops, through dark alleyways, down spiral staircases, the book of our desires, printed in purple blood. Turn the last page, in the glow of falling stars, fireworks, flaming theaters. Close the cover. Light a match.

NOTES ON THE TEXT

For this second edition of *The Book on Fire*, I have made a few small changes in the text. Several minor errors have been corrected, and the first and seventh chapters have each lost a few sentences.

The Arabic lines sprinkled throughout the text are from "The Ruins" by Ibrahim Nagi, which was set to music and became Oum Koulsoum's favorite song. The translation below is by Keith Miller. Lines used in the text are italicized.

O my heart, don't ask where love is—it was an architecture of imagination,
  and has crumbled.
Let us drink together on the ruins. Recite my sadness as long as my tears fall.
  (p. 30)
How did this love become just a tale, one speech among tormented
  speeches?
I can't forget you: you seduced me with your delicate mouth; with your
  hand, like a hand held out to a drowning man;
and with a light like that which comforts a traveler (where has that light in
  your eyes gone?).
My love, once a day I visited the tree of the bird of hope and sang it my pain.
I still sing my pain, slowly as a beggar, wisely as a judge.
My yearning for you brands my ribcage; the moments are embers in my blood.
  (p. 48)
Release my hands, give me freedom. I always give until I have
  nothing.
Ah, your handcuffs hurt my wrists—why do I clutch them when they do
  not hold me?

Unlike you, I always keep my promises. Why do I keep you captive when I have the whole world?

I can no longer see my lover. He is poised, reserved, majestic.

His steps are confident; he walks like a king. He is beautiful and proud, seductive as the perfume of a pleasant valley, and his eyes contain sweet dreams of evening.

Where are you now? In some lofty, light-filled place.

And I am love and a rambling heart: a comfortable embrace approaches you.

This yearning will be a messenger between us; a drinking companion handing us a wineglass.

Has love ever seen two such drunkards? We built so much from our dreams!

We walked on a path filled with moonlight, and our joy leapt before us.

Laughing like children, we ran till we overtook our shadows.

(p. 132)

The enchanted scent vanished, and we woke, devastated, into the day.

Our dreams had vanished with our friend the night.

The light was a tocsin, the daybreak conflagration.

We arrived at the real world and each went our own way.

(p. 174)

O insomniac, as soon as you fall asleep you remember your vow and wake with a start.

Each time the wound heals, memories reopen it.

Learn to forget, learn to purge yourself of memories.

My love, it's a matter of faith and destiny. It's out of our hands: we were created to be forlorn.

Maybe someday, after this time of separation, destiny will allow us to meet.

If someday we met like strangers, acting as if we didn't know each other,

don't claim that this sorrow was our desire: it was the desire of destiny.

(p. 20)

The line Zeinab murmurs on the corniche wall on p. 25: "These traces will not dissolve, for they are woven by the north and south winds," is from the "Muallaqa," or "Suspended Poem," of Imru al-Qais.

On p. 29, Abuna Makarios is quoting Plotinus: "To any vision must be brought an eye adapted to what is to be seen."

The quatrain sung by the passing boy on p. 54 is from *The Rubáiyát of Omar Khayyám*, translated by Edward FitzGerald.

The Italian lines on pp. 83–85 are from *Aida* by Giuseppe Verdi:

AIDA
There . . . in virgin forests,
perfumed with flowers,
in blissful ecstasy
we shall forget the world.

RADAMÈS
How could we forget the sky
that first witnessed our love?

AIDA
Beneath my sky love will
be granted us more freely;
there in the same temple
we will have the same gods,
Let us flee! Let us flee . . .

AIDA and RADAMÈS
Come with me, together we will flee
from this land of sorrow.
Come with me, I love you, I love you!
Love shall be our guide.

The line Zeinab speaks on p. 204: "I have cast fire upon the world, and see, I am guarding it till it blazes," is from the Gospel of Thomas, one of the Nag Hammadi texts, translated by Thomas O. Lambdin.

The lines Zeinab speaks on p. 215 are from "The City" by Constantin Cavafy. The translation below is by Lawrence Durrell.

There's no new land, my friend, no
New sea; for the city will follow you,
In the same streets you'll wander endlessly . . .

City of Bones

At midnight on New Year's Eve, Alexandrians move to their balconies and cast out old crockery, dolls, toys—anything they no longer need. For a few minutes, there is a tremendous cacophony, and then they retreat to their apartments to make merry for the rest of the night.

Early one New Year's morning, I walked to central Alexandria, and found it emptied of people. The streets were littered with broken pottery and glass. I felt as though I was the last survivor of some catastrophe, and that feeling was the germ of this story.

This story is not intended to serve as a coda to The Book on Fire. *It is, rather, a companion piece.*

HE ARRIVED IN THE CITY at nightfall, stepping out of the train into the echoing station, its great archways surmounted by clocks, each stalled at a different time. No other passengers disembarked and the station seemed entirely deserted. It was cooler here—his breath plumed out and he drew his coat closer. The train pulled away. He stood beside the tracks till its gnash faded, then walked down the long pier toward the paler arch of the entrance, footsteps throbbing against the walls. He had expected some odor, but there was only a whiff of salt and juniper leaves.

Outside the station the sand lay against the steps. He stood beneath a stopped clock and looked across the landscape of deserted streets and dark windows. Then he set forth into the empty city. Palm trees rustled like huge disheveled birds on either side. Above them, the windows were fanged and rayed with broken glass and broken glass lay in the street, among the drifts of paper and the wildflowers grouting the cobbles. The sand lay thickly, smoothly against all edges, softening curbs, submerging glass and broken bricks and bones, the bones that lay in the street and glimmered, pale globes and stems, in the darkened rooms. The bones had gathered more thickly in places—in certain corners, around certain palm trees, the spaces among them as interesting as the shapes themselves. The buildings rose on either side, great raw stone columns and domes, ornately knobbed and ribbed, the bashed windows like the broken lenses of spectacles. Webs and wings of char fanned from some windows and doorways. The sky seemed filled with smoke, though there was no scent of conflagration and only a little ash scurried on the sand.

It was all so changed. In the absence of eyes and hips and swinging arms and laughing mouths and footsteps his gaze floated upward, along the broken columns, tapping each star of darkness, and saw, as if for the first time, the knuckles and kneecaps of stone, stone bent into beautiful shapes, and the iron woven and welded before the dark doorways. How quickly every surface accumulated sand. Even the chains, even the leaves. His footsteps marked the soft sand with edges and patterns starkly precise in all this softness. But, bending to a footprint, he could see its fragile lip already crumbling under the urging of the breeze.

As he crested the road past the old cinema, he saw the failing light on the square of sea at the base of the road, framed between walls and the arm of the corniche. The ruined lighthouse was bulky, squarish, ragged, like a torn postage stamp sealing the pale sea to the paler sky.

He stood a while in the center of the crossroads, looking down at the patch of rustling sea, leaves scurrying across his shoes. Gulls cried. He started down the slope. Through all the streets, like a tidemark from waist height to head height, was the palimpsest of graffiti and signs and posters, the letters curling into each other, blotting and erasing in their excess, their zeal of communication. The letters and fragments of letters, dark on light, light on dark, in the dozen languages of the city, made a long tattered ribbon winding through every street, now denser, now thinner, the coiled, knobbed, slender shapes congruent with the eroding pillars, the shapes of sand-blown glass and bone. In the dusk, descending to the sea, he did not read the words. Underfoot the surf of charred paper rustled.

In the midan, the palms beat their leaves together with a thin, almost metallic clash. The fountain was dry and filled with sand and bones, and bones lay propped against the base of the statue like diminutive walking sticks. The lily garden had collapsed to stubble. He walked around the statue and down the steps and across to the corniche and stood with his thighs against the stone. The sea was unchanged, so the landscape he had passed through seemed a strange dream, and he imagined turning and witnessing the city grind, then whirl into bustle and color, like a record player churning into life, he imagined turning into the formal rainbow of flags coiling and striking and the shuddering pompoms on the bridles of horses and the blown cotton against the bodies of girls and the castanets of hooves and the bells and calls and the clapped palms of quarrels, laments on gargling radios and the brushing of soles on cobblestones and the wailing of children craving balloons. These sights and sounds rose in a single wave against the corniche wall, sprinkling his face and subsiding again into the sidewalks and the sea and he was left blotting his brow and sensing the silence curling in on his nape, huge and palpable. But, turning, he saw there was nothing to fear. An empty midan. Palm trees, statue, bones.

He had not thought beyond this, beyond walking down to the sea. Placing his palms on the stone, he eased up backward onto the corniche wall and sat looking into the city. No moon yet, only the stars shivering in their sockets.

After a while, he lifted his wrist to his face to read his watch, then sniffed, the laughter of a solitary man, and unhooked the strap and dropped the watch into the sea. What else did he no longer require?

He dropped to the cobblestones, brushed himself off, and walked across to the hotel. One of the massive earthenware pots beside the steps was smashed into a hillock of shards and earth and dry roots, but in the other, an ornamental fig still brandished a few green leaves, though the pot at its base was filled with their dry, warped companions. The door no longer turned, but the panes had been kicked in. He stepped through into the darkness of the foyer, soles crunching on glass and small bones. Here, in this trapped air, mild scents rose to his nostrils. Dust and leather and, beneath them, traces of the familiar floor polish and varnish. He could see nothing save the rectangles of windows facing the sea. Stumbling on bones, he felt his way past the paternoster to the staircase, then clutched the banister to guide himself up the steps. Even here, on the carpeted stairs, bones lay. He felt for them with his shoe-toes, nudged them out of the way. Some clattered down onto other bones, the echoes swallowed by the carpets and lift shaft. On the landing of the second floor, he realized he had walked past the first floor. There seemed no reason to stop. He continued up, on steps less cluttered with debris, and on the fifth landing felt his way door to door to the end of the hall, and entered the corner room. A shred of curtain still lingered against the light from the balcony, shifting like a hung spirit. His eyes had widened to the dark on his passage up the stairs and he took in the wardrobe, one door awry, the triangles of mirror on the carpet, the rucked clothes, bones within them, a skull on the pillow.

He moved onto the balcony and looked down across the bay, across the dark swathe of city, pale flowers of surf blooming along its ruffled edge. He kicked the wicker chair to dislodge its pelt of dust and sat looking down at the sea. In his memory the sea at night was dark. Now, against the dark land, it was full of light. The waves on the corniche seemed very loud. He wished he'd brought an apple or tangerine, even a cigarette, but he had arrived empty-handed. After a while he went inside and removed the bones from the bed, placing them against a wall, then smoothed the sheets, plumped the pillow. He lay a long time staring at the vague tracings of light on the ceiling, listening to the waves.

In the morning the room was soaked in light. The shadows dispersed, he could see how faded the cloth and furniture had become, shades of dun. The wardrobe scoured pale as driftwood by light and sand, tatters of cloth snagged on hangers within it. The carpet, save for his footprints, was pale with dust, and the shred of curtain was ivory now, sketched with the faintest tracings, like a page of manuscript submerged a long time in water. Sitting, he saw he'd ripped the bedclothes to ribbons in his sleep. The mattress beneath was stained, a brown archipelago strung along its center. He got up and moved to the balcony. The waves beat against the shore of the empty city, twigs of light stacked to the horizon. The daylight made the city more empty somehow, lack of movement clarifying the lines and angles. Sections of the city had been on fire. Across some of the facades were the wings of smoke shadow. Stones and bones lay in all the streets. Scraps of paper stirred fitfully, like fallen butterflies.

He felt lightheaded and realized he had not eaten since the morning of the day before. He walked down through the empty hotel, in the gloom of the stairwell, nudging the bones to the outside to leave a clear path along the inner banister. In the restaurant, its huge windows smashed open to the sea, plates still lay on tables, bones on some, the shapes softened and cohered by dust. On one a skull stood, looking out from grottoes of shadow onto the moving sea.

The only light in the kitchens came from the panes in the doors and a row of high square windows webbed with dust. Here too were bones, on the cluttered counters, in the great sinks. Copper-bottomed pans and enormous knives lay on the tiles. Spiders had woven their nests among upright spoon handles, but the webs seemed deserted. Here and there were clots of matter that might once have been fruit or bread, long since shriveled and dusted over.

In the great pantries at the far end of the kitchen, he rummaged blind, among crates and barrels and bones, until he turned up a jar of olives, a wheel of cheese, and a carton of rusks. Plucking a knife from the heap on the floor, he carried his gleanings back to the dining room. He dragged a tablecloth onto the floor, crockery smashing among arm bones, raising a djinn of dust that blossomed enormous, window-sashes blocking out chambers of light, then was sucked away into the hotel. He thought he could still hear the echoes of falling bones, pattering room to room. He cut a wedge of cheese, ripped the cellophane off the rusks with his teeth, opened the jar of olives, relishing the thin hiss of the cellophane, the pop of the lid. He nibbled an olive. The window at his side was entirely gone and he put his feet up on the sill. When a large wave battered the corniche, he could feel the spray against his face.

He walked up to the street of booksellers, which had been walled with spines, titles stacked higher than his head. Often in this city, he felt he was navigating a gulch, its sides intricately eroded, and this conceit had seemed even more apt on this street, the books accumulated over millennia, the lower volumes crushed, compressed, those at eyelevel fresher. The booksellers had cried their wares, books in their hands like semaphores, reciting tantalizing phrases, moments of plot, fanning the books to show the state of the pages. The books were gone, the spaces where they had stood sanded over, bones there. He imagined the wind rushing down this corridor, between empty mosques and coffeehouses, dragging at the books, tearing out brittle pages and whirling them toward the sea, the vacant bindings tumbling after. He found a single page, trapped beneath a skull, so discolored and buckled he could not make out a word. The paper disintegrated when he tried to pluck it forth, so he left it pinned under bone.

Next morning, wandering the streets behind the great central gardens, beneath the curly ledges of balconies, he came across the museum and walked up the broad flight of steps, past the ticket counter, a wad of tickets under a paperweight of finger bones. As he moved through the rooms, what struck him was the sadness of the eyes. Eyes of men and angels and winged bulls, of marble and lapis lazuli and egg tempera and mosaic, painted on wood and pottery, all gazing sadly, sightlessly, past each other at the peeling walls. What was this sad truth they at last understood? He bent to the plaques beneath the sculptures and icons, but they were illegible. Some of these faces were those of rulers, others were gods, or lesser deities, the hierarchies muddled by time and ignorance, so archangels spread their wings beside cobra-headed gods and saints saluted the goddess of the night sky. He imagined praying to these gods, these saints. He imagined the prayer that might enter those deaf ears. What common language did they speak, these gods whose names had vanished under water stain? There were rooms and rooms of them, corridors lined with sad eyes, and when a turn brought him onto a terrace, he saw that there were many more levels, and in every window he saw the silhouettes of sad faces. He felt comforted by them, by their silent sadness, by their anonymity, now, to him. Perhaps this was prayer, then, to pass beneath their still gaze and acknowledge their sadness and the ruin of their faces. Once he had known the names of some, but though sounds surfaced as he walked past certain figures, he let them sink again, subsiding below meaning.

As he wandered through the broad hallways of the museum he encountered bones, singly or in heaps, and these interested his eye as much as the marble and granite faces. Each was perfect, he saw, and realized he only saw this because they were laid at the feet of the imperfect carvings, which made bone of flesh. He picked up a thighbone and held it, sidelit by a window, and saw the easy, perfect plunge and curl of its lines.

Something in the shape compelled him and he could not drop the bone. As he exited the museum, he placed it upright in an urn filled with soil. The bone acquired a strange life, planted upright in the dim hallway, pale stalk supporting a pale, plump bud. He walked away from it, then turned back and gazed at the planted bone a long time. If that bone unfurled, what bloom might it release? He imagined the shapes of the petals, elongate, elliptical, like fingertips opening into the shadows.

He began to notice that certain interiors, whether church or mosque, café or cinema, unbuttoned his ribs and allowed him to breathe, allowed his figments to squawk and whisper in the corners, behind the wainscoting. But others, for no discernible reason, dropped cobwebs across his skull, sealed his lips and nostrils with gray gossamer, so he could not breathe and must clamber out, knocking over chairs, and only the next day would he discover the bruises on his shins. Likewise, certain vistas seemed ominous to him: a particular view from a hotel balcony looking inland, to the desert, in which the angles of the roofs seemed to lacerate the space and the gray smudge of land beyond was like a greasy thumbprint at the base of the sky. A certain curving street he could not go down. Where did the malignancy reside?

Sitting in the freeing spaces, he pondered this. Was there some shape to his spine that certain interiors altered, distorted? Or were there in fact ghosts, the memories of dire deeds resident in certain structures? His thoughts turned to ghosts and what he knew of them. He'd assumed that the scraps left after the departure of breath were only bone, but tales of ghosts were manifold. Where did they spring from, if they existed? What part of a being, what part of himself, might pass into the wind, into the shadows? Did the ghosts stay beside their bones, tethered to the bones by long fine leashes, or were they tethered to the site of the deed that did them in? Or free to roam? Could they speak? Could they reason, these ghosts, or were they merely lamentation incarnate, a thickening of the grief that surrounds us? Did they have communion, and, if so, with whom? With each other, ghostly tea parties? Or with certain individuals whose spirits were large enough or diffuse enough or warped enough to speak with ghosts? And did they take on appearances, these ghosts, could they cloak their sorrows in the seeming of a man, a girl, and go strolling? How does eternity lay its hands on moments?

As these questions rose and subsided unanswered, he picked up a bone—a bone of the upper arm, he thought—and its solidity and whiteness seemed a rebuke to his queries. He did not know the names of the bones, could not recognize more than half a dozen, but, crouching by a skeleton, he saw there were hundreds of bones, some small as dice, delicate as stamens. Did each have a name? Living in this city of bones, he must learn their names.

So the next morning he made his way to the hospital. Certain architectures that were grandiose from the outside, expansive with columns and fluted eaves, seemed cramped inside, doors locked, shut down. But the hospital, which he entered through a narrow archway, feathered into a labyrinth of shadowed hallways and snug rooms. All that morning he wandered through halls thick with bones, through rooms thick with bones, bones in places stacked like kindling, a crackling carpet of bones he walked across, a wealth of bones. The halls were so long and gently curving and mottled white he felt he was moving within bones, within the ruins of a skeleton, itself filled with skeletons, and perhaps within the bones at his feet other pilgrims wandered, restless marrow, and tiny pilgrims within them. He wandered past strange intricate machinery, all archaic now, post-historic, with knobs and levers like bones themselves under dust, and the bashed eyes of lenses and on the walls garbled tentacles of obsolete instruments. He passed weathered charts and lists of names, all faded now. He pushed through ochered glass into surgeries, scalpels upright in jars of rust, bones on the tables. In the wards, every bed was full of bones, as if whole families had inhabited each mattress, and bones lay under the beds and in the aisles, clipboards and stethoscopes among them. He passed by the pharmacy, the pretty shapes of the bottles sidelit by a nearby window, all labels nameless now, and the contents reduced to colored ash. He found in a dim hallway, rolled in a corner, sequestered from the ravages of light and time, a chart, which proved to be an exhaustively labeled etching of a skeleton. This he carried back to the hotel and hung from a hook.

Then he sorted through the bones he'd gathered, matching them to the drawing, inscribing each bone with its name in tiny cursive, sharpening the pencil with a scalpel to achieve a point fine enough to write stapes, incus, adumbrating the triquetral and trapezoid, barely sullying the ulna. The skeletons in the room lacked some bones, even when he had searched under the bed, under the wardrobe, in the folds of the mattress, so he ransacked the bones in the hallway and on the stairs till he gathered what he needed, and by nightfall a skeleton was laid before him, labeled, pieced from a dozen skeletons. Two hundred and six bones in the body. The insects of the skeleton. Stacked bumblebees of the spine. Butterfly pelvis, fat wasp tailbone, dragonfly clavicle, nesting scarabs of the wrists. By candlelight he memorized the names of the bones and their shapes, holding in his hand the distal phalanges, touching the joined bones of the face and skull, handcuffing himself to the pelvis, balancing ribs and clavicles on fingertips.

He'd not imagined the names so various, so mysteriously evocative. Temporal bone, lunate bone, palatine bone, cuneiform bones. Talus and trapezium. Sternum, sacrum, patella. Twenty-eight phalanges. The femur, with its greater trochanter and condyles, the fibula and the vomer bone. The hyoid bone of the throat. The calcaneus, the navicular and cuboid bones. The ossa coxae, or innominate bones. He had never really looked at a skull, at its curtains and folds, its ragged seams. The ripped gape of the nasal cavity, the screens within the eyesockets, the bold angle of the jaw. Turning the skull he had chosen, he heard the rattling of smaller bones within it, and the hiss of sand gathering in the chambers.

The bones he had brought together had been variously weathered, some erotically smooth, some rough as granite beneath his fingers. He handled each one, weighing them, turning them. Lying in bed watching the candles gutter one by one, then in darkness, his thoughts were crammed with the shapes of the bones, curling into each other, floating wide on a field of darkness. He could still feel their claws and nodules in his palms. He imagined, in the loosening of images before sleep, laying the bones upon his body, rib to rib, metatarsals and phalanges in place, cranium a diadem, a quilt of bones, imagined them locking into his own bones, ghosting into them, or his own skeleton rising out of his flesh.

He was not finished with the hospital. There were underground chambers, lightless, he had not explored, so he took a stash of candles. The room he sought lay in the bowels of the hospital, subterranean. He returned the next day with candles, lost his way again, and finally found the thick metal door, and behind it the machine, like a great scavenger bird hunched over the table. Along the sides of this room, cabinets had burst and their contents, black sheaves, lay in drifts across the floor. Anchoring candles at intervals along the hall and the stairwell, he ferried armloads of the dark pages up into the light: slippery bushels of thick opaque leaves. There were a number of old satchels lying about, and he fetched the largest of these and stuffed it full, then carried the x-rays back to the hotel and began holding them to the light. He found he could slot them into the sashes of the windows, so he placed a dozen at a time against the sky and sat on the mattress, looking at them. Such unexpected beauty. The areas of darkness so deep, the grains of flesh and organs like comets and asteroids, like galaxies and constellations, arcing, bunching. The bones themselves were luminous, as if on fire, the flesh like ash or dissolving salt, brushed into the dark.

He found himself at first obsessed with the bones, with naming them, but then began peering for the flesh, for the vestiges of skin and heart, the corona of face, halo around the starkness of the skull. Vertebrae like certain orchids. Some of the x-rays took on strange semblances. A pelvis became a domino, a foot an anvil, a hand a candelabra. Some seemed unblemished, but on others he could see clearly the shattered bone, shards floating in the misty flesh, splinters like snapped twigs, gray lines of less drastic fractures. He imagined moving through the hospital, the city, clutching the x-rays, till he found matches to the fractures, long healed now, or forever sundered. He had seen, within certain wards, the bones still loosely cased in plaster, some tenuously cohered by initial connective tissue. He had seen, as well, bones with the bark of healing, splintered or cracked, but never rebroken in the same place. The process of healing created a new inordinate sturdiness, it seemed, the bone determined not to allow the same trauma twice. The body shoring itself up against the future, against the repetitions of history.

Spending time with the bones, he found he could begin to read them. Clothed though they had been within sinew, skin, they told their tales, carrying only the stories of cataclysms, one or two to a skeleton. Sorting through a heap of bones, he could draw forth the chipped finger bone, the blemished patella, and imagine the stumble, the blow, that had left these traces. Few skeletons lacked such markings, so the streets, the rooms, which had seemed crowded, strewn with identical shapes, now proved, on finer examination, to be varied and wonderful as a bookshelf. In his examination of the bones some struck his fancy, and these he kept. Slender bones of children, with their extra caches that fused in adults: the ilium, the ischium, the sacral and coccygeal vertebrae, their unwelded skulls, so thin-walled. Bowed bones of the aged. And among them the bones of cats and mice and ferrets, lean, fragile, the tiny, marvelous skulls.

He could hardly have articulated why he walked through the streets with one bone and not another. Shape, texture, weight, simply the snuggle of its contours against his palm. The colors of the bones. They had weathered like stones. Some yellow, some gray, some mottled brown, some granular white, bones of ash, of salt. Sometimes he returned to the hotel laden, clutching armloads of bones, like a forager returning with firewood, dumping them in a corner of the room, sorting the bones in twilight, then candlelight. On inspection, some ceased to compel him and these he tossed over the balcony, but others he could not look at enough, he fit his palms against their hollows and swells, laid them against his cheek, in the crook of his neck, touched them with his lips. He spun clavicles on his fingertips like the narrow blades of a fan, beat time on skulls with rib drumsticks, peered through the oval frames of pelvises, wielded thighbones like sabers, candle flames washing like bright seaweed beneath their sweep. He polished them with soft cloths and the oil of his fingers, then arranged them, stacking bones in the corners of the room, in the wardrobe, on the dresser. The arrangement of the bones was of constant concern to him. Sometimes it seemed he had placed them correctly—their juxtapositions and the pockets of darkness where they overlapped satisfying—but some nights he would work long after darkness fell, beneath the fence of candles, struggling to prod the bones into positions that pleased him, on which his eye would linger.

He dreamed he was climbing a scaffold of bones, an enormous, intricate skeleton, far higher than the lighthouse had ever been, inching up the slope of the pelvis, hauling himself rung to rung of the plentiful ribs, which gave slightly beneath each footstep, then in the crevices of the vertebrae, finally into the echoing skull. He stood at last in an elliptical window-frame, peering down across the bones he had climbed, which he saw now were a constellation spread through all the sky, formed of every bone in the city, each twinkling in its place. He woke from this dream exhilarated, rejuvenated, and rushed out into the morning to gather more bones. His dream had done away with choice, but, confronted with the bones on the streets, he found he must sort through them laboriously, testing, hoarding, before he found one that he could carry away. The bones did not stack easily. Trying to create angular structures, cubes of bones, he discovered, was futile. They would slip into each other, rasp across each other, jerking him awake, as if they were only able to stand this discomfort for a short time, less than a night. So he learned to allow them to find their own repose, nudging them till they nestled into place. He tried for a while organizing them by kind, arm bones with arm bones, middens of finger bones, skulls stacked like mottled melons, but this proved both prosaic and disconcerting. The grouped skulls, even if he turned their faces to the wall, tormented him with their cohesive presence, the regularity of the stacked femurs was oppressive, like a gate, the slats of a fence, so he strove for looser groupings. Skull cradled in pelvis, skulls filled with the abraded marbles of metacarpals or the snapped sticks of carpals, ribs canting over shinbones like slender birdcages, vertebrae cupped in patellae like elaborate pastries, pairings of thighbones and ear bones, calcaneous and hyoid bone—heel and throat meeting as they never did in life. Scattering of toe bones in a shoulder blade. He labored for days in the empty room, while the light changed, trying this bone and that, manipulating them, striving for something, he could not have said what, some shape, a shape not only of bones but of the air they inhabited. The bones cast complicated shadows across the floor and partway up one wall, shadows full of shapes of light. He went back to his bedroom, which he saw now was a laboratory, a storeroom. He woke at intervals all night, returning to the neighboring room to peer at the ghostly forms in the moonlight, the worn light, bounced sun to moon to sea to ceiling to bone. The next day he dismantled them and started over.

There was no shortage of bones. No shortage of bones, days,

space. Days and days he raised his bone structures, his bone architecture, questing till the shape surprised him, till he achieved a shape that stood apart from his endeavors, that created its own life of shadows. He learned to recognize that surprise. Sometimes he repeated himself and the repetition was fruitful, spawning new forms, and sometimes the echoes died away, each duller than the last. Sometimes he felt he was digging, with breastbone hatchet, scapula spade, digging for some strange mineral, evanescent, and the seams dwindled, till he thought the mine was barren and then, when he least expected it, a stroke uncovered pockets, depths of riches. He learned to keep digging. He learned to pry into the areas of least resistance.

He slept less, ate less. He became more enamored with sunlight and shadow and their relationship. He looked at the shadows bones cast at different times of day, and the shapes his own figure cast, the shadows he sometimes thought of as an alphabet, a solitary alphabet moving through the city. In late afternoon he stood sometimes on the balcony of his room manipulating his shadow, a strange slow dance, arms raised, fingers joining and parting, torso twisting this way and that, while on an interior wall shapes of light swelled and closed, softening to suns the greater the distance between his body and the wall.

He woke from dreams of waking. He woke, and remembered waking, a dozen times, and each time into an altered room, a room of voices, room of eyes, and he could hear no single voice, could catch no individual glance. His memory was of the throngs pressing about the bed. In one of his dream awakenings he had moved to the balcony and seen the corniche crowded with souls, many more than he had remembered, shuffling in the same direction. None looked his way. But he woke at last into the empty room, into the sound of the sea, and realized he was ill. The emptiness was like a pain, a cube of pain around his skull. He shivered, though the sun lay across the floor. His eyelids scraped as though over sand, he felt scoured by wind and sand, parched. He sat up to drink a little water, lay back exhausted, crowned with perspiration. After a while he vomited thinly onto the floor. He vomited again and again, the spasms twisting his torso, pulling moans from his lips, till only strands of mucus dripped, and still his stomach contracted. At last the spasms subsided and he lay back. He was trembling and thought he ran a fever. His skin felt dry and finely textured as leaves. He slept again. All that day he slept and woke and as the afternoon wore into evening the ghosts that inhabited his dreams entered his waking moments. He was horrified by them, by these apparitions that refused to look him in the eye.

They stood in the corners of the room, at the foot of the bed, on the balcony, and their faces were just beyond recall. Looking into their faces, which were strangely hard to focus upon, he had the immediate impression he'd seen them before, but the longer he stared the more that notion faded, so he glanced face to face, roving to sustain the sense of recognition. They whispered, but he could not catch their lips moving, and the words, like the faces, never quite clarified. The evening, far from diminishing the apparitions, filled the room with them. He slept and woke, and there were always more, though he began to notice that as they grew more plentiful, they grew more transparent, as if they were manufactured of a certain quantity of their delicate substance, that spread more thinly as they multiplied. He could see through their faces the jambs of doors, the sashes of windows, the discolored paint of the walls. Those on the balcony bore clouds behind their eyes, minarets in brainpans, and one stood so the moon cradled her face. They touched only in overlapping, and they did not look at each other. The expression of their faces, which he at first took for sadness, he found, in the moonlight, to be cleansed of emotion, like the faces of deep sleepers. He did not try to speak to them. They would not have answered.

In the morning the apparitions had vanished, and with them the fever. He lay exhausted on the mattress, which was soaked with his sweat, and after a while slept again, an uninhabited sleep, from which he woke refreshed, though terribly thirsty. He rose from the bed, legs trembling, joints aching, and found water and rusks, and sat on the balcony sipping and nibbling.

It was two days before he recovered the strength to leave the hotel, and many days passed before the night of the transparent faces lifted from his mind. He wished he'd looked harder at them. He had been so horrified, had spent the hours recoiling from them, but now he wished he'd looked closer. Had they cast shadows? He did not think so, but could not be sure. When they overlapped, did they become more solid, did they draw a thicker veil across the walls, the sky? Could they pass through each other? Could they be touched? Could they hear him? At first he assumed they were only the recent dead, only those whose bones cluttered the streets and rooms of the city, but then he imagined they were all the dead, the accumulated dead, whose bones lay like roots in the earth, beneath every house, dense strata of bones through which beetles clambered. How deep did they go, the layers of bones? He imagined them pressed toward the earth's core, crushed.

How long were the leashes that tethered the apparitions to their bones? Could they venture forth across the earth's surface, or were they confined to this city, or to a certain street, a certain house? Were all of them released to wander, or only those whose work was unfinished? And what work was that? There had been children, the young.

Now, in the stark light of day, in the midans, in the empty restaurants, they seemed impossibly phantom. Where had they gone, the ghosts? Where did they live in the days, in the endless rooms of light? Did they plunge like divers, returning to their rooms beneath the earth? Or did they hide in corners, in shadows, spawning unease? Were they in fact summoned only by his dreams? They inhabited his dreams, he was certain of this, though they vanished upon waking. But he felt, each morning, the unsettling notion that he had not been alone in the room, that he had shared this space with others, and he woke searching for eyes in the corners, glances only just faded, voices only just mingled with the surf, passed beyond recognition. That lack of recognition tormented him. He feared recognition, feared the gaze he recalled, feared a voice that spoke a phrase he remembered, in a tongue and an accent he remembered, and also he feared the lack of recognition. But as the days passed, the memories of the faces, the voices, faded, as if the sand that drifted across the cobbles and paving stones, gently chafing, drifted as well through his skull, cleansing, scouring, and the apparitions, pieced of such flimsy material at the outset, cracked, thinned, and what remained were scraps, like the thinned tatters of curtains still moving in certain windows, like the wisps of flags and banners that still curled from the tops of certain flagpoles, an assortment of movement in the city, the scraps of movement. These scraps moved in his skull, flapping gently from time to time, subsiding if he stared at them.

. . .

One morning, from his balcony, he saw, calm and stunning as
a spill of blood, a pane of seawater across the lower half of the
midan, lobed into the lie of the ground, reflecting in rippled
sepia shuttered windows, ragged palms. A few bones raised
ferrules and oval slopes like islets. Among them a leaf and its
brown echo turned slowly. The breach had opened during the
night, at high tide, but the water had receded below the wall,
leaving its bright token.

Walking through the city that day, eastward, he found a
dozen jagged new lakes. In one three fish flashed like rips in a
brown curtain. The most distant incursion had tumbled away
one of the coral blocks, and the waves continued to wash in.
Where tram tracks passed under a road, seawater lay like a
river in a gorge, the reflected graffiti scored by drifting twigs.
He found the slim cataract where the sea entered this trough
and crouched by the creeping edges watching the water grout
brick and snuggle among grass blades and his toes. He saw how
the water would enter the city, stealthily, effortlessly, choosing
the easy entrances, blue benison, blue annihilation.

The initial breaching heralded a week of dramatic changes,
as the sea welled over the retaining wall and swallowed great
gulps of the littoral, the shoreline pummeled into new shapes
with each high tide. Now, descending from the hotel each
morning, he sloshed through ankle-high water before reaching
dry streets. One long morning, he moved the stores of food
from the kitchen to the second floor, hauling wheels of cheese
and boxes of crackers and dried fruit and jars of jam and olives,
stacking them in the hallway.

By the end of that week, the wall had been entirely
inundated, its curve marked now only by froth where the

incoming waves stumbled against it. The seafront buildings were footed in water. In the still mornings, when the sea was taut, the doubling of their rococo facades made an enchanted world through which twin birds sped and he imagined the reflections were in fact the roots of the houses, foundations so solid in seeming, but fractured by a breath or dropped feather. Midmorning, the breezes rushed in, ruffling the sea's surface, tousling it into soft curls.

As the waves broke against the walls, he was perched at the vanguard of a city rushing into the sea, plunging like concrete golems through the shallows, the water foaming around columns, gnashing through archways. For a few days, as the sea scoured rooms, a surf of chairs and vases and waterpipes rocked and smashed against the new shoreline, but then this debris sank or was carried away to become driftwood, driftglass, and the sea's edge was clean again. At night the noises of water rose louder and more varied. What had been the hush and wash of the waves against the corniche wall was joined by the suck and boom as they plundered the caverns of the hotel and splintered on window frames.

The wall breached, the changes again became infinitesimal, the sea's rise through the city so gradual he hardly noticed it, except when, from time to time, a higher alley overnight became a brook, or a mosque where he had sat was carpeted abruptly in saltwater. The bottom floor of the hotel flooded and every few days the water covered another step.

He walked inland, up the street he had first walked down, past the station where trains no longer arrived. Crossing the tracks, he saw that, in places, drifts of sand entirely concealed them. He walked past the station and its dark halls, into the narrower streets to the south, going downhill once more. He walked out past the last houses and stood before the sea. At first he thought the twisting streets must have turned him back on his tracks, but then, seeing the shapes of distant blue, and the smokestacks planted in the water, realized the rising sea had circled the city, had filled and joined the marshes and left him on an island. The train tracks vanished into the water, threads of light, and he imagined a train slipping into the depths like a jointed serpent. Or rising, its giant headlight like a moon surfacing, the water sluicing from its grease and paint, snorting and blowing. And what stations lay beneath the sea? And what passengers might that train carry from the alien deep?

He turned inland and climbed the hill of gardens, among the fallen fruit and unkempt grass, till he reached the highest point, climbed to the roof of the villa there, up the rickety steps of the octagonal tower surmounting it, and turned through the points of the compass, looking across his shrunken domain and the waste beyond. From this height, he could see how general the sea's invasion was. Across the channel the hospital stood on its own, smaller island, and beyond that were two more islands and then a speckling of buildings and rooftops, and then the sea. To the south the vista was submerged under haze, the smokestacks of the drowned factories like misty periscopes. The sea flashed and heaved, enormous as the sky. He was suddenly dizzy, and clutched the crumbling balustrade, then sank to his knees, forehead pressed into the pitted stone. Vertigo, he thought, and quickly descended through the villa, eyes on the steps. But when he reached the rubble in the forsaken garden, he found he was still trembling, and realized his terror had nothing to do with the height, but with the confirmation of his solitude. He walked back slowly. Every few days he returned to the eastern shores of the new island, a shorter walk each time as the water encroached.

He could sense now the movement of the water, the spaces it would fill, could anticipate the shape the shoreline might acquire in a day or a week. There was no sense of loss or diminishment, of resisting the creeping onslaught. Rather, he felt that the city welcomed the visitor into its rooms, succumbed peacefully to this new inhabitant, with its desire to penetrate even walls, even floors, its touch stronger than air, softer than skin.

As the water rose and lay in green-fingered ponds here and there, and on the tiles of the buildings, the dry air of the city was replaced by the tang of rot and stagnant seawater. Dying fish flipped idly among their motionless companions, and drying seaweed draped chair struts when the tide was out. He crouched beside some of these artificial tide pools, or straddled the windowsill of a restaurant, peering into the lively soup, the shapes of the creatures stark against the sanded marble. After his weeks with the bones and their static shapes, the variety and movement of the creatures pleased him. He watched the finger-snap concord of the tiny striped fish, flickering like candle flames blown by a breath in their minds. Shells creeping like snails, buffing a clean stripe along the tiles. The slow tumble of sea urchins. Thick, ponderous sea cucumbers, the bristling beauty of a scorpion fish, hiding behind a table leg. Sardines like dollops of mercury. These he could name, but most of the creatures he could only grip with simile. Fish like lilies, like leaves, the colors of lapis lazuli, lemons, lovebirds. Marine beings that moved like smoke, with great eyes or jaws out of nightmare and appendages whose utility he could not begin to guess at. Creatures so similar to the sand or shadows he only noticed them when they snorted, or snared a fish. The water rose, pouring new citizens through windows and doorways.

. . .

For hours, then days, he lay on the mattress watching the nets of light on the ceiling, while the sea entered the city. In the lower rooms of the hotel, the water sloshed and boomed. He began to imagine the deeps, which he had not considered. Surely other cities lurked in the blue, drowned or burgeoning. Looking across the sea, inklings of those cities rose before his mind's eye, their windows draped in seaweed. Angelfish in alcoves. In the submerged streets live shells lay like cobblestones, sharks lazing along the avenues. Utterly silent, crowded with life. The interiors blind. Cities of a thousand swaying steeples, fantastically tall, craving sunlight, surmounted by strange sea-formed symbols, arcana of seahorse and sea urchin.

In his dreams he was underwater. The sea had swarmed through the levels of the hotel, squeezing the air from the secret pockets, lifting tables and chairs in a raucous melee and juggling them against the ceilings. The fans turned like lazy propellers. Sea bass nosing painted breasts. Starfish tumbling through the windows. Lying on his mattress, underwater, breathing was more difficult but more delicious. He could feel the saltwater leaching through his limbs, suffusing them blue. All acts, even that of opening his eyes, became languid in this medium. The walls swayed within the thickness of water. The cane chair from the balcony waltzed over his head. His eyes were drenched in blue. The bones shuffled and he heard them clacking softly, like the speech of newborn birds heard a long way off and slowed by distance.

ABOUT THE AUTHOR

KEITH MILLER was born in Tanzania and has spent most of his life in East and North Africa. He has lived in Egypt since 2000. His first novel, *The Book of Flying*, was published in 2004. *The Book on Fire* is his second novel. Visit his website at millerworlds.com.

CPSIA information can be obtained at www.ICGtesting.com
Printed in the USA
LVOW12s1550160914

404330LV00001B/196/P

9 781907 737206